THE
BRIGHT
SIDE

THE
BRIGHT
SIDE

ALEX COLEMAN

POOLBEG

This novel is entirely a work of fiction. The names, characters and incidents portrayed in it are the work of the author's imagination. Any resemblance to actual persons, living or dead, events or localities is entirely coincidental.

Published 2009
by Poolbeg Press Ltd
123 Grange Hill, Baldoyle
Dublin 13, Ireland
E-mail: poolbeg@poolbeg.com
www.poolbeg.com

1 3 5 7 9 10 8 6 4 2

A catalogue record for this book is available from the British Library.

ISBN 978-1-84223-343-6

Typeset by Type Design in Caslon
Printed by CPI Cox & Wyman, Reading, RG1 8EX

Note on the author

Alex Coleman is married and lives in Dublin with the mandatory pair of writer's cats, who have asked not to be named.

Acknowledgements

I would like to express my gratitude to my agent, Faith O'Grady, for all the work she has done on my behalf and for being so consistently, almost supernaturally good-humoured. I'd also like to say thank you to Paula Campbell and all the staff at Poolbeg for their support. Thanks are due to Gaye Shortland too for making sure that the editing process was both painless and useful.

Finally, much love to my family and friends whose guidance and encouragement have been absolutely vital.

Alex Coleman

To my best friend, Sinéad

CHAPTER 1

It was a Friday the 13th, the day I caught Gerry having sex with our next-door neighbour. Not that I ever thought the two things were connected. I'd always hated all that superstitious malarkey. A broken mirror didn't mean seven years bad luck in my book – it meant a trip to the mirror shop. Still, there was no denying that I'd been having a really brutal 13th, even before I caught the pair of them puffing and panting over the back of my good sofa like a couple of knackered greyhounds. I slept in, for a start, and that always got on my nerves (no matter how often it happened). Skipping breakfast didn't bother me so much, but I really resented having to rush my shower. A rushed shower, in my opinion, was worse than none at all. You got all the hassle of getting wet but none of the benefits. It wasn't much different to getting caught in the rain. And this was a real in-and-out job: the first drops of water had barely hit the floor before I was back in the bedroom, swearing under my breath and rooting through my underwear drawer. Gerry was gently snuffling in his sleep, as usual (he was very rarely out of bed before me, even when I wasn't up on time). When we first got married, I found his snuffling seriously cute. He used to say that I'd soon change my tune about that one. But he was wrong. It always stayed cute to me, even after twenty-one years.

My day didn't improve a whole pile when I finally made it across to First Premier in Santry. When I'd started working there, about three years previously, I'd foolishly pointed out to my manager, Jenny, that "first" and "premier" meant the same thing. She'd fixed me with one of her non-smile smiles and said, "Do you really think we don't know that here at First Premier?" I discovered later that Jenny elbowed the phrase "here at First Premier" into approximately 50 per cent of her conversations. My job title was "Data Entry Operative". I liked the "Operative" part. It made me sound like a glamorous spy. It was the "Data Entry" bit I had trouble with, both as a title and, sadly, as an everyday activity. That morning, as I came through the door of our humongous open-plan office, afraid to look at my watch but knowing it was getting on for ten, I just knew that Jenny was lying in wait for me like a badly permed leopard. Sure enough, I wasn't even halfway to my desk – my work-station, rather – before she pounced.

Good afternoon, I thought.

"Good afternoon," said Jenny. This was her standard

greeting for latecomers. It was so obvious and childish and unfunny that it always made me want to cry, even when it wasn't being directed at me.

"Hello, Jenny," I said, trying my best to smile. "I'm a bit late."

She gazed back at me with the cold, unblinking eyes of a doll. "I hope everything's all right at home," she cooed then, doing a sympathetic head-tilt.

I resumed walking. Jenny followed half a pace behind, like one of those small, annoying dogs that goes *Yip* instead of *Woof*.

"Everything's fine at home," I said. "Alarm clock let me down, that's all. Dead battery or something."

"Hmmm," Jenny said.

There was something about the way she said it, some vague hint of menace, that made me stop and turn to face her.

"It won't happen again," I lied.

Jenny frowned. "The thing is, Jackie, you've said that before."

She had a point there. I'd said it many, many times before, some of them, if memory served, in the past couple of days. There didn't seem to be any point in adding that being late annoyed me as much as it did her and that I dearly wished it wouldn't happen so often. I decided instead to try the light-hearted approach. Nothing in my experience of Jenny told me she would appreciate the effort, but I gave it a whirl anyway.

"I know I've said that before," I told her with what I hoped was a loveable grin, "but this time, I really, really mean it." I held up my right hand with fingers crossed and when Jenny failed to respond, I held the left up too.

Her brow creased and uncreased. "You're aware, no doubt, of the new tardiness policy we've implemented here at First Premier?"

I half-remembered seeing an e-mail with some of those words in it. It had caused a bit of a fuss about a week or two previously. I hadn't read the thing properly and hadn't participated in the fuss. "Of course."

"Well then, you'll know all about the points system."

I drew a blank at that one. "Points system. Sure."

"Well, Jackie, I'm afraid that today's nine-fifty-seven coupled with Wednesday's nine-oh-eight, Tuesday's nine-twelve and last Thursday's nine-twenty-one puts you over the top for this month *already*. And it's only –"

"The 13th," I sighed. "It's Friday the 13th."

"Unlucky for some," Jenny said with what looked, for a change, like a genuine smile. "So you'll do it?"

I hadn't a clue what "it" was, but I knew I'd find the answer in the e-mail. "Looks like I'll have to, doesn't it?" I said.

Jenny nodded. "It's policy."

I turned and left her, hoping to God that I was merely imagining the bright bolts of pain that had started to flash along the right side of my head.

I started getting "my headaches" – I always called them that as they seemed very personal – when the kids were entering their teens. We used to joke, on the days when I felt like joking about it, that it must have had something to do with all the stereos in the house suddenly getting cranked up. But really, I had no idea what the cause might be. I didn't get them very often – four, maybe five times a year. That was plenty. Nothing seemed to provoke them – nothing that I could identify anyway. They always started the same way, with brief, shooting pains that were gone before I could even wince. Some time after that – it could be minutes, it could be hours – the party really got going; the pains returned, and this time they stayed. There were lots of suitable analogies; I usually plumped for something with white-hot six-inch nails.

As soon as I got settled in at my desk, Veronica, who sat directly opposite me, peeped over the partition and gave me an update on her battle with the kids who gathered on her front wall every night to smoke cigarettes. There had been an escalation, by all accounts. One of the kids, a girl of no more than twelve, had called Veronica a "frigid old bitch" (it was the "old" part that really hurt, apparently). Veronica had responded with something about children who dressed like little prostitutes and feared she had gone too far.

I tried to seem interested, but my mind kept wandering back to Jenny. It occurred to me that she'd had my tardiness details on the tip of her tongue. That meant that she'd looked them up in some sort of file, no doubt hoping that I'd be late, as opposed to absent, so she'd able to throw them at me. She'd even *memorised* them. I grabbed the edges of my desk and tried to think pleasant thoughts. Cute little puppies, gently babbling brooks, the last five minutes of *An Officer and a Gentleman*... I was still gripping hard and muttering darkly to myself when Eddie Hand appeared by my side.

Eddie sat at the end of our little section, facing Veronica and me. He was a forty-something bachelor who wore the same navy-blue woollen tie quite literally every day, even though he could have showed up in an Iron Maiden T-shirt for all First Premier cared. In summer he wore his tie over a short-sleeved shirt. In winter he wore it under a V-necked jumper. Every couple of days or so, I vowed to ask him why he was devoted to that one item of clothing. I never followed through, partly because I was afraid he would tell me that it had been a present from his childhood sweetheart who had died in a tragic boating accident (or something), and partly because I didn't want him to think that I was interested in being his friend. Eddie wasn't exactly the type who set the room on fire when he walked in – not unless he accidentally knocked over a candle while creeping round the edge of the group, looking for a place to hide. I wasn't proud of the attitude I had towards him. Certainly not. But I rationalised it by telling myself that most people probably had someone like that in their lives, a colleague, a neighbour, a familiar face on the bus. Someone they suspected to be a little bit sad, a little bit lonely. Someone they could possibly cheer up quite a bit, if only they'd take the time. But they didn't, and I didn't, for fear that the lonely person might start appearing on the doorstep, suggesting nights out or, worse, weekends away. Best to just smile politely and shimmy past them, that's what we all told ourselves. I smiled politely at Eddie when he showed up that morning and if I hadn't been sitting down, I would have shimmied past as well.

"Hello," he said. "Are you okay?"

I gave him a smile every bit as fake as the one Jenny had worn earlier. "I'm fine, why?"

He shrugged and cast his eyes to the right. "I dunno. You seem a bit … you know …" He pointed with his head. "Your knuckles are all white."

I loosened my grip on the desk and went into my drawer for headache tablets. "I'm okay, Eddie, really. Just a bit tense, that's all."

He nodded. "Is it because of your hair?"

On the Monday of that week I'd shown up in wicked humour on account of a weekend haircut that had gone seriously awry. My usual girl had called in sick at the last minute, but rather than make a new appointment, I'd gone ahead with another stylist. I should have known better. The replacement stank of last night's booze and seemed to be having trouble forming proper sentences ("Have you been to holiday this year, have you?" she asked me at one point). She was still drunk, I was absolutely sure of it. Long story short, I wound up with a hairstyle like Stephen Fry's. It had annoyed me for a few days, naturally, but I had more or less forgotten about it until that moment.

"No, Eddie," I said, "it's nothing to do with my hair." I wasn't at all disturbed by his contribution. He wasn't trying to be malicious or even amusing. He could see that I was upset and he knew that I'd been unhappy about my hair. He'd put the two together, that was all. He was really *asking*.

"Okay," Eddie said and smiled for a fraction of a second. He tore off then, as if frightened by a loud noise.

I watched his back as he made his way to the photocopier,

wondering if that was the longest conversation he'd had all morning. Then I told myself that I was inventing a sob story where one didn't necessarily exist. For all I knew, Eddie spent his evenings sipping champagne in fancy restaurants with a succession of sex-addicted lingerie models. When I turned back to face my computer, Veronica was half-standing again and making kissy faces. It was her firm conviction that Eddie fancied me. She seemed to have based this theory on nothing but the fact that once in a blue moon, the previous incident being a prime example, he spoke to me without my speaking to him first. He didn't do that with anyone else, not according to Veronica at any rate.

"Eddie and Jackie up a tree!" she chanted. *"K-I-S-S-I–"*

I threw the cap of a yellow highlighter at her and was pleased to see it bounce off her forehead and land in her coffee.

If I hadn't found the e-mail straight away, I might have given up and turned to the eight-inch-high pile of data that was teetering by my left elbow, waiting to be entered. My stress level would still have gone up, no doubt, but it wouldn't have instantly doubled the way it did when I got a look at the e-mail. The gist of the thing was this: tardiness had become a serious problem for First Premier and was affecting its ability to meet targets, going forward (as opposed to backwards or sideways). Management weren't callous, unfeeling monsters – as if – and could forgive an occasional five-minute slip-up here and there. However! Persistent offenders could no longer expect to get away scot-free. The new system (they called it a system four times) was points-based. If you arrived for work five to ten minutes late, you got a single point. Ten to fifteen minutes late, got you five of them. Fifteen to thirty, you got ten. Half an hour plus, you got twenty. Anyone who scored more than thirty points in a month had to do a forfeit. At that point the e-mail stopped being irritating and started being excruciating. In a breezy, matey I-Can't-Believe-We-Get-Paid-To-Work-Here! tone, it revealed that transgressors would be obliged to wear a special tardiness hat for one whole working day. Anyone who refused to play along would be excluded from all social club activities until they did what had been asked of them. They would also be named and shamed as a "spoilsport". There was a photo attached to the e-mail. It showed a dunce's cap with a letter T where the D should have been. When I finished reading, all I felt was relief. I didn't give two hoots, one hoot even, about the social club; if I really wanted to go to a pub quiz or karaoke night, I was sure I'd be able to organise it myself. And, I thought, they could name me every day until 2050, I'd still never be shamed. This meant that I could ignore the entire policy, hat and all. The relief didn't last long though. It was swept away almost immediately by bitter, jagged anger. Why hadn't they just declared that employees who were consistently late would be chucked out of the social club? Or fired, for that matter? Why bother with all the nonsense in between? Why did it have to be "fun"? It was Fancy Dress Friday all over again. That was a one-off event that had brightened all our lives a few months previously (it wasn't supposed to be a one-off; it just worked out that way). I didn't know how it had gone company-wide, but in Data Entry there were precisely three takers, out of a possible thirty-something. Jenny came as Wonder Woman and a bloke called Terry came as a vampire. They looked ridiculous, of course, mooching from their desks to the water cooler and back, but at least they had hired proper costumes. The third participant was Eddie. He came as a Roman gladiator in a bunch of kit he'd made himself out of cardboard, tin-foil and other cardboard. Not once, all day long, did he remove his helmet. It had taken him several hours to perfect, he said, and he was determined to get good wear out of it.

"Did you read this rubbish about the tardiness hat?" I called out to Veronica.

She looked up from her keyboard. I could see the top half of her head over the partition. The top half of her head looked surprised.

"Yeah," she said. "I saw it a fortnight ago with the rest of the company. Did you hear about John Lennon? Shot dead!"

I ignored the last part and went back to fuming. It was just about then that the first six-inch nail was driven into my skull. I had no sooner registered the news that my day was going from bad to much, much worse when my mobile phone jangled in my handbag. The caller was Robert, my eldest (by twelve minutes). I couldn't remember the last time he had called me and said something I wanted to hear. The smart thing to do, I told myself, would be to ignore it and get back to my impending headache. But it's never easy to ignore your own flesh and blood. And so, like an eejit, I answered the damn thing.

CHAPTER 2

Robert was an actor – a proper one. It wasn't like he was a waiter who sometimes showed up in the background of TV commercials dressed as a cereal flake or a toilet germ. He played Valentine Reilly in *The O'Mahonys*, which was a pretty big deal. The first time he told me about the part, he used the term "resident bad-boy" and I said that would be right up his street. I was trying to be encouraging and supportive, I really was. Robert didn't see it that way. He left me in no doubt that he had much preferred his father's take on the news, which was "You'll have to beat them away with a shitty stick". Gerry was talking about women, of course, and he was right. As soon as Valentine made his first appearance on the show, Robert's stock, which had always been buoyant, suddenly went through the roof. I didn't know

11

if he'd ever tried the shitty-stick approach, but he'd certainly failed to beat the women away. His latest girlfriend was a thirty-year-old fashion journalist called (honestly) Jemima. I'd only met her once, and that was by accident; Gerry and I bumped into the pair of them at the bottom of Grafton Street one Sunday afternoon. We wound up going for coffee together, during which time I formed a very clear opinion of her – she was a stone-cold bitch. Rude, aggressive, gossipy, snobby, she ticked every box, some of them twice. I tried my best to be friendly, but she kept saying things like "People who don't vote shouldn't be allowed to have children". Eventually I gave up on the pleasantries and just stared right through her. Robert called me from his apartment that night and told me that he'd been mortified by the way I had "treated" her. The tone of voice he'd used on that occasion – wounded, yet high and mighty – was the one that greeted me when I answered my mobile in the office.

"Well, I hope you're happy now," he began.

"Hello, Robert," I said. "Are you all right? Has something happened?"

He snorted. "What, you can't guess? Go on. Have a go. Something that would make me miserable and make you happy."

There was something odd about his speech. It took me a moment to realise what was causing it. "Good God," I said. "Are you *drunk*? At this hour?"

He snorted again, less convincingly this time. "I was drunk last night, if that's what you mean."

My talentless hairdresser popped into my head again. I shooed her away. "Have you been to bed?"

"Never mind the questions. Are you going to guess or –"

"Just tell me, Robert, for Christ's sake, I'm not in the mood for games. I'm starting to get –"

"It's Jemima. She's fucking dumped me."

I didn't reply for a second, hoping the delay would make me sound appalled and saddened. "Oh. I'm sorry to hear that! When d–"

"Don't give me that. Don't give me *sorry*. You're only delighted. You're grinning down the phone. I can *hear* you."

I undoubtedly would have been grinning if it hadn't been for the headache that was already settling in and getting itself comfy. Still, I decided that I could deny all without feeling too guilty about it. "That's ridiculous," I said. "I'm not grinning. Not a bit of it. Why would I be?"

He made a noise like a cat choking on a pine cone. "Even if I was blind and deaf and stupid and hadn't worked it out for myself, I'd still know you hated Jemima because Chrissy told me so, all right? You can drop the act."

My jaw clenched. So did my fingers and toes. "Chrissy told you that I … *Chrissy*? What did she say, exactly?"

"She told me she hadn't spoken to you once in all the time I've been with Jemima, not *once* without you having a go. 'She's so rude, she's so nasty, she's such a tramp, she's too old for him', I heard it all and I just want you to know that I heard it all."

I replied without pausing to think things through. But even if I'd taken the rest of the morning to ponder it, I probably wouldn't have said anything different. "That's rich coming from Chrissy," I harrumphed. "You should have heard the names *she* called her!"

Quite apart from being a low-down, dirty thing to say about my own daughter, this statement hardly constituted a cast-iron rebuttal of his original point. Nevertheless, I was surprised and a little disappointed to hear Robert issuing a bored sigh. I'd expected a sharp intake of breath at the very least.

"Chrissy and Jemima got along fine," he said. "They used to meet up in town without me sometimes." He paused, letting it sink in. "She only joined in with your bitching because she didn't want to *argue*. You know what she's like. We used to laugh about it behind your back. We laugh about all sorts of things behind your back."

There was another pause. I was desperate to fill it, but I could barely remember what day it was. In recent years I had learned to expect all sorts of abuse from Robert. Given the things he said to my face, I could only imagine what he said about me behind my back. The idea that his sister might be joining in hit me like a punch in the stomach.

"I have to go," I whimpered. "I haven't got time for this."

"Yeah, sure. Mrs Busy-High-Flying-Executive. Hasn't a moment to spare. God knows what would happen to the insurance industry if you took a few minutes off from typing in people's names and add–"

I hung up. There's only so much a person can take, even from flesh and blood. Especially from flesh and blood.

Chrissy worked at a gym in Swords. She'd been there since she left school and she seemed to like it. Actually, she seemed to love it. She was as contented in her job as anyone I'd ever known. I'd always had a problem admitting that. I was all for my daughter being happy, of course I was. It was just that I could never remember looking down at her in her crib and thinking *What a beautiful little girl – one day, many years from now, fingers crossed, she'll get a job pulling strangers' hair out of a shower drain*. I'd met her boss a few times and he always went on and on about how great she was, how motivated, how focussed, how mature for someone barely out of her teens. It was all I could do to smile at him and mumble something like "That's my girl". Gerry had a minor problem with Chrissy's job too, but his was easily explained: he couldn't stand the thought of his daughter wearing a track-suit. If Gerry had had his way, women would have worn dresses and full make-up at all times, regardless of whether they were going out for dinner or digging up weeds in the back garden. It was like a phobia with him. If you sneaked up behind him and said the words "tomboy", he lost his breath and had to have a quiet sit-down somewhere.

"Mum!" Chrissy trilled when she answered her mobile. "I was just thinking about you. You know Linda, my old flat-mate? She was away for a few days and she got the exact same pair of –"

"I was talking to your brother," I said, not caring about the interruption.

"Did he tell you about Jemima? He rang me at three o'clock this morning, absolutely *polluted*. Good riddance, I say."

"Oh? Is that what you say? Good riddance?"

"Sorry?"

I swallowed. "That's what you think about all this, is it? Good riddance?"

"Are you all right, Mum? You sound a bit –"

"Because that's not what Robert says. He says you'll be

15

sorry to see her go. He says the pair of you are great pals."

There was a pause. "Why did he say that?" Chrissy asked then in a watery tone. It was a classic response to an awkward question: giving nothing away while at the same time sounding childlike and vulnerable.

"You tell me. Could it be because it's the truth?"

"Uh ..."

"I don't know what to say, Chrissy, I really don't. You've been letting me sit there week after week complaining about that horrible girl and then running to your brother to tell him all about it? I can't, I don't –"

"Mum, listen –"

"I know Robert hates me. I'm kind of used to it at this stage. But I thought we were all right, you and me."

"We are all right! Of course we are! And Robert doesn't hate you, he just, you know, he ... You and him ... It's a phase, that's all."

"A phase? It's been years!"

"Don't get upset, please, you're going to set me off ..."

She'd no sooner threatened it than she burst into tears. Her huge, heaving sobs sounded like something out of an opera.

"Oh, stop it!" I snapped, not meaning it to sound as angry as it came out. "I'm the one who's upset here, not you."

I heard a rustle and a thump, then another rustle, a sort of groan, another thump and finally a tremendous gulp. From previous experience, I knew that Chrissy got very physical when she was upset. I could easily picture her falling around the place, dropping the phone, righting herself, dropping the phone again.

"Are you all right?" I sighed, knowing the conversation had been flipped on me. "Chrissy?"

"I'm a terrible daughter!" she whined.

I forced my voice to sound pleasant. "No, you're not. Of course you're not. I was just surprised to hear it, I felt –"

"I have to go, I can't deal with this," she said and, just like that, hung up.

"Jesus *Christ*!" I hissed into the dead phone. Then I threw it into my bag and dropped my head into my waiting hands.

The pain was rapidly intensifying now. My mouth had gone bone dry and my limbs felt like they belonged to someone else, someone who hadn't been looking after them very well. After a few minutes of sitting as still as possible, I became aware of a figure standing behind me. I knew it was Jenny before I even turned around. Her arrival seemed like something that would happen, that was all.

"It's bad enough that you waltz in late *again*," she said as I turned around. "Is it too much to ask that you log in at some point and do some, oh, what's the word … work?"

You could stab her with a biro, a voice in my head declared. *Just stab her and run like hell. No one would mind. You might even get a reward.*

"I'm not feeling well," I said. "I've got one of my headaches. I'm going home."

Jenny's eyes narrowed. "Is that so? Well, before you run off … when can I put you down for the tardiness hat?"

It must have been around then that Gerry started fumbling with my neighbour's buttons and zips.

CHAPTER 3

Before I took up with Gerry, I'd only ever kissed two boys. I met both of them in Cleopatra's, which was by far the nicer of the two discos in Ashbourne in the early 1980s. It was popular with my crowd because we were all under-age and the bouncers there would let almost anyone in, provided they weren't actually sucking their thumb at the time. Kissee number one was called Rory. I'd never seen him before that night in Cleo's (as we called it), but every time I turned around, there he was. It didn't dawn on me that this was anything other than coincidence until I felt a tap, no a *poke*, on the shoulder during the second of the three slow sets. I spun on my heels. Rory frowned up at me – he was about four feet tall – and spat the single word "Dance?" I was sixteen then and had never been slow-danced before. I thought it was about time, so I said yes. We swayed around for a few minutes in stony silence until I found the courage to ask him his name. He supplied it, then asked mine. Before I had finished speaking, he suddenly got up on tip-toe and clamped his thin, dry lips over mine. It wasn't a pleasant experience, exactly, but it wasn't *foul* either. We danced on for another couple of minutes before I ran away to tell the girls. I never learned his second name and I never laid eyes on him again. I suppose I was in shock. It was almost romantic – almost, but not quite. Kissee number two came along a few weeks later. He was called Marty Byrne and he was my first real boyfriend; we were an item for almost the entire month of July 1983. Like Rory, Marty made his initial move during a slow set in Cleo's. Unlike Rory, he was capable of conversation, inasmuch as he had deeply held convictions about the relative merits of the local chippers, which he was all too keen to share. We had a little snog while dancing, then retired to a dark corner where he told me I was easily sexy enough to be in Bucks Fizz, maybe even Abba. That didn't age well as a compliment, but at the time I was firmly swept off my feet. Ours was most definitely a relationship of two halves. The first couple of weeks were great. We saw *Flashdance* together, went for walks in the park, made a couple of return trips to Cleo's (suddenly much more fun, now that I was part of a couple). Then he started going for my boobs. I had no real objection to being felt up, as such. It was just the way he went about it, all snarly and aggressive. He reminded me of nothing so much as a hungry dog that had spotted a dropped pork chop. I tried to explain that it was a question of manners more than anything else, but he wouldn't listen. Then, one quiet Sunday tea-time, he called me up and announced that he'd started seeing "someone a bit more maturer". A few days later I saw him hand in hand with Dolores Quinn, a notorious local bike (and shoplifter – she ended up in prison, I heard). The shock of being dumped was like nothing I'd ever known. "If it feels like this when the guy's an arsehole," I wailed at anyone who would listen, "what the hell's it like when you're *in love*?" That was it for me and romance, I decided – the risks were too great. I was never going to Cleo's again – ever! Ever, ever, ever!

Teenagers ...

Every small town has its Cool Guy, its Mr Hip-and-Trendy. All the girls are mad about him; all the boys say they want to beat the crap out of him, but really, they just want him to give them the time of day in the street. When I was growing up in Ashbourne, the Cool Guy was Andrew Healey, who was a few years older than us. His family was minted. Mr Healey owned a Ford dealership and Mrs Healey, who was Spanish, was rumoured to have come from *serious* money – private-yacht-type money. Andrew was tall and lean with the whitest teeth and the deepest tan that any of us had ever seen. He wore expensive clothes and drove a brand new car – admittedly a Ford Cortina – at great speed through the reddest of lights. And, yes, there's no denying it, he was a good-looking boy, something like a young Warren Beatty. But he wasn't the only game in town, not as far as I was concerned. The first time I spoke about it out loud, I was sitting in Caroline Drumm's bedroom, listening to records and flipping through *Smash Hits*. This would have been a few months after Marty had dumped me. We were back at school then, starting our final year. But Caroline was in no mood to talk about exams or the unemployment that undoubtedly lay on the other side of them. *The Arse On Andrew Healey*, that was her topic for the day. She'd been wittering on about it for at least half an hour – not for the first time, either – and must have noticed that I wasn't really listening. Did I happen to know, she slyly enquired, that people were talking about me? They'd noticed how quiet I'd become, how I seemed to have "lost interest". Some said I was going to wind up in a convent. Others said worse. The word "lesbian" was never mentioned, but when Caroline stared in my direction and asked if I fully understood what was so great about Andrew Healey's arse, I knew what she was getting at. (For some reason, rumours about possible lesbianism were very common in my crowd). Andrew's arse was fine, as arses went, I told her. But he wasn't my type. Too flashy. Too obvious. Caroline seemed personally offended. Who *did* I fancy then, she wanted to know, getting all intrigued. I hesitated at first; I didn't want to embarrass myself. There was one guy, I eventually explained. He was a bit older than us, older than Andrew even. And he wasn't exactly the pretty-boy type. Plus, he was kind of chunky. Caroline shrieked, bouncing on her bed. Who was it? *Who*? I bit my lip for a while, considering my options. Then I rolled my eyes and muttered the name: Gerry O'Connell. I honestly thought she'd laugh at me. I thought she'd laugh at me, then I would defend my crush, then we'd change the subject. We'd part on bad terms, with her thinking she had great gossip for the girls and me thinking I had much more sophisticated taste than they did. None of that happened. Instead, Caroline collapsed back on her duvet, pulled a pillow over her face and moaned like she'd just been stabbed. It was all very confusing for a moment. And then the penny dropped: she was agreeing with me. I couldn't believe it. When she finally recovered the power of speech, she provided a long and detailed assessment of Gerry's many qualities. He wasn't pretty-boy good-looking, no, but he was – she thought for a moment – *rugged*. I'd never heard that word applied to a man's looks before, but I knew immediately that it was the right one. And Gerry wasn't chunky, she went on, he was *big*, like a real man *should be*. Even his clothes were great. All he ever seemed to wear was jeans and a T-shirt but they always *fit just right*. And his hair! It was all choppy and peaky, like he cut it himself with a Stanley knife, but it was *so incredibly cool you could die on the spot*. The best thing about him, though, she said in a husky whisper, was the way he looked at you. If you caught his eye walking down the street, you didn't know whether he was going to laugh in your face or screw you senseless on the bonnet of the nearest car. Everything about this conversation had been shocking to me, but this last bit left me slack-jawed. None of my friends ever talked about getting screwed, senseless or otherwise. We talked about so-and-so being "a ride", sure, and Andrew Healey's arse, of course, got a regular airing. But by and large, when we talked about boys, we talked about the possibility or otherwise of *kissing* them. It wasn't all we thought about, no doubt – but it was all we talked about. I left Caroline's in a funny mood. It was nice, I supposed, in a giggly, gossipy, girly sort of way to hear that she had noticed Gerry (to say the least). But it also felt as if something that was mine and mine alone now had to be shared. I was dead right on that score. Caroline had apparently taken great comfort from our little chat and from that day forth, she started dropping Gerry's name into random conversations. Every time she did it, some other girl would mutter that, actually, to tell the truth, don't laugh, she thought he had "a certain something". It was so strange. They always thought they were the only one.

My return to Cleo's, which came just after my exams, was not exactly triumphant. I'd been back in the game, as such, for about a month before I got so much as a dance, and that was from a sort of anti-Gerry. He was tall (way too tall for a half-pint like me) and incredibly skinny. It was like putting your arms around a ladder. Worse still, he had the wispy beginnings of an ill-advised moustache and the tiniest eyes I've ever seen on a human being. None of that would have mattered – at least, it wouldn't have mattered as much – if he'd been fun to talk to. But he spent the entire three or four minutes of our relationship telling me about the time a few weeks previously when he got stung by a wasp. Apparently – and this was a point he was keen to emphasise – it had really hurt. There was a happy ending to the story, though – he'd squished the little bastard with a rolled-up *RTÉ Guide*. As he mumbled on and on, I realised that I had never been less attracted to anyone in my entire life. Several weeks later, when I saw Gerry standing by the bar, the first thought that popped into my head was this: *that one wouldn't tell you if he'd done battle with a frigging bear.*

I'd never seen him in Cleo's before – I assumed he'd started going during my leave of absence. He was with a bunch of his mates and, oddly enough, he wasn't looking his best. Nothing about his physical person had changed since the last time I'd spotted him (coming out of an off-licence, carrying a bottle of whiskey), but he looked … uncomfortable. Out of place. That didn't stop me staring, though, and while I was staring, it occurred to me that looking out of place in a dive like Cleopatra's was not necessarily a bad thing. One of the guys he was drinking with was a neighbour of ours named Brendan Hunt. For a brief period around the previous Christmas, he had been my sister's boyfriend. I wasn't quite sure why it had ended, but I doubted that it was anything Brendan had done. He'd always struck me as a decent enough sort of bloke. When he caught my eye, he visibly flinched, so I smiled to let him know there were no hard feelings. Then, to my surprise, he beckoned me over. We chit-chatted for a few minutes. Turned out it was one of their number's birthday. He'd insisted on going to Cleo's, to the horror of his friends, all of whom considered themselves above such things. Eventually, Brendan plucked up the nerve to ask about his ex. I was halfway through an elaborate lie about how Melissa had seemed a little down lately when Gerry appeared at his shoulder and asked him if he wanted a drink. Brendan declined. Gerry turned in my direction and looked me over, head to toe. What about me? Was I old enough to drink? I would be soon, I told him. Seven months later, we were married with twins on the way.

CHAPTER 4

If anyone had told me when I was eighteen that one day I'd be living in a house worth half a million euros, I would have said, "What the hell is a euro?" Then I would have said, "Wow". Sadly, half a million didn't buy you an awful lot of house, not in Ireland in 2006. Ours was a bog-standard – nice, but bog-standard – three-bedroom semi on the Dublin side of Ashbourne, County Meath. Its best feature was the kitchen, which was surprisingly large. Its worst feature was the bathroom, which was only just big enough to accommodate the bath, the loo, the sink and one thin person standing stiffly upright. The bathroom had only recently risen, or rather sunk, to the worst feature position; the previous champion had been our old windows. They were seriously grotty. The frames were half-rotten and a lot of the glass was splattered with paint. Two of the smaller panes were badly cracked and all of them seemed to be permanently dirty. We'd tried to make the best of a bad lot by hanging net curtains everywhere but had only succeeded in making the place look old-fashioned and shifty. I was beside myself with delight when I finally got PVC replacements in 2001. As soon as they were in, I practically danced round the house, ripping down the nets and proclaiming a bright new day. I did worry, at first, about the front room being exposed to the street, but given our location at the end of the last cul-de-sac in the estate, I decided it wouldn't be a serious issue. And it wasn't. Not for the first five years or so. Even then, I was the one doing the looking in.

My first reaction on catching my husband in the act of infidelity was to wave. In my defence, I didn't know that he was being unfaithful at the time. That information didn't arrive until approximately three quarters of a second later.

It went like this: my headache had advanced so rapidly and so dramatically that I'd thought better of driving myself home and had ordered a taxi. When I got out at the house, I barely noticed that Gerry's jeep was in the drive. He was supposed to be shooting a wedding in Kildare and I presumed it had been cancelled at the last minute. Such were the depths of my misery that I wasn't even excited by the prospect of finding out why. I'd only taken a few steps up the path when I saw him through the front-room window and waved; he didn't see me. At that point, my thought process went as follows: *There's Gerry. What's he at? He looks like he's*

running on the spot. No, wait – he's shagging Lisa from next door.
She was so far bent over the sofa that I couldn't see her face,
but there was no doubt that it was her; I would have
recognised that beautiful blonde hair anywhere, even when
it was hanging the wrong way. I didn't faint or scream or
throw up or simply run away. I didn't do anything. I just
stood there with my hand still raised in greeting. Gerry was
wearing a tie, which he sometimes did on a whim, and it had
found its way over his shoulder. That, coupled with the
expression of grim determination on his crimson face, made
him look as if he was tackling a potentially tricky bit of DIY.
His lips were moving as he thrust back and forth and I found
myself desperately wanting to know what he was saying. Was
it something like "That's right, take it all, you little slut!" or
was it more along the lines of "Oh Christ, I shouldn't be
doing this, poor Jackie would die if she knew"? It was
probably neither. In all the time I'd known him, Gerry had
never had much to say during sex apart from "Yeah … yeah
… yeah" and an occasional "JESUS!" After a few seconds, I
found myself shuffling, zombie-like, two steps forward and
then two to the left. Now I was standing right in front of the
window. I wasn't sure if I was trying to let them know that I
was there or simply positioning myself to get a better view.
Either way, Gerry still didn't see me (Lisa couldn't, of course,
not in that position). I opened and closed my mouth a few
times, but nothing came out. Then I took another step
forward and placed my hands against the glass. Gerry raised
his head, but his eyes were now shut tight. I guessed he was
in the home straight and that seemed to snap me out of it at

last. My throat, which felt as if had closed over completely, suddenly opened and a roar came belching out of me. I made fists and slammed them hard against the glass. Gerry jumped about a foot into the air, looked me right in the eye and then put both hands on top of his head, as if I was a cop with a gun. I was grateful for the fact that he didn't move to either side – at least I was spared the sight of his old man bobbing about like a fisherman's float. Lisa took a moment to get herself upright. When she finally succeeded, a series of looks passed across her face. I thought I understood what they meant. The first seemed to be mere embarrassment: someone had been watching her having sex. The second was definitely shock: the someone was me. The third was the one that made me want to get in there and slap her gorgeous face off. It wasn't a grin or even a smile, but there was a flicker of something that told me she wasn't entirely horrified by this turn of events. Maybe she was already imagining the anecdote she'd have to tell. Gerry ducked down behind the sofa at that point and reemerged doing up his trousers. He said something to Lisa and whatever it was, it wasn't a compliment. Her response was loud and angry, but I couldn't make it out through the glass. It occurred to me then that it was high time I stopped roaring and got in there, so I stepped back from the window and across to the front door. I was still fumbling for my key when Lisa came tearing out and brushed straight past me. My instinct was to run after her and make my first ever attempt at a rugby tackle, but she was halfway down the street before I'd even drawn breath. I stared at her back, unable to think of anything sufficiently awful to scream, until she disappeared round the corner. Then I went into the house to have a word with Gerry.

He wasn't in the front room, which surprised me; wherever he'd gone, he'd gone there very quickly. I stomped through to the kitchen, feeling like a stranger in my own house – a stranger on my own planet – and found it just as empty. Then I heard a noise coming from above. When I was halfway up the stairs, I realised that it was Gerry puking his guts up in the bathroom. He sounded like one of those new-style heavy-metal singers that Robert and I used to row about: "Rorrrrr … huhhh … rorrrrrr!". I paused, mid-step, then hurried on to the landing, just in time to catch him moving on to the dry heaves. Without planning to do so, I found myself lashing out and kicking the bathroom door. The shock caused Gerry, by the sound of it at least, to choke on a gawk. For a moment I thought I'd killed him. Then I heard movement and skipped on into our bedroom. I sat on the end of the bed and rubbed my hands over my face, trying to make myself feel something (apart from the nails in my head). The toilet flushed. Gerry appeared in the doorway a few seconds later.

"Jackie," he said. His voice was hoarse and broken.

I kept on rubbing my face.

"Jackie," he said again.

I managed a reply. "What?"

As dialogue went, it wasn't great.

Here it was, the most dramatic moment of our marriage and all we could manage was *Jackie?/What?*, as if we were parked on the sofa watching the telly. He stepped into the room and I shot him a look through my fingers. He stopped dead.

"Jackie, we have to talk about this."

I dropped my hands from my face and snorted. "What are you going to say? It wasn't what it looked like?"

"No. I wasn't going to say that. I was going to say ... I don't know what I was going to say." His chin dropped and his shoulders heaved. Gerry didn't cry when his beloved dog Buddy died. He didn't cry when his mother had her stroke and went into the home. He didn't cry when the home burned to the ground with her in it. He *did* cry when the twins were born, but I took the mickey about it so much afterwards that he practically stopped talking to me. So that made this only the second occasion on which I got to see my husband's tears. There wasn't much of a comfort to be had in that fact.

"I'm sorry," he sobbed. "It was just this once, *once*, I swear to God. It will never happen again. I don't even like her."

It took a moment, but I found my voice. "You cheated on me ... with someone you don't even fucking *like*?"

"Yes. I mean, no, I –"

"You looked pretty fond of her from where I was standing."

"Jackie, please, don't ... don't ..."

"Don't what? Give you a hard time about banging one of the neighbours?"

He broke down completely then, fell to his knees, the works. I watched him rocking back and forth for a while and then I got to my feet. Slowly and deliberately, I went to the wardrobe and hauled down the suitcase that had been perched on top of it since the previous summer.

"What are you doing?" Gerry croaked.

"I'm packing," I said. "What does it look like I'm doing?"

"Where are you going?"

I gave it some thought. It was a good question.

"I'm going away," I said.

There was a rhythm to all this that made me think his next question would be "Can I come?" But he didn't have a next question. He watched in silence (bar the odd sniff) as I got my stuff together, marched down the stairs and out the front door. If he'd looked out of the bedroom window, he would have seen me realising that I didn't have my car before sneaking back in to the hall table to nick the keys to his. Headache be damned, I was getting out of there as quickly as possible.

I didn't drive very far. Half a mile outside town I pulled in at a petrol station and yanked the handbrake so hard it made an alarming *twang*. As I sucked in some deep breaths, or tried to at least, I realised that I had no memories of the journey – none. The last thing I remembered was swiping Gerry's keys, and even that seemed distant and hazy, like a dream I'd had weeks ago.

I got out of the car and walked around the forecourt in a tight circle. All of a sudden I felt an overwhelming urge to smoke a cigarette. I hadn't had one for almost a decade (and it had been *hell* to quit), but I didn't even argue with myself. I turned and marched into the shop where I bought ten Silk Cut Blue and a lighter from a sour-faced teenager who barely looked up from his magazine as he completed the transaction. As soon as I was outside again, I tore open the packet and planted a fag between my lips. It felt like such an odd thing to do – but it felt good too. I lit the end and sucked hard. For two, maybe three seconds, all of my troubles receded; even my headache seemed to turn down a notch. I thought, *I can't believe I gave this up*, and meant it.

"Idiot," someone said.

I looked to my right. A fifty-something man with an extravagant beard was staring right through me as he filled his car with petrol. He looked like one of those Open University professors from seventies TV.

"Sorry?" I squeaked.

He shook his head as if he was genuinely saddened to see that people like me were walking about in broad daylight. "It's not a very good idea to smoke cigarettes at a petrol station, is it?" he said. He was having to speak quite loudly to make himself heard over the din of the pump.

I looked down at my smouldering ciggie. It looked back at me accusingly.

"You can read, can't you?" the man said, tossing his head around. "There are signs all over the place, especially for idiots like you."

This was an exaggeration, but I didn't feel like pointing that out. It was only about twenty minutes since I'd looked in through the front-room window. My brain was still bouncing around in my skull.

The bearded man stared at me for another few seconds and then muttered something under his breath. Next thing I knew, I was moving towards him. His eyes widened and he stepped from foot to foot, gearing up for whatever was coming next.

"What did you say?" I asked when I was still ten feet away.

The man stuck his chin in the air. He was trying to hang on to the role of sensible citizen, but I could tell that his confidence was heading south.

"Never mind," he said, in a voice considerably smaller than the one he'd been using up to that point.

I was beside him by then and I leaned against the side of his car, just to annoy him.

"No, go on," I said. "You mumbled some comment. Don't tell me you're too much of a coward to mumble it to my face."

He finished pumping and slotted the pump back into its holster.

"Never mind that," I said. "I asked you a question."

"Look, I'm just trying to fill the car up, I'm not trying to start anything, so why don't you just –"

"*No*. You *mumbled* something and I want to know what it *was*."

He shrugged and tutted.

I stepped closer still and took a huge drag on the cigarette. Then I threw it in the general direction of his petrol tank. It bounced off the car about an inch from the opening and rolled away across the ground. The man's entire body went into a spasm, as if someone had just hooked him up to the mains.

"What ..." he spluttered. "You stup . . . are you ..."

"Don't tell me what I can and can't do," I said slowly and quietly. "I'm having a very bad day."

He replaced his petrol cap and shook his woolly head at me. "You're a bloody nutter," he hissed. "You should be locked up!"

I sneered at him and started back towards my car. The realisation that I had indeed behaved like a complete moron hit me like a bucket of ice water. It was closely followed by the realisation that, while behaving like a complete moron, I could have killed us both. For a moment I thought I was going to have some sort of freak-out and would indeed end the day locked up. But the moment passed. I threw the remaining cigarettes into a bin, got in the car, and drove away.

CHAPTER 5

In the normal course of events, I would have headed straight to Nancy's. She had been my next-door neighbour but one in the first proper house that Gerry and I ever lived in. For a good few months, our only real contact was on the footpath outside our front gardens, where we would talk about the weather or the incredibly noisy family on the other side of the street. Gradually though, we started to infiltrate each other's kitchens and, more importantly, to have genuine conversations. Nancy scared me a little when I first got to know her properly. It wasn't just that she was more than a decade older than me – she seemed to have done so much with her life. Voluntary work in Africa, a couple of years in London, another couple in New York, even a brief stint in Tokyo. She'd worked, at various stages, as an air-hostess, a night-club manager, a fact-checker and a hand model (I didn't even know what the last two *were*). The only thing I had done that she hadn't was have kids, and even that was more to do with youthful carelessness than pluck. Her progress from neighbour to friend to best friend was so gentle that I almost didn't notice it. But in 1994, when she finally made good on her long-dangled threat to move the fifteen miles into Dublin, I cried for a fortnight. One of Nancy's best qualities, alongside her fearlessness, kindness, sense of humour and absolute refusal to take crap from anyone, was her ability to think clearly in a crisis. There were any number of examples – the time I somehow locked myself out of the house during a chip-pan fire, the time Robert sliced his hand open with the carpet knife, the time Chrissy drank a nice tall glass of fabric softener … Nancy was always on hand to talk sense and take action. On this occasion, however, she was firmly out of reach. She'd recently acquired a "toy-boy" (David was forty-nine to her fifty-two) and they'd gone to Paris for a few days. If I'd known the name of her hotel, I would have been on the phone – or possibly a plane – like a shot. Since I didn't know it, and since Nancy refused to carry a mobile, I had to think of something else.

Several options came to mind. I could have called my old pals Cathy and Helen or my current next-door-but-one neighbour Mags (a sort of Nancy-Lite, perfectly reliable in her own way). I could even have sprung Veronica from work. But I did none of these things. Another idea occurred to me.

Right throughout my childhood, Melissa was a world-class

big sister. She joined in all of my little doll tea-parties and accompanied me on my many fairy-finding – or at least fairy-hunting – trips into the woods behind our house. When my friends complained about their monstrous elder siblings, with their practical jokes and their cruel comments, I could only look at the floor and count myself lucky. (I sometimes wondered if Melissa treated me so well because we weren't actually sisters at all. We certainly didn't look anything alike. Her hair was dark, mine was either dirty, sandy or mousey blonde, depending on who you asked. I was sallow-skinned, she was pale as a stone. She towered over me, always. And then there was the wild disparity in our body shapes. I was a robust little girl, sometimes verging on the plump. Melissa was a bean-pole when she was a *baby*.) Her finest moment, without doubt, came when I was six and she was nine. At the time my mother had a small collection of porcelain figurines, which *on no account* – that was her constant refrain – were we ever to touch or, if we could help it, look directly at. I broke this golden rule on one occasion only and, of course, managed to drop (and decapitate) the six-inch-high Edwardian lady that I had decided was my new best friend. The feeling that swept over me was a potpourri of unpleasantness. It contained not just fear and panic, although both were well represented; there was a kind of self-loathing in there too, a sense of having done something that was so awful as to verge on outright evil. Melissa discovered me in my bedroom with the Edwardian lady's body in one hand and her pretty little head in the other. Naturally enough, I was having a nervous breakdown (a very quiet one – Mum was in the kitchen directly below). Melissa listened, hugged, listened again and finally planted a kiss on the crown of my head. Everything would be all right, she assured me, before taking the broken pieces and calmly walking out. I assumed that she was going to march into the kitchen and take the blame, and was filled with gratitude and awe. But Melissa had a better plan. She did something that would never have occurred to me – she walked to the end of the street and dumped the Edwardian lady in a builder's skip. Later that night, she asked me a very good question: when was the last time I had seen Mum actually looking at any of her figurines? I admitted that I didn't think I'd *ever* seen her looking at them. Mum didn't collect figurines so she could look at them, Melissa explained. She collected them so she could have something that was hers and hers alone, nothing to do with us or Dad. The whole point of them was that no one was allowed to touch them. That was what they were *for*. She'd never notice that one was missing, not in a million years. I was stunned by this display of insight. And Mum never did notice. All that was left was my debt to my sister, a debt that she never called in.

Relations between us remained good right throughout our teenage years. We argued about little things, of course – who had used the last of the conditioner, who had ruined a particular T-shirt – but by and large we stayed pretty close. Things turned sour, for a while at least, when I became pregnant with the twins. I wasn't surprised to find that Mum and Dad were horrified. They were old-school Catholics, apart from anything else, and not so keen on the old premarital – not to mention teenage – sex. But I expected a certain level of support from Melissa – more than none, I mean. She was at university then, studying law, and her principle concern seemed to be that I would never be able to "advance", as she called it, with a couple of babies in tow. When I reminded her of my mediocre Leaving Certificate results and pointed out that the advancement ship had sailed, as I frequently did, she clammed up and gave me a look of unbearable disappointment. Her attitude to Gerry, on the few occasions when she could bring herself to meet him, ranged from frosty to openly hostile (Mum and Dad, at least, gave him points for sticking around and declaring his intention to marry me as soon as I turned eighteen). There was a time, in fact, when I was sure that our relationship had been trashed beyond repair. Then the twins were born and the thaw set in. When Melissa saw that the barrier to my advancement, the awful burden that had caused her so much concern, was a beautiful little boy with twinkly blue eyes and a gorgeous little girl with the chubbiest cheeks this side of Louis Armstrong, she seemed to forget what her point had been. Our relationship got back to normal and stayed that way until we were both well into our thirties. Then, on the night of November 29th, 2002, my parents drove into Dublin to visit Melissa and her husband, Colm. Melissa was pregnant for the first (and last) time and was feeling highly gregarious. I'd been invited over there myself every couple of days for the past several weeks and, on every occasion, had solemnly done the duty that was expected of me – smiling shyly, placing my hand on her expanding middle and declaring her "blooming" and/or "glowing". Mum and Dad brought a small gift on this particular occasion, a book of baby names. Melissa and Colm already had at least three of these – two of their own and another that I gave them – and my parents knew that. It was all they could think of, my mother confessed on the phone (during our final conversation). The gift went down a treat, Colm told me later – it was thicker than its three predecessors combined – as did the home-made pavlova that accompanied it. Even my father seemed to enjoy himself, which was something of a wonder; he was invariably uncomfortable in social situations, even those involving family. The last cup of tea was knocked back at about eleven and my parents set off for home. They were about three miles away from their destination when an oncoming van decided to overtake on a corner. The driver of the vehicle that he was trying to pass later classified the manoeuvre as "suicidal". It was all that, and homicidal too. In the inevitable head-on, Dad was killed instantly. Mum died at the scene, shortly after the ambulance arrived. The van driver made it to hospital, but he too died within a couple of hours.

I suppose any pair of bereaved siblings might have found something to fight about in the debris of such a loss. But with Melissa and me, there was an extra edge. About a month before the accident, I'd had the house to myself for once, so I decided to curl up with a *Marie-Claire* and a small glass of wine. One small glass became two, then three, then certainly four and possibly five. I'd had most of a bottle, at any rate, when I noticed the DVD that Robert had rented the night before sitting on the mantelpiece. If I'd told him once that afternoon, I'd told him six times that I was sick of paying his fines at Xtravision and still he had once again failed to leave his movie back. I tried to tell myself that this time I wasn't going to play ball. But I knew that it was pointless. Robert would be quite happy to enter into a battle of wills because he knew that the longer it went on, the bigger the fine that would be owed, and I was the one who would have to pay it. I did have a moment of doubt as I snatched my car keys from the coffee table. *You've had a glass or two of wine*, I said to myself. But the follow-up thought came quickly: *So you'll have to drive very, very carefully*. And I did. I left the movie back, having done a pretty neat job of parking in a tight spot, and headed for home, congratulating myself on my achievement. I was halfway down the main street when the door of a parked car swung all the way open right in front of me. The thing to do, of course, was to stand on the brakes. Instead, I swerved to my right, at which point I remembered – *oh yeah* – that there was traffic on that side of the road. I swerved back and caught the open door with my left wing; *then* I hit the brakes. The owner of the parked car went nuts at once and then nuttier still when I criticised his over-enthusiastic door-opening technique. He called the Guards, who chatted to me quite amiably for a couple of minutes, then breathalysed me and pronounced me over the limit. Long story short, I wound up in court and received a three-month ban, which I thoroughly deserved. I didn't tell the kids about it; I was too ashamed. We only had one car at the time and it was easy enough to think of excuses for me to stay out of it. I faked a (recurring) stomach bug that kept me house-bound for almost a month and when that finally went away, I pretended to be on a health kick; I bought new trainers and walked everywhere, glancing excitedly at the pedometer that was permanently clipped to my waist. In all probability, I could have got away without telling Melissa either. I confessed the truth to her, no doubt, because of the guilt; I wanted someone (other than Gerry, who was furious) to give me a right telling off. And Melissa certainly did. "You could have run over a child," she pointed out (stroking her tummy), as if I hadn't already thought of that. "Just so you could save a few quid on *The Mask of Zorro*." Her anger only lasted for that first conversation, however. Next time we spoke, she made no mention of my "lapse", as she had called it. She might never have mentioned it again, in fact, if it hadn't been for one unfortunate detail: the van driver who killed our parents turned out to have been plastered at the time. It was Melissa who heard it first. She passed the information on to me in an even, colourless tone. She didn't come right out and say it, but as far as I was concerned, she didn't need to. The message was clear enough: I could mourn my parents all I wanted, but I had no right to complain about the man who killed them. Not with my record.

It would have helped a lot – obviously – if one of us had said something to bring it all out into the open. But we didn't. We just sat back and let things fester between us. In the days following the double funeral, I would sometimes catch her looking at me out of the corner of her eye. I never swivelled round and asked, "What?". I knew *what?* As time went on, the dirty looks became less of regular occurrence and then disappeared entirely. Nevertheless, the damage had been done. We called each other less frequently and, even when we did, we seemed to run out of conversation within minutes. Then Melissa stopped calling me at all. Feeling rejected and small, I cut back even more on my own calls. Before long, we were speaking no more than once a month. I slowly came to accept that it would take quite a while before we were back on track. But I didn't think we were talking about years.

The bottom line is this: when I decided to call on Melissa that Friday the 13th, I didn't do it because I thought it would help me. I did it because I thought it would help *us*.

Melissa and Colm lived in Dublin – Ranelagh to be precise. Even if we'd been on proper speaking terms, I don't think I would have visited their house very often. It was just too depressingly beautiful. And huge – the sort of place you pass and think "Now who the hell lives *there*?" As it was, I'd only been over maybe half a dozen times. It had been quite a while since the last occasion, which was my excuse for driving straight past the front door on this one. After I'd hastily reversed and parked, I took a moment to compose myself. My number one concern (apart from my headache and the obvious) was that Niall, Melissa's three-year-old, would be having one of his episodes. He had been a late arrival, but the joy his parents experienced at his birth had quickly been replaced by anxiety, frustration and exhaustion. Niall was one of those babies who got *everything*. Jaundice, measles, impetigo, whooping cough; it was like he had *The Big Book of Baby Illnesses* and was working his way through it, ticking them off as he went. I think it was harder on Colm than it was on Melissa – it didn't seem right, somehow, that a consultant cardiologist should be the father of such a perfect poster-child for ill-health. The last time I had spoken to Melissa, about a month previously, she'd reported that Niall was currently quite healthy by his standards, being host to nothing more than a low-grade flu, but that his physical state was no longer the main concern. "He's gone nuts" was the way she put it. I tried to reassure her that all toddlers have tantrums. She interrupted and sneered that, no offence, I didn't know what the hell I was talking about. A tantrum was whinging and maybe rolling around a bit. When the mood took him – and it frequently did – Niall was given to outright hooliganism. He'd demolished toys and eaten picture books. He'd painted carpets and superglued locks. He'd savaged every curtain in the house with a pair of scissors that neither Melissa nor Colm had ever seen before. He'd smashed innumerable pieces of crockery and ruined several pieces of consumer electronics, some of them by throwing them through windows. Taken on their own merits, these would have been instances of bad behaviour. What raised them to the level of "episodes", apparently, was the way the child screamed throughout. It was like "a cross between a dentist's drill and a horny cat," according to Melissa. On one occasion, during a standard room-wreck, he'd screamed so loudly and for so long that he'd lost his voice for two days, only to resume screaming – and room-wrecking – as soon as he got it back. She blurted all of this out in a rush and seemed to immediately regret doing so. Nevertheless, the information had lodged in my brain. Our conversation was going to be weird enough, I thought, without that kind of thing going on in the background. With a sigh so heavy it was really more of a groan, I climbed out of the car and crunched up the gravel path to Melissa's door. Not wanting to ruin my surprise, I left my suitcase in the boot.

"*Jackie*?" she said when she answered my ring.

I made a stab at a smile. "You sound like you're not sure."

"I didn't expect to see you, that's all. You've had your hair done. It's … nice." She still hadn't opened the door more than a crack.

I thought I'd better force the issue.

"Um … can I come in?"

Melissa didn't seem at all embarrassed. She stepped back and created just enough room for me to squeeze through.

"So," she said flatly. "What brings you here?"

CHAPTER 6

I told Melissa my story at the kitchen table. Niall sat on the floor by her feet, gamely beating an old stuffed rabbit with a rubber hammer. The constant squeaks were more than a little bit off-putting, but at least they weren't screams.

I didn't want to jump right in at the good bit (as such), so I started with my headache. That was a mistake; Melissa seemed to assume that there would be nothing more to it and kept interrupting with pointless work and head-related questions. Eventually, I had to give up and skip past the preliminaries. The big moment, when it came, was less solemn than I would have liked. As soon as I had whispered the words "over the back of the sofa", Niall gave his rabbit an extra-hard thump and it was that squeak, rather than my shocking revelation, that seemed to echo round the room.

Melissa put her hand over her mouth, took it away, put it back, took it away again. I hadn't expected her to leap from her chair and gather me in a warm embrace, but I'd hoped for some sort of physical contact. There was none. On the plus side, she did, at last, start to pay proper attention.

When I finished speaking, she fiddled with her teaspoon for a moment, then said, "Jesus Christ".

"Yeah," I said. "Exactly – Jesus Christ."

"Jesus CHRIST!" said Niall.

Melissa nodded down at him then returned her gaze to me, shaking her head slowly and empathically. "I don't know what to say."

"Me neither," I replied.

"It's hard to believe."

"Believe it."

"*Lisa*. What's she like?"

"You know what? I just realised I don't even know her second name. She moved in not long after Christmas with a friend of hers. Paula. They're renting. They've kept to themselves. I don't know what they do for a living or anything. But I wouldn't be surprised to hear that Lisa's a model."

"A looker."

"Yes. She is. She sure is. Blonde, but classy blonde, you know? Mid, late-twenties. Legs up to her ears. Slim. Big green eyes. Lovely skin. Always dressed to kill. Looks like she rolls out of bed in the morning with her make-up already done."

"Stop it. You're making me sick."

"I'm making *you* sick? How do you think *I* feel about it?"

"Sorry. Go on."

"She's always had the hots for Gerry, I can tell you that much."

"How do you know?"

"I just —"

At that point Niall farted so violently that he almost levitated. He didn't seem to notice and carried on hammering his rabbit.

"Excuse *you*," Melissa said with a hint of pride. "Sorry, Jackie, he's been chuffing away like that all day. Must have been something he ate. Probably a wallet or a phone."

It wasn't a topic I was keen to explore. I hurried on. "I just knew she fancied him, right from the off. First time we ever met her was on the day she moved in. She knocked on the door, introduced herself and asked if I had any 'big strapping men' lying around to help her get her TV out of the car. I was all friendly, the way you are, said I had a big man lying around, but I couldn't vouch for his strappingness. So I called Gerry out off the sofa and when he appeared at the front door, she practically licked her lips. And you know what she said to him? Christ, when I think about it. She said, 'Your wife doesn't think you're strapping, did you know that?' Looking out from under her fringe like Princess frigging Di."

"What did Gerry say?"

"He didn't say anything, he didn't know what the hell she was talking about. Every time I met her after that, she always used to say, 'How's Gerry, still as strapping as ever, is he?' It was like a running joke. We had a barbeque in the summer. All the neighbours were there, Chrissy and Robert – not that Robert stayed long – and she stuck her head in. She was at it then too. Strapping this, strapping that. I can't believe I used to go along with it."

"Well, why did you? If you thought it was proof that she fancied him …"

"What was I supposed to say? 'Oi, you, stop calling my husband strapping!' And besides …"

"What?"

"Well … lots of women fancy Gerry. I see them all the time, on the street, in shops. Their eyes follow him when he goes past. They think I don't notice them, but I do. I've always noticed them. I'm kinda used to it at this stage. I'm sure Posh Spice gets something similar."

Melissa pulled a face. She looked as if she had something to say. When she shrugged and muttered "Suppose so" I knew that wasn't it.

We sat in silence (bar the squeaking) for a few moments.

"Anyway," I said then. "This suitcase that I packed … I was hoping I might be able to unpack it here. For tonight, at least." I tried not to feel hurt – and certainly not to show it – when Melissa's brow furrowed.

In fairness to her, she recovered quickly. "Of course," she said, then remembered to smile. "Yeah, of course you can stay here, there's a room lying free. But …"

"What?"

"Well … have you got a plan? What are you going to *do*?"

Slowly, I pushed my shoulders towards my ears. "The only plan I've made so far is to get net curtains put up again."

Melissa pulled another face.

"What is it?" I said.

"Nothing."

"No, what?"

"Nothing, honestly."

She was clearly lying, but I didn't pursue it.

"So," she went on. "Is Lisa Gerry's ... I mean, are they having an affair or what?"

"He says not. He says it was just once. He says never again."

"Do you believe him?"

I shrugged again. There was a silence.

And then, better late than never, she reached across the table and, briefly, rested her hand on mine. "It's a terrible thing," she said.

For the first time since I'd arrived – for the first time in years – I heard sisterly concern in her voice. There wasn't a lot of it, but it was there. It was a start. I thought of that bit in *The Weakest Link* where the contestant opts out, protecting their gains to date: *Bank*.

"My head's not getting any better," I said. "Would it be all right if I had lie-down for a while?"

"Oh," Melissa said, surprised. I'd only been there for ten minutes. "Oh, right. I'll show you to your room."

Niall thumped his rabbit again. "DEAD!" he declared with real delight.

"Good boy!" said Melissa.

* * *

I had wanted a lie-down because I felt weak and sick. It was nothing to do with tiredness; headaches and sleep didn't go together, not in my experience anyhow. And yet I was dead to the world within a few minutes of collapsing on Melissa's guest bed. I just shut down, like a computer that was trying to open too many documents at the same time.

Normally, my dreams were highly abstract. I woke up most mornings trying to guess the significance of the giant talking toothbrush or wondering who the old man with the spider's legs was supposed to be. But on this occasion, I had one that was fairly self-explanatory. I was sitting behind a desk in a tiny office, not much bigger than a cupboard. A succession of women trooped in and sat opposite me, their faces inches from mine, and explained how Gerry had given them the greatest sexual experience of their lives. A few of them were famous. Sharon Stone was there, for example. She told me that Gerry had "nailed" her up against a wall behind Tesco. When I woke up, I was astonished to find, firstly, that I'd been asleep at all, and secondly, that I'd been asleep for hours; it was almost seven o'clock. My headache hadn't cleared completely, but it had lost most of its teeth. I went to the bathroom to give myself a bit of a wash and tidy-up, then tiptoed down the stairs. I found Melissa in the kitchen, methodically chopping a courgette.

"Oh, you're up and about," she said. "How do you feel now?"

"Much better," I replied. "Can't believe I slept."

"Colm's home from the hospital. He's in the living room playing with Niall. Why don't you go on through? Dinner will be a while yet."

"Okay … eh …"

"What?"

"Does Colm know? About Gerry?"

"Well, yes. I had to tell him, I couldn't –"

"No, that's fine. Just asking."

"I didn't want –"

"It's fine, really. I would have told him if you hadn't."

"Okay."

"Okay then."

We looked at each other uncertainly. Then I took off in the direction of the living room.

Physically, at least, I'd always thought that Colm was Melissa's exact opposite. Where she was tall and willowy, he was short and, not to put too fine a point on it, dumpy. Even their faces seemed to have gone out of their way to provide contrast. Melissa's natural expression was serious, melancholy even. Colm's default setting was sunny and open. If he'd been an actor, he would have been type-cast as a rosy-cheeked butcher, always ready with a smile and a joke as he handed over the sausages. When I walked into the sitting room that day and got my first look at him in months, I almost choked on my own tongue.

"Colm!" I gasped. "You've lost weight!" I was pretty pleased with myself for having come up with this description of what had happened to him. What I really felt like saying was: *Colm! Are you in the final stages of a terminal disease?*

He sprang to his feet and hugged me hard. Then he withdrew from the hug and held me by my shoulders in a let's-have-a-look-at-you sort of way. "Jackie O … how are you?"

"I'm okay, Colm."

He leaned in and whispered. "I heard what happened. I'm so sorry."

"Yeah. Cheers."

"We'll talk later. If you want to, I mean. You don't have to."

"Don't WHISPER!" Niall yelled from his position six inches in front of the TV. Then he spun round and glared at us, as if to emphasise that he wasn't joking.

"Niall's watching a DVD," Colm said brightly. "Aren't you, son? Tell Auntie Jackie what it is."

The boy's shoulders drooped. "It's a DVD."

Colm tried again. "Yes, but which –"

"SPONGEBOB, SPONGEBOB, SPONGEBOB! IT'S SPONGEBOB!"

"All right," his dad said. "Calm down." He looked at me and shrugged, embarrassed.

I smiled to let him know that there was no need.

For the next twenty minutes or so, we watched the cartoon, more or less in silence.

I amused myself by trying to guess the value of the artwork on their walls. Since I knew less than nothing about art, it was kind of pointless. I based my estimate on the fact that they had real art – canvasses that someone had arted all over – as opposed to cheap prints from Roches Stores (like ours). The figure I eventually came up with was: a lot. Stuck for something to say out loud, I was eventually reduced to mentioning Colm's weight loss again. He smiled ruefully and nodded towards Niall. I took that to mean that it was stress-related, and not something of which he was particularly proud.

When the DVD finished, Colm leaped from his chair and scooped Niall up into his arms.

"Right, sunshine," he said, "let's get you into a bath and a bed. Kiss your Auntie Jackie goodnight." He swept his wriggling cargo down toward my face.

I braced myself for a punch or a head-butt, neither of which arrived.

"GoodNIGHT!" Niall yelled and planted a smacker on my cheek.

"Sleep well," I said. "Don't let the bed-bugs bite."

His face fell. As his father carried him from view, he said, "Bugs?"

CHAPTER 7

Dinner was weird. It was if I had just happened to drop in on my way past. We talked about the weather (the weather!), Melissa's impending return to the legal profession, property prices (of course), Ant and Dec, the many problems associated with hiring tradesmen, good spots for a weekend break, the late John Paul II, Jade Goody, weirdo patients of Colm's, Bono, Michael Flatley and the fact that none of us knew anyone who used cocaine, even though the papers kept telling us that practically everyone was at it. There were a couple of occasions when I almost mentioned Gerry myself, just to shatter the strangeness. Melissa was more open towards me than usual, but that wasn't saying much. The barrier between us was still there, like a pane of glass, a discreet but effective blockage.

We were halfway through dessert when the phone rang. I knew it was Gerry, somehow, even before Melissa returned from the kitchen and told me so.

"You don't have to talk to him," she said. "Not if you don't feel like it."

"Exactly," Colm chipped in. "Maybe you should let him stew for a while. He knows you're safe. Tomorrow's another –"

"No," I said, getting up. "No, I'll talk to him."

In the kitchen I found the phone sitting on its end by the knife block. It seemed to be gently pulsing, as if it was a living, breathing, quite possibly dangerous animal. I picked it up and wet my lips.

"Yes," I said. It seemed a better bet than "Hello".

There was nothing on the other end for a moment. Then I heard heavy breathing. It sounded perilously close to … heavy breathing.

"Jackie," he said eventually.

"Yes."

"Jackie … I've been ringing around for the past hour."

"Really."

"Melissa was last on my list."

"What do you want?"

He took a deep breath. "I want you to come home."

"No."

"Jackie, we have to have a … conversation."

"Do we? And what do we have to say?"

Another deep breath. "I know I've hurt you."

"Do you?"

"Jackie, *please*. I'm sorry. I'm lost here, I don't know

56

what to say. All I've got is *sorry*."

I manufactured a pause. "Not much, is it?"

"No. It isn't. I know it isn't. That's why I want to see you. I want us to talk about it properly, face to face, so I can –"

"No, Gerry. Just ... no, all right?"

There was silence for a few seconds. Then he said, "But you believe me, don't you? You believe me that it was just once, just one stupid, ridiculous mistake?"

I didn't want to get drawn into specifics – I was much more comfortable with the short rhetorical questions and general fobbing-off. But this, I felt, was something that needed an answer. "Why should I? She's been flirting with you for months, don't deny it. *Months*."

"She –"

"And you were supposed to be shooting a wedding this morning. What, do you expect me to believe that it got cancelled at the last minute so you had to come home and then you happened to bump into Lisa and things got out of hand? You expect me to believe that instead of the other explanation – that there never was a wedding and you and her were, basically, on a fucking *date*?"

"Yes. That's exactly what I expect you to believe. You got my message, didn't you?"

"What message?"

"On your mobile. I rang you this morning, but it was engaged, so I left a message. The wedding *was* cancelled. The groom's mother had a coronary in the middle of the night. She died."

I felt the ground shift beneath me, just a little. "No. I didn't get any message."

"Please, check your ph–"

"It hardly makes much difference, does it? So the wedding was cancelled. Gave you a chance to slip in a quickie with your girlfriend, didn't it? An unexpected treat."

"That's not how it was. I swear on the kids' lives."

"Don't you dare!" I howled. "Don't you *dare* swear on the kids' lives! Not about this. Not about anything. But definitely not about *this*."

"Jackie, I –"

"Goodbye."

I hung up, dearly wishing it was an old-fashioned phone that I could slam home into its cradle. Jabbing the button with my thumb just wasn't the same.

I could tell as soon as I walked into the dining room that Melissa and Colm had heard me raise my voice. It was the way they looked at me – nervously, afraid, no doubt, that I was about to break down all over them.

"Are you okay?" Melissa asked.

I retook my seat. "I'm fine."

"How was it?"

"It was … Excuse me a second."

I got up again and out to the hall table, where I had dropped my handbag earlier. Sure enough, I had eight missed calls, all from Gerry. The last seven were recent. The first was from that morning. He must have called when I was talking to Robert or Chrissy. I dialled my message service as I walked back to the kitchen.

"*Hi, it's me,*" Gerry said. "*Unbelievable – the wedding's off. The best man's just after calling me, in bits. The groom's mother took a heart attack and died in the middle of the night. Imagine that, the poor bastard. Anyway – I'm heading back to the house for a while, but I'll be in the studio this afternoon if you're looking for me. All right then. See ya. Don't work too hard. As if.*"

I put the phone down on the counter and returned to the dining room, where we did a re-run of my previous entrance.

"Are you okay?" Melissa asked again.

"I'm fine."

"Do you want to talk about it?"

I shrugged and sat down. "There's not much to talk about. He's sorry."

"I would think so," Colm said, then tucked in his chin and sheepishly sat back. "Not my place to say, but ... you know."

"He's still swearing it was just the once."

Melissa's top lip twitched. "And do you believe him?"

I shrugged. "I thought the whole wedding cancellation thing was bullshit. But it turns out he left me a message this morning. Telling me that he was on his way home. The groom's mother died, so they called it off."

"Big deal," Melissa said. "Still doesn't mean it was a one-night stand. One-morning stand, whatever."

"I know," I said. "I told him that."

"And – *and* – even if it was, what difference would that make?"

"I know that, Melissa. I said as much to him myself."

"And?"

"And nothing. He wants me to come home. That's why he called."

"What did you say?" Colm asked.

"I said no. Which doesn't mean I'll be under your feet for the next six months, don't worry. Three at the most."

Colm's eyebrows did a little dance. "Wow."

"Wow what?"

"No, nothing, just … you're holding up so well. Making little funnies and everything. I'd be a mess in your position."

Melissa gently slapped the table and said, "*Yes.*"

I gave her a look.

"You were doing it this afternoon too," she said. "Cracking jokes about curtains and Posh Spice."

At least now I had an explanation for her earlier bout of face-pulling. "Maybe that's just my way of coping," I said.

"Maybe," she allowed. "But Jackie … you haven't even cried."

She meant that I hadn't cried since arriving in her house. What she didn't know and what I had just realised was that I hadn't cried *at all*. I searched back through the day, looking for a tearful memory that I knew I wouldn't find. Nope. Nothing.

"It's the shock," I said weakly. "That's what it is. Shock."

Melissa cocked her head quickly to the side, a gesture that seemed to say, *That's one possible explanation, sure, but it's not the right one.*

"Tell me how you feel about it," she said. "The whole thing."

I gawped at her. "Tell you how I feel about it? What kind of a question is that? I just caught my husband –"

"Yes, I know you did. But, apart from the jokes, all you've

60

had to say about it is that your neighbour's really good-looking and so is Gerry."

My eyes narrowed. "What are you getting at?"

"Never mind. Forget it. Tell me –"

"No, go on. You might as well. You've come this far."

She sighed. "All right then. All right. It sounds to me like you think he's got, I don't know … an excuse. For doing what he did."

I snorted. "That's ridiculous. What do you mean, an excuse?"

"You've always had an inferiority complex about him, Jackie. About Gerry. You can't deny it."

"I don't even know what that's supposed to mean."

"You don't think you deserve him. You've never thought you deserved him, right from the start. Do you know how many times you've told me about catching other women looking at him? Over the years? When you said it this afternoon, did you really think that was the first time?"

"Women *do* look at him," I fumed. "All the time."

"You're doing it again! Who cares how many women look at him? It wouldn't make any difference if the whole country was sending him their underwear in the post! It still wouldn't give him the right to take his pick from the neighbours, now would it?"

I pushed my plate away from me, then pulled it back. "I don't know what you want me to say."

"I'm just saying it's not healthy, that's all. It's not healthy to think your husband's bound to land on someone else sooner or later, that it's inevitable. You know how you look, how you sound? *Relieved*."

My heart almost stopped. "Listen," I said through my teeth, "I've never been in this position before. I don't know how I'm supposed to behave, I don't know what I should be doing to satisfy everybody's *expectations*. But I'm plenty upset, believe me."

"Of course you are," Colm said with a sideways look at his wife. "No one's saying otherwise."

But Melissa didn't give up so easily. "Colm, how many times have you heard Jackie going on about how other women give Gerry the eye?"

"You're like a dog with a bone!" I said. "Let it go, for God's sake!"

Melissa said, "Let him answer."

Colm looked deeply uncomfortable, like a child who'd been called upon to rat out his friend. "Well, Jackie ... I have heard you saying that quite a few times. It's –"

"There you go," Melissa interrupted.

I glared at her. "There I go what?"

"You know what. You're not reacting properly –"

"*Properly*! My God!"

"– because you've got this inferiority complex. When it comes to Gerry. We've discussed it before, haven't we, Colm?"

It was probably my imagination but I thought I saw beads of sweat appearing on his forehead, just like that.

"I, eh ... yes," he said. "I suppose so. It has come up once or twice."

I shook my head. "And what? You were waiting for the right opportunity to come along so you could tell me what you think? Then it's not all bad news today. At least you got to tell me where I've been going wrong my whole life. Brilliant."

"Come on, Jackie," Melissa said, as if I was the one being unreasonable, "don't be like that. You're a good-looking woman. You always were and you still are."

"Gee, thanks. What's next? 'There's plenty more fish in the sea'?"

"That's not what I mean. You have no reason to feel inferior, that's what I'm getting at. Tell her, Colm."

He moved his lips but seemed to have lost the power of speech.

"Go on," I said. "You might as well join in."

"Maybe 'inferiority complex' is the wrong term," he said tentatively. "But I can see how, maybe, in the past, you might have felt some, I don't know … Look, I'm no expert –"

"Oh, spit it out, Colm! Jesus!"

He cleared his throat. "I can see how you, possibly, along the way, might have felt some … guilt. Maybe that's what's going on here."

My limbs took off in four different directions. "*What*?"

Ignoring me, Melissa patted Colm on the arm and said, "Yes, but the guilt is what's causing the inferiority complex. The two go hand in hand."

"What are you *talking* about?" I screeched.

Colm's head swayed from side to side. "Maybe 'guilt' is the wrong term –"

"Look," I said. "Pick a term, any bloody term, and just tell me what the hell you're getting at!"

"All right. When you met Gerry, from what Melissa tells me, he was considered quite the catch. He's still a seriously good-looking man – I mean, you're a good-looking woman, Melissa's right. And I'm sure you were lovely back then, don't get me wrong."

My eyes narrowed. "Just say whatever it is that you're going to say."

"Well … you got pregnant very quickly after you started going out."

"And?"

"Is it possible that maybe you felt … somehow …"

Melissa stepped in, her patience suddenly gone. "That you'd trapped him."

I'd thought the inferiority theory had been bad enough. This was something else. "That *I'd* trapped *him*?" I said. "I didn't get pregnant on my own, you know!"

"Of course not!" she said, all energy now, as if we were finally getting somewhere. "We're not saying that you did trap him, we're saying that may have been the way you felt. Maybe that's still the way you feel. Which is why you're not particularly bothered that he's screwing around. You don't think you have the right to be."

"I am bothered," I said slowly. "I'm very fucking bothered. And you know what else? I'm tired. It's been a long day. I'm going to get my case from the car and hit the sack."

Melissa turned away.

"Listen, Jackie …" Colm began.

"No, it's all right. Don't worry about it. I'm knackered, honestly."

"Let me get your stuff for –"

"Thanks, but I'd rather get it myself. I could do with the oxygen."

I got up and walked away, horribly conscious of the sound of my footsteps on the wooden floor. It seemed to take me about half an hour to get out of the house. I didn't take a single breath along the way. Outside, it was surprisingly warm for the time of day – *alarmingly* warm, if Al Gore was anything to go by. A couple of teenage girls were sitting on the wall next door to Melissa's. As I passed, I heard one of them saying that she couldn't wait for the party the following night. It was going to be both "wicked" and "banging". Her friend responded with at least as much enthusiasm. Their hoots and giggles followed me across the street, mocking me and my age and my clothes and my hairstyle. When I reached the car, I walked straight past it. I had no plan to go anywhere in particular – I was just glad to be putting one foot in front of the other. A couple of minutes later, I found myself outside a shop on the main road. The decision to go inside and buy cigarettes didn't seem to come from my own brain. It was if it had been taken elsewhere and then relayed to me; not so much a personal choice as an instruction from on high. I was at the counter before I gave it a thought. The thought was *Phew – thank God you brought your purse on this random, not-going-anywhere-in-particular walk.*

"Ten Silk Cut blue, please," I said to the girl.

There was a magazine rack to my left. My eye was caught by a publication called *Your Story*. Although it featured a

number of intriguing headlines: "*Haunted By My Own Dog!*";
"*Boozy Surgeon Ruined My Nose!*" The one that really sucked
me in was this: "*My Cheating Husband Will Never Stray Again!*"
I grabbed the mag and offered it for scanning.

"Six-forty altogether," the assistant said.

Peering into my purse, I realised that I had no notes.
When I fished around for change, I came up with six euros
and forty cents exactly. I took it as a sign from God that he
wanted me to inhale poisons and read crap. He had his
reasons, no doubt.

Back at the house, I stuck my head into the living room
and apologised for taking so long. Melissa nodded and then
went back to her book.

Colm said, "That's okay. Did you go for a stroll?"

"Yeah," I said. "Just a wee one. Clear the head. You
know."

"Fair enough."

"I'm off to bed then."

"Right so. Goodnight."

"Night."

Melissa closed her book with some force and looked at me
properly. "Sleep well," she said thinly.

"I'll try," I told her. "See you in the morning."

Upstairs, I flaked out on the bed and opened *Your Story*.
The cheating husband piece was by "Brenda", a woman
from Manchester who'd found a pair of furry handcuffs in
the glove box of her old man's car. She knew he wasn't
using them on her, so she confronted him. He confessed to
an affair, at which point she decided "*to teach him a lesson he*

would never forget!" (Almost every sentence ended with an exclamation mark.) Brenda's solution to her problem was to e-mail everyone on her husband's rugby team to let them know that furry handcuffs were nothing compared to some of the gizmos and get-ups he'd employed in the *marital* bedroom. "Your pal's favourite game of all," she revealed in her final paragraph, "is to play naughty schoolgirl and strict headmaster – with him as the schoolgirl!" The plan, if you could call it that, worked like a charm. The husband became a laughing stock among his friends (who forwarded the mail to everyone they knew) and wound up *"so depressed he can barely leave the house, let alone find a new mistress!"* Brenda seemed to think this was a great victory, but I wasn't so sure. She hadn't done anything to ease her own pain, had she? All she'd done was hurt her husband, which was both easy and, in the grand scheme of things, pointless.

I tossed the magazine to the other side of the room and rolled over onto my back. What was Gerry up to now, I wondered? On those rare occasions when I went out alone for the evening, I usually came back to find him sprawled across the sofa in front of an action movie, covered in a thin layer of Pringle crumbs. Tonight would be very different. He wouldn't be seizing the opportunity to revert to teenagerhood; he was more likely to be curled up in a little ball, cursing himself and wishing he was dead. At least, I presumed he was. There was always the possibility that he was next door, tearing Lisa's clothes off with his teeth. But I found that unlikely.

The simple truth was this: I believed him. I believed him when he said it was a one-off, and I believed him when he said it would never happen again. It was entirely possible for a spouse to have sex with someone else as a sort of mistake, and then never do it again.

I knew that for a fact, because I had done it myself.

CHAPTER 8

When 2002 gave way to 2003, I dared to hope that the calendar change might do wonders for my state of mind. Although my parents' accident was still horribly recent, at least now it was something that had happened "last year". But there was no improvement. I was still a zombie, slouching silently from room to room, crying more often than not. I hadn't slept for more than a couple of hours at a stretch since the accident and was stupefied by even the simplest of everyday tasks. There had been several occasions when I had been reduced to a quivering heap on the kitchen floor by the sight of a pile of ironing. Even my beloved cooking had lost all appeal; for the first time in their lives, the kids came home not to long-since perfected favourites or to bold new experiments but to boil-in-the-bag curries, oven-ready chips, frozen pizzas. Gerry was worried, and repeatedly told me so. He thought I should "talk to someone", meaning a counsellor or a psychologist. Every time he brought it up, I just shook my head and shuffled out of his sight. Talking couldn't possibly help. Nothing could. My sole consolation was that this, surely, was my allocation of misery for the next couple of decades. There would be no more bad news for a long time. There couldn't possibly be; it would be *unfair*.

And then, one crisp January day, Chrissy came through the front door in tears. The tears were not so unusual in themselves – she'd been known to come in crying because it was cold out. When I asked her what was wrong this time, she buried her head in her hands and sobbed so hard that I couldn't make out what she was saying. She'd bumped into someone or other who'd told her something or other. Gradually, I realised that she was talking about Jonathon Mullen. Then I heard the words "brain tumour" and I joined her in the sobbing. Jonathon was an eight-year-old neighbour of ours. He was quite possibly the sweetest child I'd ever met in my life. I don't think I would have liked him so much if he'd been physically cute; the effect might have been overpowering. But he had buck teeth and a big nose, and I had never seen him without a little green river snaking its way down his top lip; it was like his trademark. He was obsessed with toy cars. Most little boys like them, of course, but Jonathon was something else. He had literally hundreds, which he used to line up on the footpath outside his house, as if he was some miniature Arthur Daley. If you expressed even the tiniest bit of interest, he'd bend your ear for half an hour, holding one of his fleet in the palm of his hand and telling you all about its real-world counterpart.

"This is a Ferrari F50, Mrs O'Connell," he said to me one day. "It has a four-point-seven-litre engine and a top speed of two hundred and two miles an hour. They only ever made three hundred and forty-nine. Everyone goes on about how cool they are in the magazines. But I think they're butt-fugly."

He kicked a football into our front garden one summer's evening and took out a rampant sunflower which was far and away the most successful plant I'd ever had. I found out about this tragedy, and who was behind it, because Jonathon immediately rang the doorbell and owned up. He stood on the front step with his football under his arm, slowly shaking his head as he shifted from foot to foot. "I'm very sorry, Mrs O'Connell," he said solemnly. "I really liked that flower myself. It always looked like it was smiling."

It's stupid and wrong to think that one particular child deserves to get a brain tumour less than another, but still … that was exactly what I thought at the time.

Jonathon's dad was a tall, whip-thin forty-something called Tony. He'd been our neighbour for about two years. Gerry and I knew three things about him: he worked for Bank of Ireland, he'd moved around the country a lot, and he was a widower. His wife – we didn't even know her name at that point – had died of liver cancer when Jonathon was just a toddler. If we'd known him a little better, no doubt we'd have found it easier to call over and express our sympathies on this, the latest tragedy to befall him. As it was, it took us a couple of days to gather the courage. When we did finally manage it, we found him understandably pole-axed. He made tea and produced biscuits, as if we'd dropped by to see his holiday snaps but seemed unable to meet our eyes. His son was sound asleep upstairs. He was going to have an operation in a few days' time, but the doctors had said there was no point in admitting him before then. When Tony told us that, I could tell by his expression that he'd taken it to mean "He might as well spend a few nice days at home, just in case they're his last". Gerry and I asked banal questions and received horrifying answers. On his discovery of the problem, for example: Jonathon had been playing on his PlayStation a few weeks previously when he suddenly threw the controller across the floor. It was unlike him and Tony asked him why he was being so bad-tempered. There was something wrong with the game, he said, or the TV – sometimes he could see two of everything.

I found it difficult to ask about Jonathon's chances of survival, not just because I didn't want to hear the answer – although I didn't – but because I couldn't think of the right way to phrase the question. Eventually I settled on "Is the surgeon confident?" It was hard to tell, Tony explained; the guy was so relentlessly cheerful and positive that you wanted to grab him by the lapels and shake him. He certainly said he was confident – repeatedly. But that was little comfort.

We stayed for about half an hour and left feeling as if we had made things worse with our hopeless clichés and watery smiles. "If there's anything we can do ..." We said that at least six times, knowing full well there was absolutely nothing and it was at best pointless and at worst deeply irritating to keep asking.

Jonathon's operation came and went. It was a success, of sorts. Ninety-five percent of the tumour was removed, but ninety-five percent wasn't good enough; he needed radiation treatment to take care of the rest. Tony seemed to find this news even harder to take than the original blow. He'd been stressed to the point of breaking by the operation, but now he fell into a state of deep depression. I had started to call over every couple of days, usually without Gerry, and I saw him deteriorate right before my eyes. While his physical decline was dramatic and obvious, the thing that really worried me was the way he gradually lost the ability to hold a conversation. He wasn't just being quiet. When you spoke to him, he would nod or shake his head and his lips would move in silence, as if he understood the general concept but couldn't quite remember how to take part. He broke down one night and told me in short, stuttering sentences that he'd had several violent rages during which he'd smashed about half of his crockery and every mirror in the house. His cousin, Maria, who looked after Jonathon when Tony was at work, had seen the damage and had told him to wise up. They'd fallen out over it and now he felt more alone than ever. I reached across the table and patted the back of his hand, wishing I had this Maria character within throttling range. Once again, there was nothing I could say that might actually help. But he seemed to appreciate the contact.

As the weeks dragged by, I found myself investing more of myself in Jonathon's health than I would have thought possible. Every time I visited him in hospital, I came away cursing God and his mysterious bloody ways. When I saw my own children, I hugged them until they could stand it no more and wriggled away, complaining. One Friday night I called over and found Tony off his face on whiskey. He made no attempt to keep himself together in front of me. As I ran through my usual list of hopeless offers – to Hoover the house, do the laundry, scrub the bathroom, bring yet another lasagna – he gradually curled up into a ball on the sofa and then cried for a solid hour. I sat down beside him and … and nothing, actually. I just sat there, listening to his wails and gulps and periodically rubbing his back. When eventually I got up to leave, he grabbed my sleeve and told me in a matter-of-fact manner that he had no plan to go on living if Jonathon died. My mouth fell open. I started to protest, but he put his finger to his lips and shushed me. It'd be easy, he said. No body. No fuss. He'd just leave the house one day and he wouldn't come back. Then his face creased up and he pulled me closer. I wasn't allowed to tell anyone, was that understood? It was to be our little secret.

I got away from him as quickly as I could and ran home to Gerry. He had no doubts. "The authorities" – whoever they were – would have to be informed. How would I feel if the worst happened and he followed through on his threat? The man needed help. I knew he was right, of course, and yet I hesitated. There was still a good chance, according to the doctors, that Jonathon would pull through. And even if he didn't, there was no way to be sure that Tony would actually do anything. He'd been *very* drunk when he said it. Gerry was furious at me and said that if I didn't tell someone, then he would. We argued about it constantly. He became increasingly angry as time wore on, but I came to realise that his own threat had been an empty one; he had no intention of telling anyone. Without ever making a firm decision to do so, I wound up keeping my mouth shut. I saw Tony as frequently as ever during that period, but never found a way to ask him if he'd meant what he'd said. Quite apart from anything else, I got the distinct impression that he didn't remember saying it. I convinced myself that by bringing the subject up, I might only succeed in planting an idea that he'd never seriously considered.

And then, slowly but surely, the news from the hospital began to turn positive. The "ifs" and "buts" that had peppered every doctor's report gradually dropped away and the word "remission" was spoken out loud. Tony seemed unable to believe it and didn't show any real signs of relief until he was given a firm date for Jonathon's discharge. The day before the big event, he called at my front door. He looked like a different man, as if he'd been suffering from a demonic possession and had just had a very successful session with an exorcist. I made tea and we sat down at the kitchen table. It was the first conversation we'd ever had in which it was okay to laugh, and we did. He told me that Jonathon had *demanded* a welcome home party and had specified that the venture should be undertaken with an attitude of "Money is no objective". Tony had already been planning one, of course, but had made a great show of pretending that he wasn't keen on the idea. Jonathon went spare when he heard his dad's protestations about being broke and having no time to get things organised and ended up calling him a "complete bastard". Hadn't he noticed that his son had nearly died? *Hellooo?* What the hell was wrong with him? My smiles and giggles gradually faded as Tony related this story, and he noticed. Did I think he had been cruel? Not so. I had to understand something – he'd been sure that he would never get the chance to tease the boy again; that it would be all hand-holding and anything-you-wants until he finally slipped away. This wasn't cruelty; it was *normality*. He teared up when he said this and I found that it was contagious. Before long, the pair of us were bent double over the kitchen table. Then Tony got up and came around to my side. He leaned over me and put his arm around my shoulder. I'd been his best friend in these last few months, did I know that? Even though he had no family – no brothers or sisters, no parents, no wife – he'd felt supported and that was down, almost single-handedly, to me. He wanted to thank me, from the bottom of his heart. I had never heard anyone use that phrase before. It should have sounded corny. But it didn't. I told him he was perfectly welcome – cried it more than said it. And then he kissed me on the forehead, the way you might kiss an infant. I cried on, as did he. It was only when he leaned closer still and kissed me on the cheek that I realised what was going on. I turned my face towards him and he kissed me on the mouth. Then I was on my feet with my arms around his skinny frame. Without a word, we walked down the hall and up the stairs, where we did the things that I had only ever done with my husband. At the time, my only conscious thought was that life was fragile and brief. My parents were dead. Tony's parents were dead. His wife was dead. His son had just scraped through. Yes, it was sympathy sex. But it was myself I was feeling sorry for.

Jonathon came home from hospital next day. He had his party. I attended, with Gerry, who gave me a hard time throughout – after all the effort I'd put in, you'd think I'd be a bit *cheerier* now that the boy was home. Tony made a little speech. He singled me out for thanks and everyone applauded. I did a little bow and said it was nothing really – the real hero was Jonathon, who'd been so brave, so uncomplaining. The attention was deflected and stayed deflected. Tony and I had no time alone at the party; we were never alone again, in fact. I think that was deliberate, on both our parts. A few months after Jonathon came home, Tony called to our house one night and told us he had some news. A job had come up in the bank. It would be a sideways move, really, but he liked the sound of it and he felt he needed a new start. In short, he was off to Galway within a matter of weeks. And that was that. Our infidelity was just like Tony's suicide threat. It happened, but was never acknowledged afterwards. Despite promises to the contrary, he never made contact once he'd moved away. The house went up for sale and was bought by a man from Westmeath, who had a dozen more just like it. He rented it to a friendly Nigerian couple for a few of years, but they quickly established themselves well enough to buy a place of their own. The house went into the papers again and soon attracted new tenants. One was called Paula and one was called Lisa.

It's a funny old world.

CHAPTER 9

When I woke up on Saturday morning, I found that I had a little movie running constantly in my head – Gerry and Lisa, hard at it. I hadn't given the act itself a great deal of thought up to that point, but now it was everywhere I looked (especially on the inside of my eyelids). Worse still, my mental movie was shockingly vivid. I could see every detail, from every angle. I could hear everything too, the groans and slurps, the coos and rustles. When I emerged from Melissa's super-duper shower (which almost knocked me off my feet), I sat on the edge of bed and waited for the tears to come. They didn't. Every time I began to get upset, a new movie started up, one with similar themes but different characters; I had a starring role.

It wasn't long before I gave up and went downstairs.

I found Melissa alone in the kitchen, drinking coffee and flipping through a magazine.

"Morning," I said.

She glanced in my direction. "Hi. Just brewed up. What would you like for breakfast?"

"I'm not really hungry. I'll get a cup of –"

"I'll get it."

"No, you stay where you are, I'll do it."

"Are you –"

"Sit, sit."

I got the coffee and took a stool across the island from hers.

"How did you sleep?" she asked after a moment.

"Not very well. But okay, considering. I got a few hours."

I could tell that she hadn't really listened to my answer.

She pushed the magazine away and drew a deep breath. "I wanted to say I'm sorry," she said. "About last night."

"Oh. Right. Well, I'm sorry too."

"You've got nothing to be sorry about, Jackie. You came here after what, I'm sure, must have been one of the worst experiences of your life and I let you down."

"No, you were –"

"I should have been more sensitive. I should have just *listened*. 'Relieved' – Jesus. I can't believe I said that. I … apologise."

The word seemed to stick in her throat a little, but she got it out in the end. I gave my response a moment's thought. The right thing to say, of course, was that she hadn't entirely misread the signs, she'd just come up with the wrong explanation, that was all. But I didn't say the right thing. I said,

"Apology accepted" in the most magnanimous tone I could fake on short notice. Melissa nodded and I nodded back.

"Where's Colm?" I asked, hoping to move the conversation along to other things.

"He took Niall out to Killiney for a tramp along the beach. They'll be hours."

"God, it's years since I was out there. Does he go –"

I was interrupted by the sound of La Cucaracha coming from my mobile; I had a text. The phone was closer to Melissa than me. She slid it across the counter. The message was from Gerry. As usual, it was all caps. It read: *CAN I HAVE THE JEEP BACK PLS? I NEED IT!*

"Look," I said and passed the phone back.

Her face tightened as she read. "What do you make of that?" she said.

A thought occurred: I had no chance of making any progress, reconciliation-wise, until Melissa ditched her *Jackie's-not-that-bothered* theory. Here was my chance to kill it stone dead.

"His jeep," I said softly. "That's all he cares about. His bloody *jeep*."

"Don't get all annoyed," Melissa said. "It's not worth it."

I got off my stool and gritted my teeth. "I'm going to pop out," I said. "Do you mind? I've got something to do."

"What is it?" she said. "What are you going to do?"

I didn't answer until I was halfway down the hall. "I'm going to give him most of his jeep back."

It took me the best part of an hour to fight my way across to First Premier. I ran through a number of possible options as I drove and was satisfied, by the time I swiped my way into the car park, that I had settled on the best of them. I'd expected the place to be deserted on a Saturday, but there were a few cars dotted around the place. Overworked managers of one kind or another, I guessed; I couldn't imagine that any mere grunts like myself had popped in to enter a little extra data.

I went past my own car and parked in a space by a pillar. Then I got out and walked around for a minute or two, making sure there was no one watching. My breathing had become very shallow and my hands were shaking. Once I was sure that I was alone, I got back into the jeep and started the engine. On a sudden whim, I turned on the radio. Kate Bush was tinkling her way into "Wuthering Heights", one of my favourites. I stuck the gear into reverse and edged back out of my space. After taking one last look around, I turned the wheel to the right and rolled away – backwards. I was still in reverse. A small groan escaped me. As I moved off again, forwards this time, I found it surprisingly difficult to keep the wheel turned right. The (not very big) part of my brain that dealt with driving was screaming that this was all wrong. But I persisted. The first contact between the side of the jeep and the pillar was so jarring that I immediately stepped on the brake. I took a moment to collect myself and then tried again. The noise was incredible; it sounded like the *Titanic* going down. When the pillar reached the rear wheel arch, I reversed out of the space and drove into the one to my right. I found it easier to do the passenger side, possibly because it was further away and possibly because I was getting used to being in a vehicle that was very slowly crashing. When I'd finished and straightened the jeep up in its space, I took my hands off the wheel and just sat there, waiting for the end of the song. Kate seemed to stay out on those wild and windy moors for ages, but eventually the time came for me to get out and inspect the damage. The word for it, I realised as I covered my hand with my mouth, was "significant". I'd imagined a pair of nice clean scrapes, but the thing looked as if it had just been squeezed between two oncoming trucks. I walked around it three times on increasingly wobbly legs. It was going to cost a fortune to fix. But then again, I told myself, that was the whole point. And besides, there was no going back now. What was done was done. I bent down and deposited the keys on the ground inside the right front tyre.

"Jackie?"

I froze. The voice was familiar, but I didn't immediately attach a face. I got to my feet and turned around. Eddie from the office was standing not twenty feet away. He was looking at me the way you might look at someone who was naked and waving a sword around.

"Are you okay?" he asked.

I smiled as broadly as I could, a move which, judging by the way he flinched, alarmed him even more. "I'm fine, Eddie. How, eh … how are you?"

"I'm fine too, thank you. Um … you know you just … had a little accident? Two of them, really."

I nodded and briefly showed him my palms as if to say, *What are you gonna do?*

He stepped closer, but not too close. "You're absolutely sure you're all right?"

"Oh yes," I nodded and did the too-broad smile again. My mind raced on ahead of me. There didn't seem to be anything sensible I could say. I decided to just stand there smiling and nodding until he went away.

"I don't want to interfere," Eddie said then. "It's none of my business ..."

I did a bit more nodding.

"But I've been here for a while." He pointed his thumb behind him to the First Premier entrance. "I was in the office and I came down and I, eh ... saw you. Having your accidents."

"How come you're in work on a Saturday?" I asked. It was a ridiculous thing to say, of course, but I was pleased with how reasonable I managed to make it sound.

Eddie went up on his toes. "Me? I was just ..." He half-turned and pointed to the door again. "Y'know."

Oh-hoh, I thought. *He's up to something.* I didn't particularly care what it was, but I knew an opportunity for diversion when I saw one.

"Sounds very mysterious, Eddie." I looked at the bag he was carrying over his shoulder. "Don't tell me you were stealing stationery?"

"Stationery? No! No. I wasn't stealing stationery. I wasn't stealing *anything*."

"Are you sure?"

He nodded with great solemnity, as if I'd just asked him if he was sure he wasn't a serial killer. "Positive."

"I see. So you don't want to tell me what you're doing here on a Saturday?"

This was a shameful attempt to take advantage of Eddie's shyness. I thought he would be so disturbed by my probing into his personal affairs that he would back away from the conversation, quite possibly literally. But he didn't.

He put his chin in the air and said, "What about you? Do you want to tell me why you're deliberately driving someone else's car into a pillar?"

"It isn't someone else's car," I lied, pathetically. "It's my car."

"No, it isn't," Eddie said. "That's your car over there." He pointed to my Micra. There was a tiny pause during which I considered telling him he was mistaken. I stopped myself just before I made the small leap from pathetic to contemptible.

"It's almost my car, all right? It's my husband's, if you must know, so there's no need to call the cops or anything."

"I wasn't going to call the cops."

"Good."

He looked at me with both eyebrows raised, waiting for more information. When I stayed quiet, he flat out asked me for it. It was unlike Eddie to be so bold and I could tell that it took a lot out of him.

"How come you're wrecking your husband's car?" he said, then exhaled at length.

I thought, *To foster good relations with my sister, why do you think?* "I'd prefer not to get into it."

"Okay. Fair enough."

He capitulated so easily that I felt obliged to throw him a bone. "He upset me, that's all. Badly."

"Oh. It must have been something pretty serious."

"Yup. It was."

"Don't tell me you caught him kissing another woman …"

This, I could tell, was an attempt to add some levity. But I was unable to keep my expression neutral.

"Oh no!" Eddie said, eyes bulging. "No! He kissed someone else!"

Kissed? I thought. What planet was he on? "Eddie, please, I really don't –"

"But how could he? How could he do that to you?"

"Eddie –"

"That's disgraceful! Really, that's beyond – Are you all right? Stupid question, good man, Eddie, of course you're not all right."

"I'm fine."

"No, you're not, you're out wrecking cars. Which is understandable! You've had a terrible blow. God love you. It's just … I don't know …"

He was as exercised as I'd ever seen him. I felt like I was the one who should be doing the comforting.

"How did you find out?" he asked and then immediately raised a hand. "No, sorry. Don't answer that. I should mind my own. Nothing to do with me."

"Do you really want to know?" I asked. It was a rhetorical question, just something to say. Eddie took it seriously. He rubbed a finger across his chin, deep in thought. "Yes," he said, after an age. "Yes, I do want to know."

I went back on my heels. "Oh. You do."

"If you want to tell me, I mean. It's up to you. But I'm a

very good listener. I've had a lot of compliments on my listening. Well, a few ..."

I thought about it. Eddie was virtually a stranger. There was nothing to be gained by telling him, it seemed. But I felt a strong compulsion to justify my actions.

"All right then," I said. "When I went home from work yesterday –"

"Oh! I meant to ask. How is your headache? Jenny told me about it. Are you okay now?" He looked genuinely concerned.

"I'm fine now," I said. "When I went –"

"My cousin gets migraines. She has to sit in the dark all day with –"

"Eddie! Jesus! Do you want to hear this or not?"

"Sorry. Sorry. Tell me."

"When I arrived home yesterday I caught my husband ..." I hesitated.

"Caught him doing what?" he asked softly.

I stared at him. "Can't you finish the thought on your own?" I croaked.

"Kissing another woman?"

"No, not kissing another woman. Screwing one."

"Sex," he nodded ruefully.

"Yes, Eddie, sex. In my own front room."

"Jesus. You'd think he would have at least gone to a hotel or round to her place."

I began to think that Eddie's reputation as a listener was ill-deserved. "Yeah, you'd think that all right. But they didn't bother."

He became lost in thought again. "How are you supposed to just sit there in future watching the telly or doing a Sudoku? Knowing that's the very room –"

"All right, Eddie, that's enough."

"Sorry, sorry. Do you know her, this fancy-woman?"

"This what?"

"Fancy-woman."

"I heard you, I just … Yes, I know her. A little bit. She's our next-door neighbour."

This last nugget of information was too much for him. He put one hand on his hip and shook his head as if he'd never heard anything quite so shocking in his life. And maybe he hadn't. We stood there for a moment in silence.

Then Eddie said, "What are you going to do?"

I shrugged. "I don't know."

"But you're definitely leaving him, aren't you?"

"Christ, Eddie, I haven't really thought about it."

A look of pure confusion overran his face. "But … he took a vow."

I reached into my bag for my cigarettes. "Sorry?"

"When you got married. He took a solemn vow not to, you know …" He made a gesture that I couldn't decipher. "You know … not to go around … having sexual … with your neighbours."

We both did, I thought, as I struck up the lighter. "That's true, Eddie. But marriage is complicated."

He looked me right in the eye. "No, it isn't," he said.

And I just lost it.

CHAPTER 10

Twenty minutes later, we were sitting at the table by the window in Franco's, the tiny café across the road from First Premier. As soon as it became clear that I wasn't going to stop crying any time soon, Eddie had more or less dragged me along there. Anybody else might have thought that privacy was the order of the day, but not Eddie. He insisted that "a nice cup of tea" was the only thing that could sort me out. He must have said it half a dozen times. And it was never "tea" or "a cup of tea", always "a nice cup of tea". I failed to see the benefit at the time but had to admit that my tears dried up as soon as I sat down on the ancient, creaky chair. The tea itself seemed incidental to the cure, but I was glad of that too.

"Do you know how many cups of tea my mother used to

drink in a day?" Eddie asked once we were settled.

I shook my head.

"Have a guess," he said.

"I haven't got a clue."

"If you had to guess, though."

"Twenty."

He looked crestfallen. "Oh. Yes. That's right. Twenty."

"Sorry," I said. "I should have started with a small number and worked my way up. Kinda ruined your story."

His face brightened. "It was hardly a story. Yeah. Twenty cups of tea a day. I mean, that's an average. She didn't keep count or anything. Still – twenty! She was never off the toilet."

I trekked back through my recent memories and wondered how my decision to wreck my husband's car had led me to this, listening to a grown man telling me how often his mother urinated.

"Understandable," I said and hoped the subject was closed.

"My father was a different kettle of fish, now. You couldn't have got a cup of tea down that man's neck if your life depended on it."

"A coffee drinker," I sighed.

"No. Ribena. Gallons of it. His teeth were always purple."

I groped around for a sensible response. Eventually I came up with: "Ribena's nice."

"It's all right," Eddie allowed.

"Are your parents still alive?" I asked.

He shook his head. "No. Dead as dodos, the pair of them. My mother died ages ago. 1983. Dad died in 1999. Which was a pity, because he was really looking forward to the millennium."

"Was he religious?"

"Sorry?"

"The millennium. Lots of religious people thought Jesus was coming back."

"Oh. Right. Not my dad. He just liked fireworks. He really wanted to see the big display in town. His last words were 'Fireworks'. Last word, really, I suppose."

I searched his face for clues that he was joking. There were none. Not only was he not joking, he didn't seem to realise that there was anything funny about what he'd said.

"I'm sorry to hear that," I said. "I lost my parents too. Both at once. A car crash."

"That's awful," Eddie said. "Still – nice and quick."

I shot him a look, but he didn't seem to notice.

"That can't have been any fun for you," he said then.

"No. It wasn't. I don't want to talk about it. I shouldn't have mentioned it."

"Sometimes it helps to t–"

"*No*. I don't want to, all right?"

I'd lost my temper. That happened a lot when the subject of my parents came up. I was about to apologise but Eddie didn't give me a chance.

"Mine took forever to go," he said. "You don't want that, believe me. It's exhausting. And, don't get me wrong, very hard, emotionally and all. But mostly it's exhausting."

He'd taken off his jacket when we arrived. I had found myself looking at the T-shirt he was wearing underneath and suddenly realised why: it was the first time I'd seen him without his navy-blue woollen tie.

For the want of something better say, I mentioned it. "No tie today, Eddie?"

He looked down at his T-shirt, which had presumably been black at one point and was now mid-grey, at best. "No tie?" he said, puzzled. "Sure it's Saturday."

"I know. But you don't have to wear a tie Monday to Friday. You still do. Every day."

"You don't like my tie," he said. It was a statement, not a question.

"It's not that," I said, afraid that I'd hurt his feelings. "I'm just saying. Most men don't like wearing a tie unless they absolutely have to."

Eddie rolled one of his shoulders. "It's an office. I think you should make a bit of an effort when you work in an office." He paused, but not for long. "Why don't you like my tie?"

"I *do* like it," I insisted. "I just wondered …"

"What?"

"How come you wear the same one all the time?"

He frowned. "You've really got it in for my tie …"

"No, honestly. I'm sorry, forget I said anything."

For the next thirty seconds, he stirred his tea in silence, gazing down at it along the length of his nose. I got the impression he was preparing to say something significant and for one terrible moment was sure it was going to be something about a childhood sweetheart after all. In the end, he stopped stirring and said, "I like it, that's all. It goes with everything."

"Of course it does," I said, relieved. "It's a *lovely* tie. I really wasn't trying to –"

"Ah, I know you weren't, Jackie. I'm a bit sensitive sometimes. Don't mind me. Anyway – the main thing is, you've stopped crying."

"Yeah. Thanks for … you know. Looking after me."

"No problem. I still can't believe it. What he did. Your husband."

"Me neither."

"He must want his head examined. Fooling around on *you*."

I raised my cup to my face and hid behind it for as long as I thought plausible. When I dared to look out, I saw that Eddie was gritting his teeth, his eyes half-closed. He was clearly regretting that last contribution. The best way forward, I decided, was to change the subject as quickly as possible.

"What about you?" I said. "You never married?"

"Me? No."

That apparently, was the end of that. But his previous comment was still hanging over us. I tried a second change of subject. "So – are you going to tell me what you were doing in the office on a Saturday?"

His eyes flitted down towards his bag. He seemed to realise his mistake and immediately snapped his head around in the direction of the till.

"What's in the bag, Eddie?" I asked.

"Nothing," he said. "Nothing at all."

"Come on. I told you my thing." This seemed to carry a lot of weight with him. While he wrestled with his dilemma,

I pressed home my advantage. "Whatever it is, it can't be as big a deal as mine, can it?"

His tongue emerged to moisten his lips. "It's nothing," he said again.

"I'm intrigued now," I told him. It was the truth.

"Nothing," Eddie repeated a third time.

"Okay. If you don't want to tell me ..."

He made a gentle smacking noise with his lips, as if he was beckoning a kitten. I stayed silent, guessing that he was now considering telling me his terrible secret but wouldn't appreciate being pushed into it. Nothing was said for a minute or more. If I'd been with anyone else, I would have found the silence highly embarrassing. But with Eddie, somehow, it didn't seem so bad. By the time he spoke again, I'd drifted back to my own business. His sudden reanimation made me jump.

"If I show you and you laugh, you and I won't be friends any more."

Up until that point, I hadn't thought we *were* friends. But then again, for all I knew, neither had he.

"I won't laugh, Eddie. I promise I won't." I really meant that, but as soon as I said it, I was seized with fear. What if I couldn't help myself? Who knew what he had in that bag? It might have been his collection of Action Men.

"The monitor on my home computer is broken," he muttered. It sounded like something a cold war spy might have said to establish contact on a bench in Prague.

I had no idea how to respond – *Modern appliances are often unreliable?*

"Right."

"So I had to come in to work to get on the Internet."

"I see."

He frowned, sat back, sat forward again. "You *promise* you won't laugh?"

I drew an X on my chest with my finger. "Cross my heart, hope to die."

Even that didn't seem to convince him. He bit his lip and gave it yet more thought. Then, just when I was about to tell him to forget it, he suddenly dived under the table and started rummaging through his bag. He reappeared with a sheaf of paper, which he deposited carefully on the table.

"All right," he said miserably. "Take a look before I change my mind."

As I picked up the papers, Eddie began to hum. He didn't seem to be aware that he was doing it.

"Are you sure?" I said.

"Look, look. Go on."

I turned the pages towards me and read the headline *How to Talk to Women*.

"It's advice," Eddie said quickly. "Nothing sleazy or anything."

I nodded that I understood and cast my eyes down the page. The first line I read was *It's important to remember that women aren't just men with different bodies – they're practically a whole other species!*

"I got stuff from a few different sites," Eddie said. "Just to get a good overview."

I nodded again and flipped forward a few pages. *Women*

love talking about clothes – why not pick up a copy of Elle *or* Vogue *and get hip to the latest fashion trends?*

"It's pathetic, isn't it?" Eddie said and dropped his head into his hands. "You think it's pathetic. You think *I'm* pathetic."

I did another flip forward. *Compliments are vital. If you can't think of anything she deserves to be complimented on, imagine you're sitting with your favourite movie star and proceed accordingly.* That was enough for me. I dropped the printouts and looked at Eddie. "Of course I don't think you're pathetic," I said. "Everyone needs a few pointers once in a while. I'm just not sure that these particular pointers are all that great."

He blanched. "Why not? They made sense to me, the few I saw."

"I just don't think it's a good idea to have a strategy in mind for this kind of thing. It's more confusing than helpful. Um … are we talking about women in general or is there someone specific?"

"It's someone specific."

I wasn't sure if it was the way he said it or the way he looked at me, but I was suddenly convinced that this conversation was about to take a very awkward turn.

I was already preparing my defences when he added, "She's called Margaret. I met her in my cooking class."

"Oh! Right. I didn't know you were into cooking." It was a silly thing to say – I didn't know anything about him, really. "Me too. I'm never out of the kitchen."

"Yeah. You made a cake for Veronica's birthday that time. Chocolate. It was unbelievable."

"Thanks."

"I'm not bad at it either, if I say so myself. But I didn't really join up for the lessons. I joined up to … you know …"

"Meet someone"

He squirmed. "Yes. To meet someone."

"And now you have. That's great, isn't it?"

"No. It isn't. It's terrifying."

"What's she like? Tell me about her."

"She's short. A bit fat."

"Eddie!"

"What? She *is*. But she's got nice eyes. Very kind face. And she's funny, she's always cracking me up in the class. *Brutal* cook."

"So. You're planning to ask her out, is that right?"

"I already did."

"Really? And?"

"She said yes. We're going out for dinner tonight."

"But that's fantastic! She obviously likes you back."

"Don't worry, I'll soon fix that. We've only ever spoken in the class, and there's always something obvious to say there. 'How did your curry turn out last week?', you know, that kind of thing. When it's just me on my own, I'll make a balls of it, I know I will."

"Nonsense. Just be yourself." When I heard myself saying that, I recoiled a little. I got in there again before Eddie could protest. "I know, I know. Everyone always says that. But it's true. Look, she wouldn't have agreed to this date –"

He moaned. "Oh God. It's a date, I'm going on a *date*."

I ignored him. "She wouldn't have agreed to this date if

she wasn't interested. You've got this far without the Internet. Please – put your printouts in the bin and just be your– … just be natural."

"I don't know, Jackie. I've got a bad history with being natural."

"You'll be fine. Has it been a while?"

He looked up, aghast.

"Since your last date," I clarified.

"You could say that."

"When was it?"

"1993."

"I see."

"Her name was Alice. She was a district nurse, looked after my dad for a while when he had his bowel thing."

"Where did you take her?"

"Just for a drink. I thought it might help, being a bit tipsy. Not her! I didn't mean –"

"I know."

"I meant me. Loosen the tongue sort of thing."

"And?"

"Oh, it loosened it all right. I told her … Jesus …"

"Go on."

"I told her that it wasn't just me who fancied her – Dad thought she was 'a real little ride'."

"Oh. I see."

"Bad enough to tell her – but to give her the exact quote! 'A real little ride.' I did an impression of him and everything." He screwed his face up into what I presumed was an approximation of toothlessness and said it again in a thick Dublin accent: "'A real little ride.' I could tell she was disgusted, but I couldn't stop saying it. 'A real little –'"

"All right, Eddie, I get it."

"See? I can't stop now even."

"So your date went downhill from there?"

"You can say that again. Once I got on to the subject of my father, I couldn't get off it. He was all we had in common. I wound up … Oh God …" He buried his face in his hands and didn't emerge for some time. "I wound up asking her about other impacted colons of her experience. Was Dad's very bad or had she seen worse?"

"What did she say?"

"She said it was about average."

"No, I mean, did she say anything, like … Did she complain?"

"Not as such. But then again, she didn't stick around long enough. She had two drinks – one and a half, actually – and legged it."

"Still, you learned a lesson. When you see Margaret tonight, you're not going to mention colons, are you, impacted or otherwise?"

I meant it as a small joke. Eddie didn't seem to take it that way. "Christ, I hope not. But I can't promise."

"Do you know anything else about her? Outside of cooking?"

"Not much. She's never been married either, I know that. She told me so on the first night of the course. Tell you the truth, I think she had the same idea as meself. Meeting someone, I mean."

"Is she a Dub?"

"Yeah. From Drumcondra, I think, but I don't know how I know that. She must have mentioned it at some stage."

"And you're a northsider, aren't you?"

"Finglas."

"There you go. If all else fails, you can do a bit of reminiscing. Dublin in the rare oul' times, that sort of thing."

"Are you saying I'm old?"

"No, I –"

"I'm only forty-five. And Margaret's younger than you are."

I did my best not to look astonished, but I could tell by Eddie's sudden frown that I had failed.

"What?" he said.

"Nothing, nothing. Good for you."

"She's not a teenager, you know. About thirty, thirty-two, I'd say."

This changed everything. I'd had a very clear image of Margaret in my head; sensible cardigan, bag of Murray Mints, subscription to *Ireland's Own*. Now I didn't know what to think.

"Anyway, her age doesn't matter. The principle's still the same. Show a bit interest in her, Eddie. Ask questions. And not yes or no-type questions – something that will get a bit of a spark going. Find out about her history, where she's been, what she's done with her life. You might find that you've got lots in common. Throw in a few details about yourself, but don't bang on and on. It's not rocket science. I mean, you're talking to me just fine, aren't you? Forget about these bloody websites."

"You're right," he said. "I know you're right. I'm over-thinking it."

"Exactly."

"What about jokes? I've been practising a few. There's a good one about a leper who enters a talent –"

"I don't know, Eddie. I think funny anecdotes are a better bet."

"I haven't got any."

"The one about the district nurse was pretty good."

He gave me a mock dirty look.

"But you probably shouldn't tell her that one," I added, just to make sure.

"I *know*."

I looked at my watch. It was time to make tracks. "Listen, Eddie, I really have to run. Thanks again for your … support. And for not calling the cops on me."

"Don't mention it. Thank *you* for the advice. I hope you feel better soon. Well, obviously, I know you're not going to feel great, are you, after that kind of thing, but I hope –"

"I know what you mean, Eddie. Thanks." I got up from the table, wrestling with a sudden whim. *What the hell*, I thought, and went into my bag for a pen. "Here's my mobile number," I said, scribbling on his printout. "Give me a bell and let me know how you get on with Margaret."

He looked up at me with real gratitude. "I will. I definitely will."

"Good luck," I said and left him.

On the way back to my car, I texted Gerry and told him where he could find the jeep.

CHAPTER 11

The front door opened within two seconds of my ringing the bell. Either Melissa had been waiting behind it the entire time or she'd done some serious sprinting.

"Where *were* you?" she said, and then in a much softer voice, "You were ages, I was worried."

"I'll tell you if you let me inside."

She stepped out of the way. "Sorry, sorry. Go on into the kitchen, I'll put the kettle on."

I glanced behind me as I went down the hall. She had a curious expression on her face. I didn't recognise it at first – and then it dawned on me: she was eagerly anticipating having a conversation with me. I'd forgotten what that looked like.

Melissa shook her head almost continually throughout my

story and even managed a guttural "Nooo!" at one stage – the crashing the car into the pillar stage, obviously. She was clearly shocked by my actions but excited too. Every so often, she would realise that she wearing a smile and abruptly wipe it off.

"How do you feel now?" she asked when I was finished. "Better?"

That was the answer she wanted to hear, so I gave it to her in a thick mumble. "A wee bit, I suppose."

"Don't tell me you feel bad about it. Jesus Christ. You were bound to lash out after what you've been through."

"Maybe."

"And he probably *expected* you to do something. Chances are he won't even be all that shocked."

"You reckon?"

"And even if he is! So what? You're not thinking straight. How could you be?"

"I'm *not*. I'm not thinking straight."

"Of course not. Look at you, you're a bag of nerves."

I'd been fiddling with my cup, rather than drinking from it. In truth, I was full of tea and didn't want any more. But, once again, I let Melissa think what she liked.

"And you finally had a good cry, that's progress," she said. "Even if it was in front of some stranger weirdo."

"Eddie's not a *weirdo*," I said, regretting my earlier description of him. "He's just a bit shy and …" I couldn't think of another word that did the job.

"Whatever," Melissa said. "Listen, maybe you should have a lie-down. Just twenty winks."

I looked up, stunned. "Just twenty winks" was a phrase from our childhood. My mother used to say it to us all the time when we'd done too much running around and were getting cranky: *I think it's time for twenty winks.* Later, Melissa and I adopted it for our own ends. We'd mumble it to each other over the phone when we'd been out and were a little worse for wear: *"Can't wait to get home and have twenty winks."* She hadn't said it to me in years.

"Yeah," I said. "Maybe just ... twenty winks."

I half-expected her to catch on to what she'd said and, somehow, take it back. But she didn't. "Up you go," she said. "The boys should be back soon. We'll have a nice dinner later and you can just chill out."

I didn't need a lie-down, but I wanted to keep the moment alive.

"Thanks," I said and got to my feet. "That sounds nice."

God help me, I even yawned.

Upstairs, I read Brenda's article in *Your Story* again, imagining how my own tale of adultery and revenge would sound if it appeared in those hallowed pages. That quickly became depressing, so I lay down and stared at the ceiling for a while. A few minutes later, Colm and Niall arrived home. Niall was very excited and making lots of noise. I could tell that Melissa was trying to calm him down and knew that it was because I was resting – or was supposed to be at least. The guilt was substantial, but manageable.

After half an hour or so, the doorbell rang. I heard footsteps, then voices, then an ominous silence. *Christ*, I thought. *It's Gerry. He's come to throttle me.* Someone came padding up the stairs. There was a faint tap at the door.

"Come in," I said. "I'm awake."

Melissa stuck her head in. "You've got a visitor."

I closed my eyes and put my hands over my face. I wasn't ready for this.

"It's Robert," she said.

My eyes flew open and my hands fell away. I sat up and looked at her.

"My *son* Robert?"

She nodded and retreated.

I bounded off the bed and took a look at myself in the mirror. The words "hedge" and "backwards" sprang to mind. I rearranged my hair as best I could and poked at the bags under my eyes which was, of course, pointless. Eye-bags don't do a damn thing when you poke them.

When I made it down to the kitchen and saw Robert leaning somewhat awkwardly on the counter-top, I realised how long it had been since I'd seen him – it must have been more than a month. He had hair, for a start, an inch or so of it. Last time we'd met, he'd had it cropped right down to the scalp. But that wasn't the only change. He was heavier now, not fatter but bulkier; time well-spent in the gym, I guessed. I'd never seen him look so much like his dad.

"Here she is," said Melissa, who was sitting on a stool, trying to look casual. "I'll leave you to it, go see what my boys are doing."

"You don't have to go," I said quickly. "Stay, stay."

There was a good chance, I thought, that Robert would

say this was all my fault – I wanted a witness in case things got out of hand.

I turned towards him and gave him a small smile. "Hello there."

He stood up straight and marched towards me. Long before it was necessary to do so, he threw his arms wide. As he gathered me close to him, he put his mouth to my ear and said, "The bastard. I could fucking kill him."

Surprise and relief did battle for control of my brain. Surprise carried the day, but not by much. I backed out of his embrace and asked, "How did you find out?"

He ran his hand around his jaw – an ancient habit – and said, "I rang him this morning."

"And, what, he just confessed?"

"Not straight away. I could tell something was up and when I asked him if he was okay, he told me the whole thing. Fucking *tool*."

"Don't swear, Robert." His language was just one of the many subjects we rowed about. When I brought it up, Robert usually pointed out that I wasn't averse to an occasional volley myself and I usually told him not to be cheeky. This time he said nothing.

"Anyway," I went on. "What did he tell you?"

"He was all over the place – I couldn't even make him out at first. Kept saying he was stupid, that he'd done a stupid thing, he was a stupid man, why had he been so stupid. There were a lot of 'stupids' in there."

"But what did he say happened, exactly?"

I wanted to hear his precise description because I'd often

wondered how I'd have confessed myself, if that had ever become necessary. Robert looked down at me for some time before he answered. I knew it was uncomfortable for him, but I held his gaze. I really wanted to know.

"He said he'd been unfaithful. And you'd caught him. It was just once, he kept swearing that, like, all disbelief."

"What couldn't he believe? That he'd done it or that I'd caught him?"

"Both, I think."

"Did he tell you who she is … was … is?"

His eyes darted around for a second. "Yeah … *Jesus*. She's not much older than me. I see her out and about sometimes, you know. In town. In clubs. Surrounded by men."

"You're impressed with your dad."

"No!"

"It's all right, Robert. She's very beautiful, I know that."

"Jackie! You're doing it again!" This was from Melissa, obviously.

"Doing what?" Robert asked, looking from his aunt to me and back again.

I gave her a pleading look. *Not now*. She backed down.

"Nothing," she said. "I think maybe I will … after all …" She slid off her stool and left us alone.

"We might as well sit down," I said to Robert. "Would you like a cup of coffee or anything?"

"Christ, no," he said as he took a seat. "Are you joking me? I feel like I'm going to fucking split. How could he do this? What's the matter with him? Aren't you even angry? How can you be so calm?"

I glanced towards the open door, hoping Melissa hadn't heard him.

"Of course I'm angry!" I barked. "What kind of a question is that? Jesus, Robert, do you really think –"

"Sorry, sorry. That was a stupid thing to say. But what are you going to do?"

"Well, in the short-term, I've wrecked the jeep – in the long-term, I don't know."

I could tell by Robert's face that he had heard and understood the sentence but couldn't quite grasp the meaning. His features rippled and contorted as he struggled to bring the concepts of *Jeep-wrecking* and *My mother* together. It looked as if his whole face was chewing. I tried not to feel pleased about his reaction, but I couldn't help myself.

"You did *what?*"

"Wrecked the jeep. Well, damaged it, anyway. Scraped it against a pillar. Both sides."

A grin slowly formed. It was the same grin that his alter-ego, Valentine Reilly, used on vulnerable young girls who knew better but couldn't help themselves.

"Good for you," he said. "Fuck him. What about her? Lisa? What are you going to do to her? She's got that nice Beamer, hasn't she, you could have swiped Dad's yoke up against it. Two birds."

"I've got no intention of doing anything to her, Robert. She's not worth it."

"No. Suppose not. The *bitch.*"

I drifted away for a moment to the alternative universe where Robert was telling Gerry that there was no point in taking revenge on Tony – the *bastard*.

"Does Chrissy know?" I asked.

"Yeah. I phoned her."

"At work?"

"Yeah, well, I thought she should know right away."

"And?"

"And what do you think? She went nuts. Roaring and crying. I had to hang up on her in the end, there was no point to it."

"Robert! For the love of –"

"It's all right, I called her back a few minutes later. She was still bawling, though. I'm sure she's stopped by now. She'll be winding down anyway."

"She's her daddy's little girl. This will hurt her very badly."

He did another jaw-rub, then picked at his jeans. "Yeah, well …" Just for a moment, his man-on-the-up persona dropped away and he looked like what he was, a twenty-one-year-old who'd taken a kick in the guts. I tried to think of something comforting to say, but the words didn't come easily. I was no longer used to comforting Robert, that was the problem. If he'd thrown one of his patented jibes at me, I'd have had a comeback to hand in a flash.

"And you too, of course. I'm sure you're not exactly thrilled."

His recovery was immediate and total. "Don't mind me, I'm grand."

"Two pieces of bad news in two days though. First Jemima and now this."

"Shit happens. It happens quite a lot, I've noticed."

"Do you want to talk about it? About her, I mean. What went wrong?"

"No. I don't want to talk about it. And I don't want to tell you what went wrong."

"You never know, Robert, I might be able –"

"*No*, all right? It's not … Just, no. Leave it."

He'd raised his voice to the level he usually used when snapping at me about this or that. The experience was so familiar, it was almost comforting. I lowered my eyes and felt my head dropping, my shoulders getting rounder. It was the reaction of an animal that has been mistreated in the past and has learned to fear a certain tone.

"Ah, Christ," Robert said, "I didn't mean to shout at you." He sighed. "She said I was too young for her. That was her reason. I don't know how it took her four months to work it out, but there you go."

This was the most personal information, in both quantity and quality, that he had given me in an age.

"I'm sorry," I said. "I really am." This wasn't even a lie. At that particular moment, I actually *was* sorry. "But she's right. You were too young for her. Or rather, she was too old for you. I said as much, didn't I? Plenty of times."

For a moment, Robert seemed ready to go for me again. But he swallowed whatever he'd been about to say and changed the subject.

"So," he said. "How come you came to stay with …" He cocked his head towards the door. "I would have thought you'd be straight over to Nancy's."

Robert and Chrissy both knew that Melissa and I had

fallen out after Mum and Dad were killed, but they didn't know the specifics. Gerry had once told me that they assumed it was something to do with the wills. We'd agreed not to correct them.

"Nancy's in Paris," I told him in an unnecessary whisper.

"Right. I knew there had to be a reason. And how are you getting along with Rumpole of the Bailey?"

This was a nickname that he and Chrissy had come up with years ago when Melissa was still practising law. It shouldn't have worked. She was a delicate Irishwoman, not a beefy British man and as far as I knew had never even seen the outside of the Old Bailey. Still, it had always cracked me up.

"Shhh. She'll hear you. We're getting along fine."

"Yeah?"

"Yeah. I mean, y'know ... all right. So far."

At that moment, La Cucaracha came weedle-eedling from my bag.

"Text," I said and hopped off my stool. "Might be from Chrissy."

It wasn't. It was from Gerry. *FOUND THE JEEP*, it read. *I UNDERSTAND. I'M SORRY. I LOVE YOU. PLEASE COME BACK*.

My knees buckled and I only just made it back to my stool upright.

"What is it?" Robert asked. "Mum?"

I showed him the message. He read it without expression. Then he said, "Wow. He *must* be sorry. He loves that fucking car."

"Christ … " I said mournfully.

"What? Don't tell me you feel guilty?"

I wanted to deny it, but I found that I just couldn't.

Robert became very animated. "Now listen. Between the pair of you, there's only one who should be feeling guilty and, lemme tell you, it ain't you."

"I know that," I said, each word sticking in my throat like a cowboy's spur. "He's the one who … I didn't …"

"Shhh. Don't upset yourself."

But it was too late. I'd upset myself.

"Please don't cry," Robert begged.

I tried to stop, but the tears kept coming. Robert reached across, patted my knee and sat back again. It was quite obvious that he hadn't a clue what to do or what to say. I felt sorry for him, which made me cry all the harder. After a minute or so, during which time he just sat there wringing his hands and staring at the counter, he suddenly leaped from his stool and more or less ran from the room. He returned seconds later with Melissa.

"What is it now?" she said as she arrived at my side. "What happened?"

"She got a text," Robert said. "From Dad. About the car. Saying he understands." Now that he had a woman on hand to help, he was all chat. "She feels guilty. She's pretending she doesn't, but she does."

I thought, *Melissa's going to say I've done nothing to feel guilty about.*

"That's silly," Melissa said. "What have you got to feel guilty about?"

I sobbed my biggest sob to date.

"So you damaged a car!" she went on. "Big deal! He had an affair!"

"It wasn't an affair," I blubbed. "It was a one-off. He made *a mistake*. People do that! He's a good man!"

She took a tentative step towards me and, ever so slowly, as if afraid she might get scalded or pricked, she placed her hand between my shoulder blades. When she had satisfied herself that she was in no physical danger, she started to rub up and down, as if she was trying to burp me. It was surprisingly pleasant. She stopped when I showed her the phone message and then she started again, harder than ever.

"Now, Jackie. Let's not take any backwards steps. No excuses, no get-out clauses. You're entitled to your anger. If he 'understands', well, good for him. That shouldn't make you feel any differently about it."

"Yeah," Robert said, emphatically. He moved closer and put his hand on my shoulder.

"Okay," I said, miserably.

Melissa started her strange rubbing again. I cried on for another few minutes, not sure if I was doing it because I felt bad about Gerry or because I felt good about having Melissa and Robert's sympathy. Either way, I wasn't proud of myself.

* * *

I expected Chrissy to call over that night, but she didn't. She phoned instead, not long after Robert left. It wasn't really a conversation, as such. I did all the talking. Chrissy just cried. In the end, I managed to arrange a time for us to meet by making suggestions and then interpreting her sniffs and moans as yeses or nos. The time and place we settled on, as far as I could tell, was the café in Arnotts at two the next day. I didn't like hearing my child so upset, but it was nice to be the one doing the comforting for a change. It was honest work.

Colm disappeared that evening to attend some golf club do. Niall stayed up until way past his regular bedtime; he was engrossed in a finger-painting session which Melissa was reluctant to disturb on the grounds that it was a creative activity, as opposed to a ruinously destructive one, and made a nice change. He showed me some of his compositions and, in fairness to him, reacted well when I failed to recognise the subject of a single one ("Is that a space-ship?"; "No, it's a CLOWN!").

After he went to bed, Melissa rose from her chair and asked me if I wanted a drink. I wasn't sure what she meant; I doubted that she was talking about something alcoholic. We hadn't shared so much as a glass of wine since Mum and Dad died. I told her I could murder an orange juice and waited to see if she'd try to press something harder upon me. She didn't – she returned with two OJs and got settled in again. I realised that we were staring down the barrel of our first couple of hours alone in God knew how long and felt a shot of adrenaline course through me.

For the next hour or so, Melissa's attitude was like that of a nurse who'd been lumbered with an extra patient whom she could have done without. She was perfectly civil (Was I warm enough? Cool enough? Did I want another glass of orange juice? Another cushion? Was *Heartbeat* all right or did I want to watch something else?) but still, hardly chatty. I wasn't exactly full of beans myself. Every time I thought of something to say, I gave it a trial run in my head and found it too frivolous, too perky. I was the wounded wife, I reminded myself; it was not traditionally a speaking role. Gradually, however, Melissa began to open up. She started small with observations about TV commercials and such-like but really came to life when she got on to the subject of her neighbours. The couple on their left had lived there forever and were two of the most unpleasant people she'd ever met. He was a retired civil servant and she was a retired head-mistress. They were both desperately keen on capital punishment and managed to crowbar it into almost every conversation, as if it was the burning issue of the day. On Ash Wednesday the previous year, they had set upon Melissa as she emerged from her car and demanded to know why her forehead was cross-free. At first, she'd tried to explain that she hadn't made it to mass yet – a lie, she never went – but eventually she'd lost her cool and told them, more or less, to piss off. They hadn't spoken to her (or Colm or Niall) since and she was perfectly happy with that. The couple who lived on the right were much more fun. He was a director of television commercials and she was a bigwig in the National Museum. They were middle-aged but acted twenty years younger. They had no children but plenty of parties; Melissa had once spotted Jeremy Irons coming out of one. One afternoon the previous summer, Melissa had seen the husband walk the length of his back garden in a miniskirt and heels, turn at the bottom, and come straight back the way he came, like a sentry on duty. He glanced up as he turned and saw her at the bedroom window. She dived out of the way, but it was too late. Half an hour later, he showed up at the front door (in jeans and a T-shirt) and told her everything. His wife knew and didn't mind, so long as he didn't do it in public. She'd kill him if she knew about his occasional jaunt down the garden and back, which he did once in a while to "ease the tension". Melissa promised to keep mum but to this day had a terrible urge to tell the neighbours on the other side, just to see what would happen. I took great delight in these and other similar stories, but was saddened to think that I hadn't heard them before. What else had happened in her life that I didn't know about?

The conversation – or rather, the monologue, for I was careful to restrict my own contributions – went on until well past midnight. It never strayed beyond the trivial, but that was fine by me. I hadn't missed having deadly serious discussions with my sister. I'd missed talking shite.

CHAPTER 12

As soon as I walked into the Arnotts café on Sunday afternoon, I realised that I had made a mistake with the venue. I'd thought *Coffee-Town-Arnotts*, without pausing to consider how crowded it would be, which was very. It would be hard enough to talk Chrissy down off the ceiling without doing it in front of an audience. She was there before me, as I'd expected – she was one of those people for whom "on time" meant "ten minutes early" – and had taken a table for two by the wall. I nodded and waved as I approached, hoping that she would at least let me get settled before she started sobbing. She rose to greet me and squeezed me hard, kissing me on the cheek.

"Mum," she said by way of hello.

"Hi," I said. "I knew you'd get here first."

We hugged for quite a while. People were looking at us, no doubt wondering what the big deal was. I tried to imagine what I'd have guessed in their shoes. Bereavement, probably. Then Chrissy let me go, wrinkled her nose and said, "Have you been smoking?"

"No!" I said, faking shock. "Don't be ridiculous!" In fact, I'd just had three fags in a row, each lit with the butt of its predecessor. I felt quite nauseous.

Chrissy sat down, gesturing around the table. "I got tea for two and a couple of muffins. Is that okay?"

I worked my way out of my jacket and took a seat, my eyes locked on hers. Not only was she not crying, she didn't look as if she was about to start. It was such a surprising development that I couldn't help but comment.

"You look grand," I said. "I thought you'd be, you know … upset."

She tucked a strand of hair behind her ear, then joined her hands as if in prayer. "I'm all cried out," she said. "Seriously, I think I'm dehydrated."

There was a protracted silence.

"It's hard to know what to say, isn't it?" I ventured then.

She nodded in agreement. "Yeah. It is."

"It must have been an awful shock for you. When Robert called. You at work and all …"

"Yeah. It was."

"And did you go home or –"

"Yup. Told them I felt sick. Which was the truth."

"Ah, Chrissy. Are you all right now?"

She grabbed a knife and cut a chunk off her chocolate-chip muffin. "I'm fine," she said and popped it in her mouth.

At that point, I began to get a nervous feeling deep in the pit of my stomach. She wasn't herself. Not by a long way.

"Never mind me," she said then. "How are you? That's the main thing."

I took a moment and chose my words with great care. "I'm very shocked, obviously. Bad enough that he did … what he did. I could have done without catching him at it."

Chrissy cut another piece of muffin, finished chewing the first and then went to work on the second. When she'd swallowed it down, she said, "I can't even imagine. I don't want to think about it. I *refuse* to think about it."

I poured myself some tea, wondering how to proceed. "Have you spoken to your father yet?"

She gave her head the tiniest little shake and said, "No, I haven't spoken to him. I'm never speaking to him again."

I looked up and straight away I knew that she wasn't being colourful. It wasn't just a figure of speech, like "I'm going to kill him when I get my hands on him". She meant it. That didn't stop me from saying, "Come on, Chrissy, you don't mean that."

"Yes. I do."

"No, you don't."

"Yes, I do."

"No, you don't."

"Yes –"

"What is this, panto? You're being silly, Chrissy, stop it."

"Watch my lips, Mum: I. Am. Never. Speaking. To. Him. Again. Ever."

"Don't be so –"

"No, I'm sorry. That's it. We're finished, me and him."

My head spun. "What is it, are you trying to help *me*? Because that doesn't help, dear. Far from it."

Once again, she took a bit of muffin before replying. It was as if she was getting some sort of strength from it. "I'm not saying it because I think it's what you want to hear. It's the truth, that's all."

"But you love your dad. You and him were always –"

"I did love him. Right up until yesterday."

"Chrissy!"

"I'm sorry, but that's the way I feel."

I slumped in my seat, defeated. A question formed in my head. I let it bounce around for a while before I gave it voice. "And what if it was me?"

"What do you mean?"

"Me who'd done the … dirty. Would you stop loving me too?"

"I'm not answering that."

My palms dampened. "In other words, yes, you would."

"I didn't say that. It's a what-do-you-call-it question – rhetorical."

"Hypo–"

"Hypothetical, I mean. I'm not answering hypothetical questions about what I'd do if it was you for the simple reason that it's not you, is it? It's *him*." She said this with real anger in her voice, so much so that a little old woman at the next table looked across for a moment before returning to the piece of toast she'd been encasing in butter.

I didn't know what to say.

"I've been presuming something," Chrissy said then, "and now I'm starting to think I've got it wrong."

I swallowed. "What's that?"

"You *are* leaving him, aren't you? I mean, you *are* getting a divorce, right? Right?"

"God, Chrissy, it's only been two days. I haven't thought about it yet."

"But you must have done! How can you not have thought about it? You have to leave him. Of course you have to leave him! How could you trust him after this?"

"I don't know …"

"Every time you left the house, you'd be thinking –"

"That's enough."

"I'm just saying –"

"I said, that's enough."

She pouted for a moment, then said, "You know what, Mum … I know you're in shock and all, but I have to say, you're not doing yourself any favours by being like this."

"Like what?"

She waved her hands around. "All passive and easy-going. You can't let him walk all over you."

"No one's walking over me, Chrissy."

"You're allowed to get angry, you know."

"I am angry."

"Well, it doesn't show."

"You obviously haven't heard about the car, then."

She blinked at me. "What car?"

"Your father's. The jeep. I wrecked it."

Her eyes took over her face. "What? How? When?"

"I took it when I left the house on Friday. And yesterday morning I drove it into a pillar. Well, along the side of a pillar. Right and left. Ruined it."

She reached across and grabbed my hand. "Great! That's fantastic! Well done, you. He'll go nuts, he loves that bloody jeep."

"He didn't go nuts. I got a text from him. He said he understood and wasn't mad."

The wind left her sails, but not for long. "He's just saying that. I guarantee you, he would have been gutted."

She smiled. My child was positively delighted by the thought of her father being gutted about something. My heart felt like a piece of coal.

"I really don't think he was. There wasn't even a hint of anger in what he said. None." I ran a hand over my forehead, which suddenly felt numb and tingly.

"Oh, Christ," Chrissy said. "You feel *bad* about it, don't you? Mum!"

I made no reply.

"Not only should you not feel bad," she went on, "you should be thinking of what else you can do for revenge. What about *her*? You'll have to do something to get back at *her*."

I exhaled as if for the last time. "That's what your brother said."

"Well, he's right. You can't let her get away scot-free. She's got it coming to her."

"No, Chrissy. I don't want to get involved with her at all."

"But you have to!"

We were back to square one. "No, I don't. Nothing's going to change if, I don't know, I throw a brick through her window, is it?"

Chrissy sat back and took some tea. "She'd have a broken window," she said then. "Better than nothing."

I let that one just hang in the air for few seconds. Then I said, "How are things with you anyway? How's work?

She grimaced. "'How's work?' Mum!"

"What?"

"We're having a crisis here! You can't be asking me about work! Who cares?"

"I'm only making conversation."

"Jesus! We've already got a topic of conversation – the end of your marriage, remember?"

I collapsed back in my seat and slapped my hands to my face like Macaulay Culkin in *Home Alone*.

"I'm sorry," Chrissy said as she realised she'd gone too far. "I didn't mean to sound so –"

"I have to go," I wheezed and rose from the table.

"No, don't go," she said. "Please. You just got here." Her voice was cracking.

"I'll talk to you later."

"Mum, please!"

I grabbed my bag and jacket and scarpered. More fool me, I looked back as I threaded my way between the tables. Chrissy was bent over her teacup, crying into her hands; just the way I'd expected to find her when I arrived. I should have gone back. But I didn't. I hurried on towards the exit.

Outside on the street, I paused and considered my

options. After a moment's thought, I turned right and headed towards St. Stephen's Green, where I planned to take a breather and clear my head. It had been a while since I'd been in town at the weekend and, as ever, I was overwhelmed by the sheer volume of human traffic. It didn't seem possible that all of these people knew exactly where they were going and how to get there; it looked too chaotic, too random. If I'd suddenly noticed that they were all carrying bits of leaves on their backs, I wouldn't have been at all surprised.

In Stephen's Green, I took a seat on a bench near the bandstand, next to an old man. He had a tremendous beard which he stroked continuously, making a loose fist at his chin and then drawing it down to where the fuzz ran out, in the centre of his chest. I turned my head a little and watched him from the corner of my eye. *It must be so nice to have a beard like that*, I thought. *A little security blanket that you can never lose.* Then I had one of those moments where you catch a glimpse of yourself from the outside and snapped my head forward again. Jealous of an old man's beard ... These were strange days indeed. After I'd been sitting there for fifteen minutes or so (and had nauseated myself all over again with a fresh string of cigarettes), my mobile rang. I didn't recognise the number and didn't think of Eddie until I heard his voice.

"Jackie? It's Eddie. Hand. From work. "

"Hello."

"Oh. You sound upset, are you all right?"

"I'll be fine. In a while."

"Do you feel any better today? No, of course you don't, what a thing to say. Have you –"

"Never mind me," I cut in. "How are you? How did it go last night?"

"That's what I want to talk to you about. Oh – sorry. I didn't – sorry."

"Hello?"

"Sorry, Jackie, I just stood on a wee boy's toe."

"Where are you?"

"I'm in the Jervis Centre. Buying clothes."

That sounded significant, but I chose not to pursue it for the moment. "I'm in Stephen's Green," I said. The next sentence was out before I was aware that I'd even had the thought. "Why don't you come up and meet me?"

"*Yes*. Yes, I will. I'm done here anyway. Where are you exactly?"

"On a bench to the right of the bandstand as you come from Grafton Street."

"I'll see you in twenty minutes. Is that too long? Can you wait?"

"Sure. But give me a clue. Was it okay, the date?"

"I don't know. That's what I want you to tell me."

"Oh. Okay. See you soon."

"Great. Thank you. Thank you. Thanks very much. Bye."

He hung up. I put my phone away and realised that I was greatly looking forward to the distraction of seeing him and would have stuck around if he'd been an hour away. Eddie. Hand. From work. Strange, strange days.

CHAPTER 13

Eddie arrived less than ten minutes after we got off the phone.

"Jesus," I said. "Did you fly?"

"I ran," he gasped, which was patently the truth. He was badly out of breath and his entire face was covered with sweat. There was a little droplet hanging from the tip of his nose. "I'm not used to running."

"Sit down," I said and made to get up.

But the bearded man beside me waved a hand in the air and said, "Don't get up, stay where you are. I'm away to watch the match." With some difficulty, he got to his feet. "You shouldn't be tearing around the place like a blue-arsed fly," he said to Eddie as he turned to leave. "Man in your physical condition."

Eddie looked down at his heaving belly. If any counter-slurs occurred to him, he kept them to himself.

"Come on," I said. "Sit down, tell all."

"What about you, first," Eddie said as he took a pew. "Are you sure you're all right?"

"Yeah. I just met my daughter. Didn't stay long."

"Oh. Right. Taking it badly, is she?"

"You could say that. I'd prefer not to talk about it."

"Okay. And what about the car? Did your husband pick it up?"

"He did, yeah."

"He must have hit the roof."

"Nope. He sent me a text saying he understood."

"Really?"

"Yup."

He gazed off across the park, lost in thought. "I suppose you felt awful guilty."

I spun towards him. "*Yes*. What made you say that?"

He shrugged. "You're a good person. Doing bad things wouldn't come easily to you. Not that I think you did a bad thing! I mean –"

"I know what you mean. And I'm glad to hear you saying it. I've had nothing but grief from everyone else."

"Who?"

"My son, my daughter, my sister. They think I'm being too soft."

"Don't mind them."

That, apparently, was the beginning and the end of his advice. Still, it made me feel a bit better. I shouted down the voice in my head that told me I didn't deserve to feel better because (like everyone else) Eddie was comforting me without knowing all the facts.

"You're right," I said. "I should … not mind them. Come on, tell me how it went with … eh …"

"Margaret."

"Margaret. Start at the start. Where did you take her?"

"The Firefly."

"Eddie! Big spender."

"One of the papers had a write-up about it last week. Said it was fantastic, so I thought I'd push the boat out."

"And?"

"Well, I'll never see the boat again, that's for sure. It's gone over the bloody horizon."

"Worth it though?"

"Oh yeah, it was lovely. Very elegant and all, but they didn't make you feel like you didn't belong there. I've been to a few other nice restaurants, on my own I might add, and they all treated me like a bloody competition winner. *Eat this and clear off.*"

"Were you nervous?"

He held a hand in the air and quickly shook it back and forth. "I could hardly do my shoelaces before I left the house. But she was nervous too. It was one of the first things she said to me, so that helped."

"Good."

"And I followed your advice. Asked her lots of questions, found out loads. There wasn't one awkward silence, not one."

"And what exactly did you find out?"

"She's thirty-three. Shares a flat with a pal of hers. Works for Aer Lingus. Loves cats. Hates spiders. Big into music but nobody I've ever heard of, except Elvis and Johnny Cash. Oh, and Frank Sinatra. Hasn't travelled much but wants to. Had her appendix out last year. Only child, just like me. Very close to her mother and father. Reads a lot. Loves Roddy Doyle. She met him a few times and thought he was very nice. She tried to write a book herself once but gave up after a few weeks. Plays the piano a little bit. Can't stand Bertie Ahern. Her favourite film is *The Shawshank Redemption*. When she was little girl, she had a hamster, but her cousin stood on it. She once got burgled three times in a fortnight. She doesn't believe in UFOs, but she does believe in ghosts. She hates *Big Brother*, but she always watches it anyway. She has very little interest in learning how to cook. And she's always liked older men."

He allowed himself to smile when he came to this last detail. I melted a little bit. It was just so cute.

"Wow," I said. "You did a lot of listening."

"I did a bit of talking as well. But not too much. It was going so well that I didn't want to ruin it."

"Is there a 'but' coming, Eddie?"

"Yes. Well, no. Kind of. That's what I want to talk to you about." He put his hand to the back of his head and gave it a vigorous scratching.

"Did you say something you shouldn't have or –"

"No, not at first anyway. I was really proud of myself, Jackie. And grateful to you. God knows what I would have been like if I'd gone in there armed with a load of old guff I got off the Internet. I did fine, honest. Right up until the very end."

"Oh? What happened then?"

"We finished up in the restaurant and went outside, still chatting away, still getting on great, getting more comfortable, you know? Taking the mickey a bit. At least *she* was taking the mickey out of *me*."

"About what?"

"My shirt. She said her grandfather had one just like it."

"Ah. Hence the shopping. I don't see any bags …"

"I didn't buy anything. I was halfway to the counter with a shirt when I realised it was almost exactly the same as the one I wore on our date, only the check was a bit bigger. You and her would get on great. She laughs at my shirt, you laugh at my tie."

"For the last time, I *like* your tie."

"Anyway. So there we were on the street, chatting away good-o. It wasn't too late, so I thought maybe we'd go and get a drink, you know, keep the thing going."

"But she wanted to go home. Eddie, you shouldn't read too much –"

"No, no, it wasn't that. Just the opposite. I suggested going for a drink and she said 'Wouldn't you rather come back to my place?' Like, she stepped all close and everything when she said it." He shook his head as if he couldn't quite believe that such a thing had happened.

"I'm not sure I see the problem," I said. "You like her, don't you?"

"Oh yeah! Yeah." He smiled. "She told me this great story about a chap at work who went to Greece with his wife ... Well, I'll tell you some other time. But she's ... lovely, she's really lovely."

I took a deep breath. "I think I know what you're telling me, Eddie. Are you saying that it's been a while? Since you ... y'know. With a woman."

He rolled about on his hips and clasped his hands together. "This is a big, it's a big ... I don't know why I'm telling you. Sorry, sorry, that's not true. I do know why I'm telling you. Because you're helpful and kind and ... knowledgable. But you can't laugh."

I patted his knee, confident that I had his number. "I didn't laugh at your Internet printouts, did I?"

"No. You didn't."

"Eddie, maybe it'd be easier if I said it for you."

"Maybe."

"Are you telling me you're a bit ... inexperienced?"

He recoiled as if I'd slapped him. "You could say that."

I gave him time to elaborate.

He leaned forward and stared down at the ground. "Jackie, I've never even kissed a woman. Let alone ... anything else."

My first thought was that I should be very quick about saying something supportive. But nothing came to mind. I peeled my tongue from the roof of my mouth, where it had suddenly lodged, and made a noise along the lines of "*Uhwehuhum*".

"It's a shocker, isn't it?" Eddie said, still staring at the ground. "Forty-five years of age. Pathetic."

I recovered the power of speech. "It's sad, that's what it is."

He looked up at me. "Oh. I didn't think you were going to agree with me."

"No, Eddie, Jesus, I mean it's sad as in heartbreaking, not sad as in ... *sad*. How did ... I don't understand how ..."

"Just never happened. What can I say?"

"But when you were a teenager . . .?"

"Not when I was a teenager, not when I was a twenty-something, not when I was thirty-something ... and so on."

Right on cue, a young couple walked past hand in hand.

I spoke up quickly, hoping to distract his attention. "Could be worse. I had twins when I was a teenager."

His reply was instant: "That's not worse, Jackie."

I was about to protest but thought better of it. He had a point. "You just didn't go on dates, is that it?"

"That other woman I told you about? My dad's nurse?"

"Yeah."

"That was in 1993. The last time before that was about 1988, maybe even 1987, I'm not sure. And *that* was my first ever. I've been on three dates in my life."

I tried not to look shocked. "But, dates aside, surely there was a game of spin-the-bottle or some drunken –"

"Jackie. This is hard enough without you not even believing me. Trust me. I'd have remembered if it had happened."

"I'm sorry, Eddie. That was a stupid thing to say." I saw an opportunity to compliment him then and grabbed it. "I'm just saying, with all the creeps and losers out there, I'm surprised that's all, I'm surprised that a kind, decent bloke like you has … missed out."

He didn't reply. I guessed that the same thought had occurred to him long, long ago, but he was too modest to agree.

"So finish your story," I said. "She asked you back to hers …"

"And I just panicked. I know what you're going to say. You'd think I'd have jumped at the chance, but –"

"I wasn't going to say that. You must have been really on edge. The unknown and all that."

He gave me a half-smile. "See? I knew you'd get it. She asked me back and my stomach churned. We'd been getting on so well and now all I could see was me making a complete mess of it. She'd be able to tell as soon as I … started. There's just no way she wouldn't be able to tell. Is there?"

This was a real question. I was determined to give a good answer. "There is such a thing as a natural, you know. I remember when the kids were about twelve, we all went out to play pitch 'n' putt one day. We were all hopeless, except Robert. Now I'm not saying he was getting holes in one or anything, but you could tell by looking at him, the way he swung the pitcher or whatever it's called – he was just naturally good at it. People were telling Gerry and me that he could be a professional golfer if he kept it up. Which he didn't, of course. He never keeps anything up, that one."

Eddie didn't look impressed. I wished I had a better example than pitch 'n' frigging putt.

"I don't think I can rely on being a natural," he said. "Not at this. Not at anything."

His confidence in me was obviously shaken.

I tried a different tack. "Well, how about this: for all you know, she's just as inexperienced as you are."

That was no good either.

"I know for a fact she's had at least one boyfriend," Eddie said, "because she told me about him. He was a real scumbag. Went out with her for a few months then dumped her over the phone and never gave her CDs back. Even if he was the only partner she's ever had – which I severely doubt – she's still a long way down the track ahead of me."

"You never told me how it ended."

"Sorry?"

"On the street outside the restaurant."

"Oh. I just made up an excuse."

"What did you say?"

He made a face like someone sucking a lemon. "It was the first thing to come into my head."

"Go on."

"I said I had a tummy bug."

"That's not so bad."

"Yes, it is. When people say 'I've got a tummy bug' what they really mean is 'I've got the raging squits'."

He had me there. I could think of nothing to say but "Hmmm".

"So not only did she have to toddle off home on her own, she was left with an image of me glued to the pot all night with bad guts."

"Well, people do get sick, Eddie, it's not a sin."

He ignored that. "And I'll tell you what was worse. She started asking all sorts of questions. Why hadn't I mentioned it before? How come it hadn't been bothering me up until then?"

"And you said what?"

"I said it had been coming and going all day. There was more imagery she could have done without. What the hell's the matter with me? Last time it was Dad's impacted colon and now it's my dose of the trots. Every time I go out with a woman – every decade or so – I wind up on the subject of … bums."

"It's unfortunate. I'm not saying it isn't unfortunate. So how did you part?"

"Once I finished answering her diarrhoea questions, I just sort of backed off, waving. She looked awful confused. She took a little step towards me again so I turned and … well … sort of … ran away."

"You're exaggerating for comic effect, I presume …"

He shook his head miserably. "Not really, no."

"You *literally* ran away?"

"A wee bit, yeah."

"Oh." I gave it some thought. "Well, we've got one thing going for us at least."

"We?"

"You, then."

"I prefer *we*."

I melted again. "We've got one thing going for us and that, if you ask me, is the very fact that you used that particular excuse."

"Don't follow."

"For a start, it's embarrassing –"

"It sure is."

"No, I mean it would be embarrassing if it was true. So that gives you a lot of leeway for acting a bit … odd. And, number two – so to speak – it helps explain why you ran off at the end. You needed the loo."

Eddie chewed on this for a moment. "Let me see if I've got this right. You're saying that, assuming she answers the phone to me, I shouldn't avoid the whole diarrhoea thing, I should try to use it to my advantage."

"Exactly."

"To be honest, I had my heart set on avoiding it."

"Tough. Eddie, you can't call her up and act like nothing peculiar happened. She threw herself at you and not only did you not take her up on it, you started babbling about your tummy and then ran off. I guarantee you she's sitting at home today thinking *He could have just told me he wasn't interested, there was no need to start making up silly excuses*."

"Oh God …"

"I haven't finished yet. Then she'll be thinking *On the other hand, no man in his right mind would tell you he had a tummy bug i.e. the raging squits if it wasn't actually true*. You see?"

He looked out across the park again and I saw the beginnings of a smile. "Yeah … yeah, I see what you're getting at." He turned towards me again. "You're *very* good at this."

"It's just common sense, Eddie, really."

"Yeah. I've never been too good on the old common sense. Em . . . Jackie?"

"What?"

"Are you in a hurry to get back home? Back to your sister's, I mean? Sorry."

"Not really, why."

"I don't want to impose much more, you've been a great help and God knows you have enough on your plate without –"

"What is it, Eddie?"

"Well, I was wondering, seeing how I'm so nervous and all … I was wondering if maybe you and me could practise it together first."

A thin squeal escaped me, followed by "Eddie! Are you out of your mind?" I jumped to my feet and grabbed my bag. It was only then that I realised what he meant. "Oh! Oh. You're talking about the phone call."

He blinked at me, deep in shock. "The phone call, yes. What did you think I meant?"

I sat back down again. "Y'know. I thought you meant … y'know . . ."

He looked more shocked than I had felt. "*No!* No. No, that's not what I meant. Oh God. No. *No.*"

"So you want to practise the phone call?"

"Yes. The phone call. Not … anything else."

"And you mean actually practise it, like a rehearsal? Not just talk about it?"

"Like a rehearsal, exactly."

It sounded childish. But it sounded fun too. "Okay. I'm game. Do you want to start?"

Eddie made a fist, then stuck out his thumb and little finger. He held the hand up to his ear and said, "Ring, ring!"

The urge to laugh was almost overwhelming, but I resisted it. I made a hand-phone of my own and held it up to my ear.

"Hello," I said. "Margaret speaking."

CHAPTER 14

When I got back to the house and Melissa asked me how it had gone with Chrissy, I hesitated. We were just starting to get along. If I told her what had happened, there might be a row. I couldn't imagine her being very impressed with the way I'd walked out on my crying daughter. On the other hand, I mused, there was a chance for further bonding here. I was the one who'd been offended, after all. And I was the one having the crisis. I quickly decided that it was worth the risk. We sat down in the living room and got ourselves comfy while Niall quietly made confetti of a colouring book on the rug.

To my relief and delight, Melissa saw my side of the Arnotts incident. Chrissy should have been more supportive. Chrissy should have been more understanding. Chrissy should have been more sensitive. This was a ricochet from her own reaction on Friday – I understood that – but still, I lapped it up. My big fear, I explained, was that my relationship with my daughter was going to go the way of my relationship with my son. It wasn't just today. I'd also learned that she'd been pretending to share my low opinion of Robert's girlfriend while laughing about it behind my back. This was the way it had started with him: small disagreements, small deceptions. Melissa and I had never talked about any of this, naturally enough – on those rare occasions when we had spoken, I'd thought it wise to stay off the topic of feuds – but she'd been dimly aware that all was not well. Now she wanted details. I started with Jemima, explaining how Robert had seemed to like her precisely because I didn't. Melissa sympathised and probed further. Go back to the beginning, she said, back to the first sign of trouble. I was more than happy to oblige.

"It's hard to say when things started to go wrong," I told her. "We just … I don't know … We just seemed to start getting on each other's nerves. Little rows, but lots of them."

"When was this?"

I thought, *Funnily enough, it was around the time you and I fell out.* "Towards the end of his schooldays."

"And what were the rows about?"

"Well, lemme think. Steven Morris for one. He was this tiny wee guy from Dunshaughlin that Robert started hanging around with in sixth year. If you only saw a photo of him, you'd know you couldn't trust him."

"Eyes too close together, were they?"

"Yes! I know that sounds stupid, but ..." I paused, aware that I wasn't doing a very good hatchet job. "It wasn't just the way he looked, it was the way he moved about too, all slippery and slidey and sneaky, like he was on castors. But mostly it was the way he acted, what-do-they-call-it ... over-familiar. The first time I met him was in our house, in the kitchen. Robert pointed at me like I was a stain and said out of the corner of his mouth, 'Steven, my mum, my mum, Steven.' Your man slipped over towards me and said, 'What's your first name?'"

"Ooh," Melissa said. "Don't like that."

"Neither did I. It's Jackie, I told him, but Mrs O'Connell will do fine."

"You were just right."

"Made no difference. He always called me Jackie, every time. Actually, once or twice, it was Jackie O. I didn't want to look like an old bat, so I let on I didn't care."

"The tosser."

"That wasn't the half of it. He used to help himself to biscuits *out of the cupboard*."

"Jesus."

"Honestly. One time I caught him walking out with our newspaper under his arm. He said he 'thought we were finished with it'. I didn't want to say to Robert, flat-out, that I thought his friend was a dick, but he knew I didn't like him. So that was one thing. Steven Morris."

"What else?"

"All the usual suspects. His bloody awful music, stupid

haircuts he got, his unbelievable untidiness, that horrible earring that he quickly removed, thank God."

"But isn't that always the way with teenagers?" Melissa said. "I'm sure Chrissy had the same faults."

"What are you getting at?" I said sharply – more sharply than I meant to.

"Nothing."

"Are you trying –"

"Nothing, Jackie, I wasn't getting at anything. Go on."

"Listen, even if I did give out to Chrissy about, I don't know, the state of her room, she'd just roll her eyes and, at worst, mutter something under her breath. Robert would always go for me, screaming and roaring, then storm off and not speak to me for a few days. Then there was the famous hash incident, of course."

"Tut-tut."

"Tut-tut is right. This was in the summer after he left school. There was already tension because he said he had no intention of going to third level, he wanted to pursue his acting. He'd applied to a few courses because we'd stood over him and made him, but we knew he wasn't going to go, even if he got accepted – which, later on, he was. Anyway, I was cleaning his room one day – I mean, I was moving the piles of rubbish about – he'd go mental if I threw anything out – when I came across this little wooden box. Very ornate, nothing like you'd expect our Robert to have. I opened it up, not snooping, just curious, because I couldn't imagine what he was using it for. And inside there was this little brown lump about the size of a clove of garlic. I wouldn't have known what it was if there hadn't been a packet of Rizlas with it. Even then, it took me a minute to work it out. I showed it to Gerry and he hit the roof. You know what he's like about drugs."

Melissa rolled her head about on her shoulders, neither nodding nor shaking.

"There was a huge row, a real top-of-the-lungs job. Just Gerry and Robert – I kept out of it. But still, I was the one who took all the flak. He blamed me, Robert, for invading his privacy, that was the way he put it, and most of all for getting his dad involved. It wasn't long after that when he started talking about moving out. And that was when the trouble really started."

"Yeah, I remember you telling me about it."

I was taken aback. I'd almost forgotten that she wasn't a total stranger.

"It just seemed too soon," I said, recovering quickly. "He was only out of school; he wasn't even nineteen. He'd got a job in a call centre by then – a *call centre*, you can imagine how proud I was – so he wasn't entirely broke, but he had no idea about budgeting or anything like that. And practical things, he was hopeless at, just hopeless. He had trouble changing a light-bulb. He couldn't work a washing machine, he certainly couldn't cook. I'd tried to teach him a few things, but he wasn't interested; I'd get as far as 'Peel an onion' and he'd be off. I was sure the whole thing would be a disaster. And, of course, when I pointed this out I was the worst in the world."

"It wasn't a disaster, though. He managed, didn't he?"

"Well, he *managed*, yeah, but ... Look, I suppose the real

reason I didn't want him to move out is because I knew that would make it even harder for the pair of us to get back on good terms. Gerry said it would work out just the opposite, that he'd get a dose of reality and realise how much I'd done for him at home, blah, blah, blah. Gerry was wrong. I was right. Once he moved out, things went from bad to much, much worse. And quickly too. He never called me, never. And when I called him, he used to just *sigh* down the phone at me, like he couldn't believe what an idiot I was."

"Did you visit him much? In … where was it?"

"Portobello. I did at the start. The place was a tip, as I knew it would be. I wouldn't have thought it was possible that Robert could have found a house-mate who was even lazier than himself, but he managed. Derek something-or-other, worked in the call centre. *He* could barely make a cup of tea. At least Robert knew how that miracle was achieved. He had an awful girlfriend around then too, worse than Jemima even. I can't remember her name, but she was hideous, all tattoos and piercings and ripped stockings. I asked her what she did for a living once and she said, 'Drummer', just the one word. I said, 'Bummer'."

I waited for Melissa to say something supportive or at least smile at my joke, but she didn't.

"I stopped going over there in the end," I went on. "There was no point, he barely spoke to me. Sighed a lot, as usual but no real sentences. Gerry used to go on his own sometimes, you know, take Robert out for a pint."

"PINT!" Niall yelped.

I jumped a foot.

"Yes!" Melissa said, as if the boy had just suggested a cure for cancer. "That's right. Pint!"

"Next thing you know," I said, getting back on track, "Chrissy's talking about moving out. Anything he could do, she could do better. I did blame him for that, I must say. I didn't want to, but I couldn't help it."

Melissa nodded. "Have you any idea why, though? Why he was being like that?"

"I used to think it was because his acting hadn't taken off and he was just frustrated. But when he got the part in *The O'Mahonys*, he all but thumbed his nose and stuck out his tongue at me. I said he'd never get anywhere and look at him now kind of thing. Then he went right back to treating me like dirt."

I fell silent. My problems with Robert had always sounded intensely dramatic in my head. Now that I was talking about them out loud, they seemed so dreary.

"*Did* you say he'd never get anywhere?" Melissa asked.

"No! Well, I warned him that it was an unstable business. Lots of times."

"Hmmm. And you've got *no* idea why things went wrong? Not a clue?"

My back went up again. "No. Why?"

"Well … you don't think maybe … you were being a bit of a nag?"

I blinked in surprise. "*Me*? A nag? No. Why? What do you mean? A *nag*?"

"Maybe not. I'm just guessing. It sounds to me like you did a lot of complaining, that's all. Didn't like his friend Steven —"

"You called him a tosser yourself!"

"I'm not saying he wasn't one." She gave me a challenging look, then continued. "You didn't like his friend Steven, you didn't like his girlfriend, didn't like his haircuts or his music and all that rubbish, didn't like his choice of career –"

"It was hardly a career, working in a call-centre!"

"I meant acting."

"Oh." I could think of nothing else to add.

"You didn't like his flat, didn't like his flat-*mate*, didn't –"

"All right, I get it," I said. "I think you're wrong."

She stared at me. I stared back.

"Okay," she said amiably. "So I'm wrong."

"Okay then."

"Fine."

"Good."

We sat in silence for a few moments. I wondered if Melissa was thinking what I was thinking – were we on the cusp of a proper row? Was all the progress we'd made about to be undone? For my part, I was determined that it would not be.

"Still," she said then. "All's well that ends well, eh?"

"I don't follow you."

"I mean, he's all right now, isn't he? With you?"

"*No*," I said. "God, no. Friday morning, over the Jemima thing, he was effing and blinding at me like he was getting paid for it."

"Oh. But he turned up yesterday, didn't he? He seemed very concerned, I thought."

I had to be careful here. "I was glad to see him. And yes, he did seem concerned. So maybe there's hope."

Belatedly, Melissa seemed to join me in realising that we were uncomfortably close to talking about our own fledgling reconciliation. I was greatly relieved when Niall threw down the tattered remains of his colouring book and announced that he wanted to hear a story.

"A story?" Melissa said. "I don't know. Have we got any storybooks?"

"Yes!" Niall cried. "LOADS!"

"And who's going to read this story? Mummy or Auntie Jackie?"

"It's been a while since I read a story," I said nervously. I didn't know if I was talking to the child or his mother.

Niall stared from one of us to the other for a few seconds, then fixed his gaze on me.

"YOU read it," he said and pointed at me like that bloke from the army recruitment posters.

The tale Niall chose, after ten minutes of deliberation, was *The Three Little Pigs*. He handed me the storybook (which was a replacement for another volume that he'd flicked through, then thrown against the wall) and sat down at my feet. I smiled down at him and he frowned back. Just for a moment, he reminded me of Gordon Ramsay.

"*The Three Little Pigs*," I began.

"I KNOW," Niall fumed.

I glanced at Melissa. She gave me a little y*ou'll-be-fine* nod.

"*Once upon a time,*" I read, "*there was a mother pig who had three little pigs. The three little pigs grew so big that their mother said to them, 'You are too big to live here any longer. You must go and build houses for yourselves. But take care that the wolf does not catch you.'*

I paused to clear my throat. Quite honestly, reading the words "Once upon a time" had caused a bit of a lump to develop. It had been so long.

"Hurry UP!" Niall screeched.

That cleared the lump at least.

"Now, now," Melissa said. "You have to be patient, sweetie."

"The three little pigs set off," I continued. *"They said, 'We will take care that the wolf does not catch us.' Soon they met a man who was carrying some straw."*

Niall waved his arms around, and not in a good way.

"What is it?" I asked him, trying not to sound annoyed.

"Where's the wolf? I want the WOLF!"

"The wolf doesn't come into it just yet," I said.

"He'll be along in a minute," Melissa added.

Back to the book I went. I read quite well, I thought, all things considered. I did separate voices for each character and really went to town on my huffs and puffs. Right throughout, I was aware that Niall was growing ever more displeased, but I tried to tell myself that it was the subject matter and not my delivery that was upsetting him; pigs number one and two do get eaten, after all. The wolf was just beginning to realise that pig number three was a smarter cookie than his dead brothers when Niall suddenly blew his top.

"The WOLF!" he roared, his face crimson. "I want the WOLF!"

"The wolf"s here now," I said. I didn't want to make the child feel stupid, but there was no other way of putting it. "That was him blowing the houses down, remember?"

Niall made fists and stared at my feet. "The other wolf," he said slowly. "The wolf in the dress. I want the wolf in the DRESS!"

Melissa cottoned on before I did. "No, honey, that's a different story. That's *Little Red Riding Hood*."

"Ah," I said. "Case of mistaken identity. Tell you what, we'll finish this one and then I'll read you that one. Is that okay?"

It was a more than reasonable offer, I thought.

Niall disagreed. He screamed and flopped onto his side as if he'd been shot. Then he curled up into a ball. Before I knew what was what, he was in the grip of a full-on episode.

"Brilliant," I said under my breath.

Credit where credit is due – Melissa was dead right: an episode was nothing like a tantrum. There was a time, about twenty minutes after Niall had issued his first scream, when I thought we might need to call an ambulance. Or the Guards.

"*No need!*" Melissa roared over the din. "I used to think that too. But it'll pass, don't worry. He'll burn himself out in a minute. Well, maybe not a minute but soon enough."

The screaming was just as she had described it, only worse. And louder. It was accompanied by a frantic flailing of all four limbs which eventually became so threatening that we decided to restrain him. It took us quite a while to get him onto a sofa, where Melissa sat on his ankles while I held him by the wrists. He bucked and writhed and snapped his teeth at the thin air, periodically roaring something semi-comprehensible about the wolf in the dress.

"It's nice having someone to help," Melissa shouted. "I can't get him into this position on my own." She was perfectly calm, engrossed in the task at hand as if it was baking a cake or sewing a button on a shirt.

"He's very purple," I yelled, nodding at Niall.

"Yeah. That goes away, don't worry about it."

I must have relaxed my grip then because his right hand broke free and, before I could even gasp, he'd grabbed the TV remote control from the cushion beside him and thrown it into the fireplace. The fire wasn't lit, but that was hardly the point.

"*Niall, honey!*" Melissa cried. "*That's not very nice!*"

I caught his wrist again before he could do any more damage, but he clearly felt that he had scored a little victory; for a couple of seconds, the screaming was replaced by giggling. Then he screwed his face up into the same tight little knot of anger and went right back into it. God knows how long he would have kept it up for if he hadn't been interrupted by his father's return home.

Colm had gone into his office to "catch up on some paperwork". I'd never trusted that phrase. It always sounded so obviously bogus to me, like "I walked into a door" or "The cheque's in the post". I assumed that Colm had been doing what Gerry did when he used those words; he'd been in the pub, watching football in peace. On the other hand, the man was a cardiologist. For all I knew, he was drowning in life-or-

149

death paperwork. Either way, his arrival had a remarkable effect on his son. When he stuck his head into the room, it was as if Niall had been suddenly unplugged. He went limp, then stretched and, to my astonishment, *yawned*, as if he'd just come to the end of a vigorous but enjoyable work-out.

"What's going on here then?" Colm asked.

"Usual," Melissa said, arching her back. "I'll put the kettle on."

"KETTLE!" Niall yelled and clapped his little hands in glee.

"Yes!" Melissa said and tousled his hair. "Kettle!"

Colm dropped his briefcase and sat down beside his son. "Were you being naughty?" he asked. Niall shook his head; Colm nodded his, then turned towards me and said, "So – how are you?"

Apparently, the crisis was over.

"I'm fine," I said. "But I'm not sure about …" I nodded down at Niall.

"Ah, he's grand," Colm said. "Aren't you, soldier?"

"I'm a GRAND," Niall declared.

"Tea or coffee?" Melissa asked and moved towards the kitchen. I got up and followed her.

"Coffee for me," Colm said cheerily.

In the kitchen I closed the door behind me. "Uh …"

Melissa turned to face me.

"Is that it?" I asked.

"Is what what?" she smiled.

"With Niall …"

"What do you mean?"

"I mean … no discussion, nothing?"

"Discussion?"

"Well … don't you think it's something you should … investigate?"

Her smile became fixed. "We're used to it at this stage, Jackie. I know it looks alarming, but you saw for yourself – he snaps right out of it."

"But you're the one who calls them 'episodes'. You gave out to me a while back when I used the word 'tantrum'."

She flapped a tea-towel. "That was ages ago. I was a bit panicked that day, that's all. As I say – I'm used to them now."

"I know, but –"

"There's no need for a 'but', Jackie. Honestly."

I regrouped and tried again. "There doesn't seem to –"

"You know what it is," Melissa said, folding her arms (an ominous sign, I thought). "You haven't been around very young kids for a long time. You've forgotten what it's like, that's all."

"I haven't forgotten anything," I said coldly. There was an uncomfortable silence. "Look," I said then, "I don't mean to be critical –"

"So don't be."

"I just think –"

"Jackie. Let it go."

The words hung over us for a moment.

"Okay," I said slowly.

"Good. Now – tea or coffee?"

* * *

I had a sudden urge to cook that night. It had been a few days and I was missing it badly. Melissa wasn't keen on the idea at first. She did a lot of (unconvincing) flapping about my status as a guest in her house, but I persisted. Eventually, she took me aside and confessed that she didn't want me showing her up in front of her husband. I wasn't sure how to react to that. Backing down, I thought, would be tantamount to saying *Yeah, you're right, I'm much better than you are – you'd never live it down if Colm got a taste of my cooking.* Digging my heels in, on the other hand, would make me look like an insensitive clod. I thought about it so hard and for so long that Melissa eventually took the decision out of my hands. If it meant that much to me, she sighed, I could go ahead – but I was to do my best to make mistakes. I spent a happy hour cobbling together a mushroom risotto and while it was far from my finest work, I was reasonably chuffed with the results. So was Colm. He started insisting that I write down exactly what I did for Melissa (he put great emphasis on the word "exactly"), but when she caught his eye, cleared her throat and raised her chin in one fluid movement, he suddenly seemed to lose his voice. Niall was impressed too. After much prompting from both parents, he gruffly allowed that his dinner was "a nice colour".

Gerry rang again that night, at almost exactly the time he'd called on Friday. This time it was Colm who answered. When he told me who was on the phone, there was a deeply weird moment where I almost bounded out of my chair, eager to tell him that I was making progress with Melissa and, as an unexpected bonus, with Robert too. But I stayed put, telling Colm to explain that I wasn't in the mood to talk and would be in touch soon. I could see that he wasn't happy about being the bearer of bad news, but fair play to him, he trooped off and did as I had asked.

It was a little awkward when he came back. The next topic of conversation seemed to have been chosen for us, but no one, least of all me, had any stomach for it. We pushed our coffee cups around in silence for a while, periodically smiling to each other as if to say, *This is great, isn't it? Nope, no tension here. Nosirree.* Finally, Melissa leaned across the table and said she had an idea. Why didn't we all go to the zoo the next day? She'd been promising to take Niall for ages, Colm wasn't working, and I … She ran out of steam at that point, but only for a second. It would be good for me, she eventually declared; it'd blow the cobwebs away. Frankly, I'd been half-thinking of going to work and had been wondering how to bring it up without setting Melissa off on the *Jackie's-not-that-bothered* track again. This was a much better idea; I couldn't remember the last time we'd been on any kind of outing together. It might be the perfect opportunity to consolidate our progress to date. On the down side, however, it would mean prolonged exposure to Niall. He'd been set off on one by the wrong kind of fictional wolf – who knew how he'd react to a real-life tiger? There was only one way to find out, I guessed.

CHAPTER 15

On Monday morning, I didn't even hear the phone ring before Jenny picked it up. Her lightning-fast response to the merest hint of a beep was something I'd noticed before while sitting miserably in her office. She seemed to pride herself on it, as if it was proof of her dazzling efficiency.

"Jennifer Moore," she said in a somewhat sultry tone of voice. I guessed she was waiting for a call from someone she fancied. The "Jennifer" was new too.

"Jenny?" I said. "It's Jackie O'Connell."

"Oh. Jackie." There was considerable disappointment in her voice. "Let me guess –"

"I won't be able to come in today," I said, not wanting to give her the satisfaction.

"Really?"

"Yes. Really."

"Headache, wasn't it?"

"Yeah. Awful."

"That's a pity. Poor you."

"Yeah." There was something coming, I could feel it.

"Headaches can last for hours, can't they?"

"That's right."

"Or a whole day, sometimes."

"Bad ones, yeah."

She paused for dramatic effect. "I didn't know they could last for *four* days."

Attack, I decided immediately, was the best form of defence. "What are you implying?" I growled. "Are you accusing me of faking it?"

"No, no –"

"I can hardly *see*, Jenny. And if you must know, it isn't the same headache, I've had several over the weekend. They've been coming and going."

"Okay, Jackie, keep –"

"I must say I find this very offensive. Does Trevor know you carry on like this?"

Trevor was her boss. In my three years at First Premier, I'd laid eyes on him maybe four times.

"Now wait a minute –"

"No, you wait a minute. I'm *sick*, Jenny, I'm sick and I'm not coming to work. You can take it that I won't be in for several days, in fact. I'm … badly … weakened. And next time I call in like this, please do your best to be sympathetic and if you can't manage that –"

"I'm sorry, Jackie, okay? I apologise."

I did some heavy breathing, pretending to be recovering my composure. "Fine then," I said. "Believe me, I would rather be going to work than spending all day in a darkened room vomiting into a bucket."

I was quite pleased with that bit. As I'd hoped, it killed off any interest she had in continuing the conversation.

"I have to go," she said feebly. "Hope you get better soon."

"So do I," I said and hung up – just in time too. A smile had started to form and if I hadn't got off the phone, she would surely have heard it in my voice.

The day was off to a great start, I couldn't help but think.

* * *

The drive to the zoo was memorable for one reason only. The entire way, from the front door to the parking spot in the Phoenix Park, Melissa sang "We're Going to the Zoo". She only knew the chorus: *"We're going to the zoo, zoo, zoo! How about you, you, you? You can come too, too, too! We're going to the zoo, zoo, zoo!"* In fairness to her, Niall was absolutely delighted with this mini-concert and joined in with an occasional "YOU, YOU, YOU!" or "ZOO, ZOO, ZOO!". She'd almost lost her voice by the time we crossed the river, but her enthusiasm remained undimmed. I tried to remember the last time I'd sung myself hoarse to entertain a child. On the way to Wexford on an ill-advised day-trip in about 1990, I concluded. The child was Robert – Chrissy was never bothered by long car journeys – and the song was "Puff, the Magic Dragon". I suddenly felt very old.

"We're here!" Colm said, somewhat redundantly, when he was finished toing and froing. "Everybody out!"

"*Yay!*" said Melissa.

"YAY!" said Niall.

I thought about saying "Yay!" too, but by the time I'd decided that it was appropriate to join in, it felt like it was too late.

It had been quite a while since I'd been to the zoo – a decade, at least – and I simply could not believe how much it cost to get in.

"They can't be serious," I said as I stared, goggle-eyed at the price list.

Melissa and Colm weren't bothered, and not just because they were minted.

"That's what things cost," Melissa said simply.

"Have you been to a *circus* lately?" Colm added.

Once inside (Colm paid), we trooped off to the left. Although we had a map, Melissa decided it would be more fun if we just wandered aimlessly. I wasn't a big fan of aimless wandering, as a rule, but kept my mouth shut. The first enclosure we came across was home to a group of macaques. I didn't know that when I caught sight of them, of course. Like Colm and Melissa, I pointed and said, "Look, Niall! Monkeys!", as if I'd been expecting the zoo to be full of hamsters and kittens and couldn't believe my luck. The macaques were just being macaques – they had little choice in the matter – but it was hard to shake the feeling that they were putting on a show, dangling from beams, tight-rope walking, chasing each other only to turn round and leg it when their prey was cornered. I was completely captivated (as were they, of course – best not to think about it). Colm and Melissa seemed equally thrilled. Niall, on the other hand, wasn't at all impressed. No matter how much we pointed and ooed, he kept the same blank expression on his face, not quite a scowl but a long way from a smile. He did say, "Monkeys" at one point but he said it the way you might say "Rain" before going back in for an umbrella. For that reason, we didn't stay long *chez* macaque. No more than five minutes had gone by before we shuffled off towards the tigers. Or tiger, I should say. There were three of them in there, according to the information plaque, but only one was receiving visitors. My God, he was impressive though. He was sitting on an old tree trunk with one paw dangling down and he had that superior look on his face, the one that all cats, big or small, seem to sport most of the time: *Yes, I am this cool. Get used to it.* Melissa and I offered fresh murmurs of astonishment and delight as Colm read aloud from the plaque, but Niall stayed mute. He was standing right in front of me, leaning against the glass with his forehead bearing the weight and for a moment I thought he'd actually dropped off. Then he turned and looked up at me. His eyes were wide and unblinking, his mouth agape.

"It's a *tiger*," he whispered in a voice filled with awe.

I nodded. "Yup. He's big, isn't he?"

Niall returned his gaze to the main event for a moment, then came back to me. "It's a *tiger*," he whispered again.

"Isn't he lovely?" Melissa said.

"It says here he eats nine kilos of meat a day," Colm said. "Imagine that, Niall."

Melissa tutted. "Oh for God's sake, Colm. Niall doesn't know a kilo from a hole in the ground."

Colm bristled. "I'm just saying . . . it's a lot of meat."

"Fine, but leave the maths out of it."

"It's hardly *maths*!"

"Units of measurement, then ..."

Colm shook his head. "Maths ..."

While this mini-argument was blowing up and then immediately dying down, Niall moved his feet closer to the glass and then spread his arms and legs, as if that could get him closer to his new god. I hunkered down beside him. Just as I did so, the tiger yawned, possibly because he was exhausted by being so cool and possibly because he wanted us to get a load of his teeth.

"He *yawned*!" Niall marvelled.

"He must be very sleepy," I said. "Maybe he's been running around a lot."

Niall turned. His nose was almost touching mine. "Does he eat people?"

I thought about it for a moment and decided to tell him the truth, mostly because the truth was more fun. "He might if he was very, very hungry," I said. "He'd rather have something else, though. And don't worry, he can't get *us*. We're safe."

He blinked at me and I could practically see the information settling into his brain. "I would *hate* that," he said solemnly. "Being eat by a lion. Tiger."

"Me too," I agreed. "It would be no good at all."

"He's got a name," Colm said then. "Do you know what it is? Go on, have a guess."

Niall gave it some thought. "Niall?" he ventured.

Colm's head dropped. "No. Turlough. Turlough … the Tiger." He seemed to realise slightly too late that his son didn't appreciate being asked to guess something that he had no chance of getting right.

It was a tumbleweed moment. I was reminded of my twenty-fifth birthday party when Robert squinted up at me and asked me my age. When I challenged him to guess, he bit his thumb for a moment, then said, "Sixty?" Asking children to guess things is a mug's game.

We watched Turlough for another few minutes, during which Niall's devotion only seemed to grow. It wasn't easy getting him to move on. We managed it, in the end, by making outlandish claims about the animals around the corner. The word "magical" was used more than once.

Over the course of the next hour and a half, I tried to discern a pattern in Niall's response to the animals but without success. He thought the spider monkeys were "boring", but the colobus monkeys were "lovely". The lemurs were "funny", but the orangutans were "sad". He found the hippos mesmerising but didn't even slow down at the giraffes; he toddled right past, waving his hand dismissively, as if to say, *Yeah, yeah, long necks – I get it*. The zebras were his least favourite of all. He did pause by their enclosure but only long enough to deliver this damning indictment: "Stripey horses." He said it with such an air of finality, as if nothing ever needed to be said about the species again, that I instantly cracked up. Niall looked at me from the corner of his eye, checking to make sure that I wasn't laughing *at* him. Once he had satisfied himself that I was not, he joined in, his little shoulders rising and falling with each guffaw.

Predictably enough, the dining facilities at the zoo weren't up to much. When lunchtime came around, we had flavourless sandwiches, which somehow managed to be both limp and hard, and bottles of water that cost as much as the average cocktail. Colm kept Niall amused with impressions of the animals we'd seen so far (he did a particularly fine macaque), while Melissa and I put our heads together to bitch about the woman three tables over. She had two kids with her, both of whom were horrendously fat. The mother was no pipe-cleaner herself, but the kids were like something from a documentary. They were tucking into quarter-pounders and chips, pausing periodically to suck on jumbo Cokes, the kind that come in buckets.

"I feel like going over," Melissa whispered. "Bloody idiot. It's practically child abuse. They're, what, about six or seven years of age? They must be twenty stone between them."

"A bit of junk once in a while does no one any harm," I agreed. "But those two must be living on it. *Must* be."

"They've bars of chocolate there too, look – and crisps. That's dessert."

"They probably wouldn't know an apple if it ran up and kissed them."

"It's disgusting, that's what it is."

"Disgraceful."

"What would Jamie Oliver say?"

"I *know*."

Yes, we were being horribly judgmental and no, it was none of our business in the first place, but I was really enjoying myself. In days gone by, Melissa and I had regularly joined up to bitch about a third party; it was practically a hobby and one I had sorely missed. I was greatly disappointed when she dropped the subject and started telling me about the deli near her house, whose greatness was only slightly marred by the fact that it was run by the rudest man in the world. I tried to feign interest, but my attention kept wandering back towards the fat children. They were having a bit of a row because the little boy – the young boy, rather – had stolen some chips from his sister's stash. This, despite the fact that he had plenty of his own in front of him. I couldn't quite hear what she was saying but, whatever it was, she really meant it. She had a face on her like a clenched fist and seemed to be having difficulty forcing the words past her teeth. I'd been watching for a few seconds before I became aware that I was being watched back. When I flicked my eyes slightly to the left and saw the mother staring at me, I jerked my entire body towards Melissa and started nodding furiously, as if I was thoroughly engrossed in what she was saying. Just as I began to hope that I'd got away with it, the mother pushed back her chair and rose steadily, like Godzilla coming up from the depths. I allowed myself to believe that maybe, just maybe, she was going to one of the two tables between us, both of which were empty. *For more salt*, I thought. *Or more ketchup. Or more napkins*. She wasn't, of course. She was coming for me.

"You," she said as she arrived in our airspace. Before I could even blink, much less respond, she brought her palm down on the table in way that sounded like it must have hurt. "Yeah, *you*."

I looked up at her.

"What's your problem?" she said.

"Excuse *me*," Melissa puffed. "You're frightening my son."

In fact, Niall was looking at the new arrival without the slightest trace of apprehension. If anything, he seemed to be enjoying her obvious fury.

"And what about my son and daughter?" the woman hissed. "What about *them*? Are they not entitled to have their lunch in peace without people staring at them like they were animals in a zoo?" Her mouth puckered as she remembered where she was. She carried on regardless. "Just because they've got a weight problem, that doesn't give anyone the right –"

"I'm sorry," I said. "I wasn't looking over because they're – because of their weight. They just caught my eye because they were arguing."

"Bullshit!" she cried. "You're lying."

"Steady on there!" Colm said, putting his arm around Niall's shoulders. I sneaked a peek at the other table. The kids had stopped arguing and resumed shovelling food.

"First of all," Melissa said, "don't you dare call my sister a liar. And second of all, if you're all that concerned about your children's weight, then maybe you shouldn't be buying them burgers and chips and great big flippin' Cokes."

"Who the hell do you think you are?" the woman spat (literally – a small globule landed by the remains of Colm's sandwich). "I'll feed my kids whatever I want to feed them. And for your information, they happen to *like* burgers and chips and Cokes."

She said this with such confidence that it took me a moment to realise that it was nonsense. Melissa got there way ahead of me.

"Oh, well that's all right then!" she said. "Sure it doesn't matter what you give them so long as they *like* it, isn't that right? For a minute there, I thought you were force-feeding them rubbish against their will. But they *like* it, you say? God, I *apologise*. I had no idea, *please* forgive me."

I got the impression that the woman wasn't used to dealing with sarcasm on this scale. It seemed to defuse, or at least confuse, her for a long couple of seconds. Then she returned her attention to me and started barking again, this time at even greater volume. "You're so bloody smug, aren't you? Little Miss Perfect, passing judgement on everyone else's shortcomings. Have you taken a look in the mirror yourself lately?"

This, I desperately hoped, was a reference to my hairstyle and not my face. I decided immediately that it was not worth responding to.

Melissa decided otherwise. She cleared her throat and leaned forward on her elbows.

"If I were you," she said softly, "I would apologise for that remark. Then I would turn around and walk away. Right now." And then she smiled, sort of. I felt goose-bumps popping up on my arms. Right before my eyes, she'd turned into Tony Soprano.

The woman's eyes narrowed. She sucked on her lips for a moment, then turned and walked away, mumbling something under her breath. I didn't quite catch it but, whatever it was, it wasn't an apology. Despite the tension in the air, I felt mildly giddy – had my ears deceived me or had Melissa fallen back into the role of protective big sister? The fact that I'd only required her help because I'd been staring at some unfortunate fat children seemed beside the point.

There was no doubt about it. We were really getting somewhere.

* * *

Our afternoon in the zoo was much like our morning. We adults pretended to be wildly enthusiastic (and knowledgable) about each and every one of the animals, while Niall, for no obvious reason, veered between near-hysteria and abject boredom. He was greatly impressed by the sea lions, for instance (sample quote: "Look at his flippy-floppy feet!") but regarded the elephants with folded arms and a decidedly grim expression. "They're enormous, aren't they?" his dad said in an attempt to raise the excitement level. "Yeah," Niall sighed from the depths of his push-chair (his little legs had long since failed him), "really, really big." He had no time for birds of any kind, no matter how extravagant but did at least three tours of the reptile house.

Eventually, exhaustion overran him completely and we made our last stop of the day, in the zoo's shop. For the first five minutes or so, all was well. Niall skipped from aisle to aisle, pointing out items of interest, which Colm duly picked up. Melissa and I hung about by the entrance, each of us long since ready to call it a day. When we heard a sudden howl, Melissa seemed to think, as I did, that it had come from a nearby animal enclosure. The truth dawned only when we saw a cardboard box appear from behind a display and strike the ceiling. We rushed over and found Niall on his side, enthusiastically kicking his father who, try as he might, couldn't get close enough to lift the boy back onto his feet. The screaming started just as we arrived and attracted the attention of the few shoppers who had missed the flying cardboard box.

"*Niall!*" Colm hissed. "*Get up! Please, son! Please!*"

"JIGSAW!" Niall roared in response. "JIGSAW, JIGSAW, JIGSAW!"

"He wants a jigsaw," Colm explained, as if we hadn't grasped the essentials of the current difficulty. "But it's for ten-year-olds and up."

"JIGSAW!" Niall insisted and lashed out with his foot again, this time catching a stuffed gorilla square in the kisser.

I was about to hunker down and start negotiations, reasoning (with no great confidence) that he was unlikely to lash out at a stranger the way he lashed out at his dad, but Melissa spoke up before I could make my move.

"All right, Niall," she said soothingly. "Get your jigsaw and we'll go."

Her son was on his feet in a flash. He grabbed the box that had recently rebounded from the ceiling and ran off in the direction of the cash register.

I bit my lip and wondered if I should say anything. The answer, I quickly decided, was yes and no; yes, I should but no, I wouldn't. There was no way I was going to risk annoying Melissa. So I kept my trap shut and faked sudden interest in a range of Dublin Zoo keyrings.

On the way back to the car, Melissa asked me if I'd had a good time.

"Of course!" I said. "I had a lovely time."

"Are you sure?" she asked, slowing down.

I slowed down too and then we both stopped. Colm looked over his shoulder, but kept pushing the buggy.

"I'm sure," I said. "Why?"

She shrugged. "Ah, I don't know, I just started to feel guilty. After the weekend you've had, I thought maybe you were secretly fuming that we'd dragged you out for this."

"Don't be silly," I said. "It was great. Better doing this than moping around the house."

"So long as you're all right."

"I am," I said and smiled at her.

She smiled back. Then she gave my shoulder a little rub. I patted the back of her hand and she withdrew it, embarrassed.

We turned forwards again and walked off, each of us pretending that nothing had happened.

CHAPTER 16

We got back to the house at about four. Colm went out to do a bit of gardening, which, Melissa swore, would involve nothing more than mowing the lawn, then poking at various under-performing plants while frowning. Niall went – or rather was put down – for a much-needed nap. Feeling at something of a loose end, I decided to have a bath. It was there, lying up to my nose in what felt like very expensive bubbles, that I suddenly remembered it was a Monday; *The O'Mahonys* would be on at seven thirty. When I finally dragged myself out of the water (which took a lot of willpower), I sat on the edge of my bed and stared at my mobile for a few minutes. My reconciliation with Melissa was going great guns. Did I dare to try and push things with Robert? When he first got the job on the show,

I'd called him twice every Monday night, once to say how much I was looking forward to it and then again to tell him what I thought. No matter how sincere my congratulations, no matter how clever my criticisms of the script and his fellow actors, he always treated me like a phone company cold-caller. There was one occasion, after a quite spectacular bout of rudeness on his part, when I actually said, "Can I speak to the person who pays the bill?" He didn't get the joke, of course, and took it as further evidence that I was simply not worth talking to. I gave up trying in the end, just as I had given up calling over to his flat.

On this occasion, I decided to split the difference with a text. *Looking forward to the show*, I wrote, *Love, Mum x*. I dropped the phone onto the bed and started to get dressed, wondering if I dared hang out the window for a crafty fag. A few seconds later, when I was halfway into a pair of jeans, it rang. I hopped across and picked it up. It was Robert. My heart began to hammer. I poked the green button.

"Hello?"

"Hi, Mum. It's me."

"Hi. How are you?"

"I'm fine. I got your text."

"Good, good. Seven thirty?"

"Yeah. Same as ever. So … how are you feeling?"

I bit down on the first reply that came to mind, which was "Not bad at all". And then I heard myself saying, "I haven't been feeling great today, to be honest."

"No?"

"Not really. Things have just caught up with me a bit, I suppose."

"Bound to happen," Robert said quickly and uncertainly. "Bound to."

"Yeah …. Is there any chance …"

"What?"

"Ah, I'm sure you're busy."

"No, what?"

"Well … is there any chance you could nip out and meet me? Just for a coffee. It might do me good to have a chat. Won't take an hour, I swear. You'll be back in plenty of time to watch yourself."

He hesitated but not for very long. "I wouldn't mind a proper drink," he said. "How about that?"

"Okay," I said. "Where?"

* * *

Downstairs in the kitchen, I reminded Melissa that this was *The O'Mahonys* night. She made a big show of pretending that she already knew because they never missed it. I let her make a fool of herself for a while and then told her it was all right, she could drop the act.

"I keep meaning to watch it," she said meekly. "And I have caught it a few times. Vincent – isn't that right?"

"Valentine," I corrected. "Valentine Reilly. He's no good."

"I knew that much. I saw one where he stole money from his girlfriend's purse."

"That was Nicola. She was about five girlfriends ago. And

having a few quid nicked from her purse was the least of her problems. He got her pregnant and then cheered when she had a miscarriage. He crashed her car and said it was joyriders. He beat the crap out of her ex-boyfriend because he smiled at her in the pub. He drowned her cat in the toilet because it scratched him. I could go on."

"He must have some redeeming features," Melissa said.

I nodded. "Apparently … he's very good in bed."

"I see."

"Listen," I said then. "I'm going to pop out for a while. I'm meeting Robert for a, y'know … chat."

"Oh. Okay. Are you going around to his?"

"No. He fancies a pint. We're meeting halfway. Leeson Lounge."

Her face shimmered. "Right. Are you … walking?"

"No," I said as evenly as I could. "I'm driving. And not drinking. Obviously."

She smiled quickly – too quickly – and returned to the bonsai she'd been pruning.

"Enjoy," she said.

* * *

Robert arrived at the pub fifteen minutes late, as I had guessed he probably would; in matters of punctuality, as in so much else, he was his sister's polar opposite. When he walked in, two women who were perched at the bar (and evidently had been for some time) made audible squeaks, eyed him up and down, then put their heads together to giggle like schoolgirls, which they were most certainly not – they were my age, at least. As he nodded hello and asked me if I wanted a drink, I found myself feeling faintly unwell. I had no trouble guessing what they might be saying to each other and dearly wished I could make my imagination a little more PG. I told Robert that I was fine with my sparkling water and watched with some surprise as he ordered a glass of red wine. The women at the bar clammed up and stared hard at each other while he was beside them, which was a relief; I'd half-suspected that one (or both) of them was going to proposition him there and then.

"Wine?" I said as he retook his seat. "I thought you were a Guinness man."

He shrugged. "Dunno what to tell you. I got a taste for it, that's all."

"You'll be on the caviar next," I smiled. Robert didn't smile back. He was, I presumed, on the cusp of taking offence. "Good for you," I added hurriedly.

"So," he said then. "Has he been in touch?"

"Your father? He called, yes. But I didn't speak to him."

"Right. Are you planning on speaking to him?"

"I suppose so. Yes. I'll call him … soon. Have you been talking to him yourself?"

"Have I *fuck*."

"Language, Rob –"

"I was talking to Chrissy though."

"Oh."

"She feels like shit. She told me so. I think she only told me because she wanted me to tell you."

I took some water. "I see."

"I got the impression she's afraid to call you."

"Well, there's no need for that. What did she say, exactly?"

"She didn't go into a lot of detail. She said she was a bit hard on you. Gave you grief about being too cool. Said something about your marriage being over. And then you bolted."

"I did, yeah. I'm not proud of it either. I'll give her a call and get it all sorted."

"I'm sure that'd go down well."

"And what about you? How are you … feeling?"

There was a long pause, punctuated by a large gulp of wine on Robert's part and another sip of water on mine.

"I'm still mad. Fucking furious, actually." Another pause, shorter this time. "But he's my dad, isn't he?"

"Yes, Robert. He is."

"So what am I supposed to do?"

I mistook this for a rhetorical question at first. When I realised that it wasn't, I said, "You're not *supposed* to do anything. Just … play it by ear."

He made a noise with his lips. "Yeah, but …"

"Go on."

"It's just that … Chrissy says she's never talking to him again."

"I know. She told me."

"Oh. I didn't know that. I thought it was something she came up with while she was talking to me. But …"

"But you don't feel that way."

"No." There was an element of fear in his voice.

"Robert, she obviously didn't tell you this much either: I

was very upset when she said she was finished with your father. *Very* upset."

The fear turned to relief. "Really?"

"Of course. Why would I want my children hating their dad? Never mind what he's done to me. He's still your father, like you said."

That middle bit stuck in my throat a little. But I got it out. Practice makes perfect.

"Don't get me wrong," Robert said. "I could kill him."

"I know. Please don't."

He laughed, briefly. It was a sound I hadn't heard in a long while – the non-sarcastic version anyway. "Anyway – what about you? You said you're not feeling the Mae West. Did something happen? I mean ... something else?"

I shook my head. "No. Nothing specific. I just . . . I don't know. I thought it would be nice to see you."

"Christ," he said. "Now I feel all pressurised."

"Don't worry, Robert. I'm not expecting you to make it all go away."

"Phew! Probably just as well."

I began to smile, then aborted the move, replacing it with a deep sigh. "I haven't slept a wink since," I said.

"No shit," Robert replied. "Sure how could you with all this going on?"

The best course of action, I quickly decided, was not to backtrack over the lie, but to fully embrace it and run like hell. "Yeah. As soon as my head hits the pillow, my mind starts racing, you know?"

"I bet."

"I start wondering …" At that point, I hit a spot of trouble. I'd launched into a sentence for which I had no ending.

"What?" Robert said softly. His tone was so sympathetic that I almost cracked and told him I'd been sleeping perfectly well and had just had a pleasant day at the zoo where his aunt and I had almost *hugged*. Instead, I closed my eyes and allowed my head to droop. As I struggled to think of a way to elaborate on my deception without making myself sick, Robert reached across the table and placed his hand over mine.

"It'll be all right," he said in a voice that was so much like his father's that I lost my breath. Before I knew what was what, I felt tears streaming down my face.

"Come on, Mum," Robert whispered. "Don't cry. Everyone will think it was something *I* said."

I smiled through my silent sobs for a moment and then made a serious effort to get myself under control. When I had achieved a small degree of stability, I looked up and saw that Robert was on the edge of tears himself. That did it; I took a deep breath and cleared my throat. Equilibrium was soon restored.

"I'm sorry," I said sincerely, dabbing my eyes with a napkin.

"Don't worry about it."

"I didn't drag you out here to give you a sob story." Another lie: that was exactly what I had meant to do.

"You didn't drag me anywhere," he said. "I wanted to come."

I withdrew my hand and placed it on top of his. "Thanks, son."

"What for? I didn't do anything."

Just then, the nearer of the two women at the bar slid off her stool and began to slowly step towards us. I noticed before Robert did and looked up at her expectantly.

"Excuse me," she said, slurring slightly, as he turned to see what had caught my eye. "I don't want to be a pain in the arse … but are you Valentine Reilly out of *The O'Mahonys*?"

"That's me," Robert said and stuck out his hand.

The woman shook it for what seemed like several minutes.

"I can't think of your real name," she said when she finally relinquished her grip. "It's driving me mental."

"Will I give you the initials?" Robert teased.

He was good at this, I thought. Slick.

"Go on," the woman said, enjoying herself immensely.

"R O'C."

"R O'C … O'Connell! Something O'Connell, that's right." She turned to her pal at the bar, who, for some reason, had been pretending she wasn't even watching. "Maggie! It's something O'Connell! Begins with an R!"

"*Robert!*" Maggie cried instantly, pointing at my son as if he might not have been sure himself.

Robert clapped. "Correct. Congratulations."

"It was on the tip of my tongue," the woman said. "C'mere, we were just finishing up – would you ever do us a photo before we go?"

"Sure," Robert said.

For the first time, the woman acknowledged my existence. "Maybe you'd take it for us," she said. "Don't worry, we're not going to steal him away from you."

"You couldn't if you tried," I said. "I'm his *mother*."

I expected her to say what practically everyone said in this situation (or the corresponding one with Chrissy), which was "You don't look old enough." But she didn't say that. She said – with an air of considerable satisfaction – "Ahhh! I was wondering ..."

Robert suppressed a grin as she withdrew her mobile phone and switched the camera on.

"You just press the middle button," she said cheerfully as I snatched it from her hand.

"*Thanks*."

Maggie hopped off her bar-stool and the three of them arranged themselves in a tight bunch. Both women put their arms around Robert. Most of the pub was watching proceedings by now. I felt slightly embarrassed and took the photo quickly – too quickly for Maggie's liking.

"Aw!" she said. "You barely looked! Do one more."

"Two," her friend added. "Just to be sure."

I took the shots and handed back the phone.

"Thanks," the women said. They spoke as one; each addressed her gratitude to Robert.

"Any time," he said. "Will you be watching tonight?"

"Definitely," they said, once again speaking simultaneously.

And then, amid a flurry of handshakes and cheek-pecks and compliments, they were gone.

"Sorry about that," Robert said as we retook our seats.

I'd found the two women – or more correctly, their

obvious lusting over my child – quite annoying. But there was an upside to their intrusion, I now realised: way ahead of schedule, I could stop pretending to be more miserable than I was, while still giving Robert credit for the improvement.

"Don't apologise," I said. "I've never seen that happen before. It was ... cool. I keep forgetting that you're famous."

"Well, now, I'm hardly *famous* famous. It's not like I can't walk the streets."

"Won't be long though. Wait'll you see."

He tried not to show that he was tickled by the idea. I was reminded of the time when he was eleven or twelve and my mother pointed out that he was turning into "a little heartbreaker". He was too young for girls then and made a big deal of slapping the compliment away. But he'd been unable to keep his mouth straight. The same difficulty plagued him now.

"Will I get you another glass of wine?" I asked, just to change the subject and put him out of his misery.

"I'll get it," he said, jumping to his feet. "Another water?"

"I'll have a Diet Coke this time," I said. "Might as well go mad."

He nodded and went to the bar.

We took our time over that second round, and over the third as well. Robert did almost all of the talking – out of nerves, I suspected. Like his Aunt Melissa, he wasn't used to being alone with me. I listened intently as he trotted out one harmless anecdote after another (most of them featuring various nutter neighbours in his apartment block), smiling and frowning when appropriate. When we realised that we'd been sitting there for an hour and would miss *The O'Mahonys* if we didn't leave soon, I offered him a lift. He declined, but he did so politely, pointing out – ha-ha – that he just wanted some air and wasn't trying to get away from me or anything. We said goodbye on the pavement and briefly hugged. I thanked him for cheering me up, a statement that only felt like half a lie.

"Will I give you a call after the show?" I asked just as we were parting.

"Sure," he said.

I smiled and turned away, feeling a little light-headed.

Will I give you a call after the show?

Sure.

It was like old times, only just the opposite.

* * *

I got back to Melissa's to find her putting the finishing touches to dinner. We ate and cleaned up and got comfortably installed in the living room just in time for the seven-thirty deadline. Niall had been roused from his nap to have a bite, but he was clearly still exhausted and had to be tucked up again within half an hour. (There was an awkward moment when he announced that his mother's chicken curry smelled "funny" and wondered if I would be cooking again any time soon. I quickly changed the subject to tigers.)

"We'll be seeing him again," Colm said, as the opening credits rolled. "There's no way he's going to sleep all night."

"Shhh," said Melissa, as if she was missing something already.

179

The show's first couple of minutes were embarrassingly dull. I let them slide by without much interruption; there didn't seem to be any point in getting into detail about every last storyline and character. Then the scene changed to a small office. Henry O'Mahony was sitting behind his desk, making dinner arrangements with his mistress. *The O'Mahonys*, I had always thought, was a County Wicklow version of *Dallas*. But while the Ewings had made a huge fortune from oil, the O'Mahonys had made a small one from construction. Like Jock and Miss Ellie, the senior members of the family were honest, hard-working types. Francis was an old-school gent and his wife, Theresa, was quietly devoted to her man and her two boys. They had a Bobby-like son in James, who worshipped his father and worked every hour God sent. Henry, on the other hand, was J.R. He was mean and cunning and ruthless and got all the best lines; they might as well have given him cowboy boots and a Stetson.

"Robert owes this guy money," I explained quickly. "I mean, Valentine owes him money. He got into a poker game he shouldn't have gone near and ended up writing an IOU for five grand. Henry here bailed him out, but he hasn't seen a penny of it since."

Sure enough, Henry's phone call was interrupted by a knock on the door. It was Valentine, looking very sheepish.

"Oh, he looks so well!" Melissa said. "So handsome!"

The scene was no more than a minute long and, frankly, was one that we'd all come across before. Henry pointed to the calendar on the wall behind him and asked Valentine if he'd mind reading out the date. Nervously, Valentine did so.

Henry played dumb, saying he was sure he remembered something about a payment of some kind that was supposed to have been made by this date. Was he dreaming or had the money failed to materialise? Valentine ran through the usual assurances; there had been unexpected complications, but things were getting back on track. He'd have the cash in a matter of days. Henry said he sincerely hoped so. He hated having to hire muscle. It went wrong so often. These guys were animals, had no sense of restraint. You asked them to rough someone up and next thing you knew, the someone was in a box. No need for muscle, Valentine whimpered, the debt was as good as paid.

"Very good!" Colm said when it was over. "He does the accent very well."

"The other guy was good too," Melissa added. "Menacing. But Robert was better."

This was pure flattery, of course. Still, I was happy to hear it.

"Your man who plays Henry is a really nice guy," I said. "He was on *The Late, Late Show* a couple of months ago. Couldn't be any more different from his character. He gets letters from old ladies giving out about all the terrible things Henry does and telling him he should be ashamed of himself."

"What about Robert?" Colm asked. "Does he get many letters?"

I had no idea. It wasn't the sort of information that would have come my way.

"Oh, yeah," I said. "Loads. Mostly from girls, you know ..."

"Good man," Melissa said. "He'll be off to Hollywood next. Like Colin Farrell."

"I don't know about that," I said, unable to keep the smile off my face.

Robert didn't make another appearance until after the commercial break. This time he was in the pub, talking in a low and serious voice with his best friend, Dodger. I felt the need to do a little more explaining.

"This guy's a bit like Valentine, only without the charm. He's not that bright either. And he has no morals whatsoever."

Right on cue, Dodger said he might have a solution to Valentine's money worries. His plan wasn't exactly legal – in fact, it was highly illegal – but the risk was small. Was Valentine interested? He was.

"This isn't going to end well," Melissa said when the scene was over.

"No," Colm agreed. "Definitely not."

"God, I hope they aren't writing him out," I said. "He can't go on forever, I know, but I'd hate to see him going too soon. Off to jail or worse …"

"Nah," Melissa said. "He'll be grand."

We watched until the end, but Valentine didn't appear again.

Niall did though, shortly after eight.

He still looked and sounded wrecked, but he said he couldn't sleep. Melissa and Colm made a big fuss and reached for one of their zoo purchases, the jigsaw puzzle. I said I'd go and put the kettle on.

Out in the kitchen, I took a few deep breaths and dialled Robert. It rang and rang and rang. But he didn't answer. I hung up when his voicemail came on. *Too good to be true*, I thought as I busied myself with mugs and spoon. *I knew it*. And then my mobile chimed. I dropped the packet of chocolate digestives I'd been failing to rip open and pounced on it. My skin tingled when I saw who was calling.

"Hello, Robert," I said.

"Mum. Sorry, I was on the land line there, couldn't answer."

"Don't worry about it. So! You were just great, son. And you *looked* great. Melissa said so too. Very handsome."

"Cheers. I thought I fluffed a line in Henry's office, the one about his suit."

"No, no, you were perfect."

"I don't know. It was supposed to sound all agitated and nervous, but I think it came out cocky, like I was taking the piss."

"Well, I didn't think so."

This was already just about the most in-depth conversation we'd ever had about *The O'Mahonys*. And it quickly got even better.

"Maybe you're right. Karen didn't say anything and she's usually not shy about setting us right. That's the new director. Mick walked out, did I tell you?"

"Oh. No, I didn't know that." I didn't know because he never told me *anything* about work. I'd never even heard of Mick.

"Yeah. A row about money, everyone says. Good riddance,

if you ask me. He was a miserable bastard. Karen's much nicer. Bit of a perfectionist, but I suppose she's only being professional."

"Oh, yeah. You have to be professional."

"Yeah."

"I don't suppose you want to tell me what happens next?"

"Nope. You'll just have to watch."

I heard a smile in his voice and hoped he'd heard the smile in mine.

"But you've seen the scripts and everything, haven't you? I mean, nothing bad …"

"Sorry?"

"This isn't the beginning of the end of Valentine, is it? Because –"

"God, no. Onwards and upwards. The stuff we're shooting now, all this debt business is over and done with."

"Good, good. I was worried."

There was a pause. "Were you?"

"Yeah. I was. Characters get written out, even I know that." I caught my breath. If I'd said that a week previously, Robert would have said something like "You'd love that, wouldn't you? Typical."

"Not this one," he said. "If anything, I'm getting more to do. It's going pretty well, if I say so myself."

Relief went through me like a shot of adrenaline. "That's great. Well, keep up the good work."

"I will. Uh … have you spoken to himself yet?"

"No. Tomorrow. I'll do it tomorrow."

"All right. Listen, I'm away. Big night out tonight. Again.

We had a big night out last night too. *Very* big. Actually, now that I think about it, I might stay in. No – to hell with it, I'll go."

Now he was volunteering *social* information. It was almost too much.

"Have fun either way," I said. "And well done again. I'll talk to you soon."

"Okay. Good luck."

"See ya."

We hung up and I went back to getting the tea together, dancing on the spot.

* * *

Back in the living room, we had the tea and biccies and all three of us joined in helping Niall with his jigsaw. He wasn't downstairs for more than half an hour before his eyelids started to droop. Melissa put him to bed again, for good this time, and then we settled in to watch the movie on Channel 4; some cop thing with Denzel Washington. Colm and Melissa seemed to enjoy it, but it washed over me without leaving a trace. I was too pleased and excited by the day's events to pay proper attention. At eleven or so, I was suddenly overcome with exhaustion; the good kind, the kind joggers are always claiming to experience. I made my excuses and padded off to bed, feeling genuinely happy. Not *happy given the circumstances*. Plain old happy.

And that was it – the high point. It was all downhill from there.

CHAPTER 17

I woke late on Tuesday morning, at around nine fifteen, and was downstairs less than five minutes later, having showered and dressed at speed.

"Hiya," Melissa said, as I entered the kitchen. "Sleep okay?"

"Fine, thanks. Where's Niall?"

"He's doing one of his colouring books from the zoo, with one eye on the gorillas DVD that he got at the zoo, while wearing his *I've Been To Dublin Zoo* T-shirt."

"Good for him."

"He'll be high as a kite for a month. Now – cup of tea? Cereal? Toast?"

"Cup of tea for sure," I said. "And maybe –"

The doorbell rang. Melissa looked at me as if *I* had done it with some kind of remote control.

"Who's that at this time of the morning?" she asked, then dropped her tea-towel and stomped off down the hall. She seemed to greatly resent the interruption and if the caller had been a salesman or ticket-seller, I'm sure she would have given them short shrift.

But it wasn't a salesman or a ticket-seller. It was Gerry.

My initial reaction, when I heard his voice, was to jump down from my stool and bounce on my toes like an athlete getting ready for the long jump. Then I took a step towards the other door, the one that led to the dining room.

Niall was coming from the opposite direction; we ran smack into each other.

"Hello," he said.

"Hi there."

He held up his colouring book. "I did a lion," he said. "Look!"

Not knowing what else to do, I hunkered down beside him. "Oh, that's lovely, Niall! You did a great job."

Melissa appeared then, pointing behind herself with her thumb.

"Uh … Gerry's here," she said. "He wants to talk to you."

I stayed hunkered down. "Right."

And there he suddenly was, peering over her shoulder.

"Hi," he said.

Melissa stepped into the room. Gerry stayed put. I suddenly thought of Adam Clayton. I saw him in town one day, walking down South William Street. There was nothing remarkable about him, but I gasped as he went by. Purely because he was so familiar, he seemed somehow more *there* than everyone else, as if the rest of us were only in 2-D.

Looking up at Gerry that morning, I experienced a similar sort of effect.

"Hi, yourself," I said, horribly aware of the catch in my voice.

"Come on," Melissa said to Niall. "Let's go and watch the rest of your DVD."

He grimaced furiously. "But I was showing Auntie Jackie my COLOURING book."

"You can show her later, if you haven't ripped it up or set fire to it. Come on." She left, dragging him behind her.

I watched them go, then realised it was probably time I stood up. My knees cracked as I did so. I felt ridiculous.

"I haven't come here to argue," Gerry said, stepping into the room properly.

I gave him a quick once-over. He looked pale and spent.

"Why are you here then?" I asked him.

He scratched the stubble on his chin. "I just wanted to let you know . . ." He closed his eyes and shook his head.

At that moment, I would have bet the house that he was going to say, "I'm leaving you for Lisa." I was heading for the floor again. I just knew it.

"Chrissy did a stupid thing last night," he said.

The room spun. I teetered back on my heels.

"What do you mean, stupid? What kind of stupid?" One possible answer occurred to me immediately. It turned out to be the right one.

"She took a little revenge," Gerry said. "On … our neighbour."

"Our *neighbour*? What, are you afraid to use her name?"

He nodded as if to say, *I deserved that*. "Lisa, then. Chrissy put a brick through her living-room window and threw a tin of red paint over the roof of her car."

I felt a little finger poking me in the ribs. I'd said something about window-bricking in Arnotts. "Oh, for Christ's sake! When was this?"

"About three this morning."

"How do you know it was her?" I asked, knowing it was a useless question.

"Well ... she didn't plan it very well. She threw the brick first, *then* did the car. Lisa was at her bedroom window like a shot when she heard the noise and she recognised Chrissy. She started hurling abuse and Chrissy hurled some back. She didn't even run. She just stood there in the drive."

I let my head drop and wearily trudged towards a stool. "Terrific," I said. "You might as well sit down."

Gerry did so. I looked at him across the island. He could have phoned me with this information. There'd been no need for him to show up in person. He was using it as an excuse, I realised. I considered calling him on it but decided that there was no point.

"So, what are you telling me? She's in jail?"

"No. The Guards weren't involved."

"How did *you* get involved?" I asked. "I can't imagine you woke up. And I doubt that Chrissy told you."

"No, eh ... no. The other ... uh ..."

"Lisa told you."

"Yes."

"Knocked on the door for a cosy wee chat, did she?"

"No, Jackie. She kicked the shit out of the door for a very

uncosy wee shouting match. She *wanted* to call the Guards, but I wouldn't let her. And she made a lot of noise about the repair bills too."

I tutted.

"It was the first time I'd spoken to her," Gerry added. "Believe it or don't, it's up to you. But it's the truth. If I had my way, I'd never have spoken to her again."

"Yeah," I sneered. "After the way she treated you."

He chose to ignore that.

"What about Chrissy?" I said then. "What did she have to say for herself?"

"To me? Nothing. She'd gone by the time I knew what was happening. I called over there first thing this morning, but she wouldn't answer her door. Or the phone."

"Right. I'll go now. Tuesday's her day off, she might still be at home."

"We should go together."

I froze. He noticed.

"We don't have to go in the same car," he said wearily. "If you don't want to."

"It's not that … Gerry, she told me …"

"What?"

"She told me she doesn't want to talk to you. I mean … ever again."

He frowned at me as if he didn't quite follow. "That's silly. I'm her father."

"I know that. But she's very upset. And angry."

"I'm her *father*," he said again. It was the only argument he had.

"I think it's better if I go on my own," I said. "Just for today. Just until … just for today."

"No," he said and slowly shook his head. "Everybody's mad at me, everybody hates me. Fair enough. I deserve it. But I'm not running away from my responsibilities. This is my daughter we're talking about. I'm going."

"But you've already tried to talk to her and she wouldn't. What's the point in going there again?"

It was as if I hadn't spoken.

"I'm going," he said bluntly, "and that's all there is to it."

I was tempted to point out that he was in no position to be getting pushy. But I didn't.

"All right," I said. "Separate cars."

* * *

I should have let him pull out first. This was the thought that ate away at me throughout the entire journey from Ranelagh to Chrissy's flat in Swords. If I'd let him pull out first then I would have been able to lag behind and would eventually have lost him – or rather let him lose me. Instead, I had to drive the whole way with Gerry and the car I had ruined permanently visible in my rear-view mirror. I realised my error at the very first set of traffic lights. As I stared miserably into the mirror, wondering how I could have been so stupid, I was horrified to see Gerry raising his hand and – briefly, tentatively – nodding his fingers, one by one, like a child. What else could I do? I waved back. The moment reminded me of Friday morning and my peek through the front window at home. All these inappropriate waves … *If this was a movie*, I thought, *then that would mean something*. I made a shameful effort to get away from him by slowing up at amber lights and then racing through, but it didn't work and made me so nervous that I abandoned the idea after a couple of goes.

It was just after eleven when we arrived at our destination. I got out of the car and walked across to the main doorway. When Gerry joined me, we nodded meaningfully at each other like a couple of detectives about to raid a drug den. But that was where the analogy broke down. Real detectives would have said a few words to each other. Gerry and I stuck with the nodding.

Chrissy's building was small and squat and frankly ugly. According to the buzzers by the front door, it contained fourteen separate flats, which didn't seem possible. Chrissy was in number three, on the ground floor. I jabbed the appropriate buzzer and was surprised when she answered almost immediately. Somehow, I had imagined that it would take a while.

"Yes?"

"Chrissy? Chrissy, it's me. Mum. Your mother."

Silence.

"Chrissy, I –"

"Come in."

The door clicked and opened half an inch. The intercom went dead. I had planned on saying, "I'm here with your dad", just to remove the element of surprise. Now my chance had gone.

"After you," Gerry said and held the door open.

As ever, I became quite alarmed during the short walk from the entrance to Chrissy's front door. She paid a small fortune in maintenance fees, but wherever the money was going, it sure as hell wasn't on maintenance. The walls of the communal corridors were grubby and chipped, the carpets badly stained. There was a funny smell, not unlike that of a dog's basket.

Chrissy poked her head out of her apartment while Gerry and I were still coming down the corridor. She didn't look all that happy to begin with, but once she saw that I was not alone, she bared her teeth and disappeared inside again. The door slammed before we reached it. I decided to go with the no-nonsense approach.

"Chrissy!" I shouted, banging the door with my palm. "Open up right now."

There was no reply. Gerry stepped forward and gave the door a gentle little knock.

"Come on, love," he said (so softly that I doubted his audibility). "Let's just have a chat."

Still no reply. I tried the thumping and shouting approach again, which meant that we were back in detective mode, this time as good cop and bad cop.

When Chrissy once again failed to respond, I looked to Gerry and said, "This isn't working. Maybe you should wait in the car."

I expected an argument, but he merely nodded once, quickly, and turned away. All of a sudden, I was furious. A great many factors had contributed to my current predicament, of course, but my daughter's stubbornness was the one I lighted on.

"Chrissy!" I roared as Gerry disappeared from view. "I'm not kidding, open this bloody door right now! Your father's gone, it's just me. *Open up. Now.*"

I heard movement straight away, but she must have just been pacing around; ten, fifteen seconds went by before she returned to the door to reopen negotiations.

"You're taking little trips together?" she said incredulously. "Jesus Christ!"

"We came separately," I said in a sort of shouty sigh. "And he's *gone* now. Open up!"

There was another series of rustles, and then finally she did as I had asked.

"Is he really gone?" she said through the crack she'd opened in the doorway. "Don't lie to me."

"No," I said. "He's standing behind me and as soon as your guard's down, we're going to force our way in."

She squinted at me.

"Yes," I clarified. "For Christ's sake ... he's gone."

"Good," she said, opening up properly. "Because I might throw up if I have to look at his face."

"Don't talk about your father like that," I said, stepping in and slamming the door behind me. Chrissy jumped, startled not so much by the sudden noise, I suspected, as by my attitude. I forged ahead while I had the initiative. "If you think I'm grateful to you for what you did, you've got another think coming. I'm not. Far from it. I'm disgusted. Did it ever occur to you that I might have enough on my mind without you turning to crime on top of it all?"

She rounded on me. "Did it ever occur to *you* that I didn't do it for you?"

So much for the initiative, I thought. "What do you mean? What did you do it for then?"

"I did it for me," she said and flopped down on the sofa. "And you know what? I feel better for it."

The wind left my sails. I did a quick lap of the room, then sat down beside her. "Better how? Explain it to me."

"Just … better. I've *done* something."

"Smashed a window and wrecked a car . . ."

"You can talk."

"I wrecked your *father's* car," I said. "That's different." It would have been a reasonably pathetic contribution if I'd ended it right there. Sadly, I puffed myself up and added, "Furthermore, I didn't smash *any* windows." In fairness to Chrissy, she didn't go to town on me. On the other hand, she didn't need to. "When did you decide to do it?" I asked then, hoping to move things along. "It wasn't when you were talking to me, was it?"

She looked genuinely lost. "What?"

"On Sunday, in the café. I said something about breaking a window. I said it would do no good, but I did … mention it. I was afraid that was what gave you the idea."

"No! God, no. I don't even remember you saying that. I wasn't thinking straight on Sunday." She paused for a moment. "And I'm sorry I said … you know. I'm sorry I wasn't a bit more … sensitive."

I sighed and patted her knee. "That's all right. I'm sorry I walked out on you."

"Don't worry about it."

"It's been a tough few days for all of us."

"Yeah."

"Yeah …"

It was going fairly well at that point, I thought. I should have got up and left it at that, even though I'd only been in the room for two minutes. Instead, I did a bit of basking in the moment. That was when Gerry knocked on the door again.

"Let me in, Chrissy," he whimpered. "Please … please …"

He sounded pathetic. I'd never heard him sounding pathetic before. I didn't care for it. Chrissy reacted to his intervention by jumping to her feet and pointing an accusing finger at me. "You said he'd gone!" she snarled.

"He did go. But he obviously didn't go very far."

"*Please!*" Gerry begged. "Please let me in." He knocked again, which made him sound even more wretched.

"Let him in, Chrissy," I said. "This is stupid."

"What's the matter with you?" she said. "How can you be on his side in anything? I'm starting to worry about you, Mum, I really am."

I got to my feet. "Chrissy, let him in."

She folded her arms, as if that in itself provided another barrier to entry. "No. I will not."

"Right, then I will," I said and stepped towards the door.

Chrissy nipped around me and spread herself across it like a goalkeeper facing a penalty.

"Don't you dare," she said. "This is my private property."

"Chrissy, you're being ridiculous. You'll have to talk to him at some point."

"No," she insisted. "Never again."

"*Please!*" Gerry called through the door.

For a moment, all was silence. We had reached a stand-off.

"All right," I said. "Have it your way. But if you're not going to let your father in, then I'm leaving."

"Fine by me," she said in a childish tone and stepped aside.

It had genuinely been my intention to leave, but now that she had left me an open goal, as such, I had a sudden change of heart. Instead of grabbing the handle, I flicked the lock. Gerry started to come in, but Chrissy had other ideas. She turned and put her shoulder to the door, trapping his foot in the frame. He yelped; she pushed harder. I grabbed her then and pulled her away, using more force than I meant to. As Gerry sprang through the door like a man being chased by wolves, she looked at me as if I'd slapped her. In the few minutes since I'd seen him, he seemed to have aged a decade. Even Chrissy was shocked; I could tell. She soon got over it though.

"*Get out, both of you!*" she roared, and then she started to cry.

Frankly, I'd been surprised that she hadn't started sooner, what with her track record. Still, it wasn't easy to watch. Gerry moved stiffly towards her, as if his knees were giving him trouble. She danced backwards like Muhammad Ali.

"I thought you let me in," he said.

She drew breath for another roar. This one was even more impressive: "*Get! Oouuuttt!*"

I imagined my hair blowing back, like in a cartoon. Gerry

collapsed onto the sofa at that point, not because he was trying to gain a territorial foothold, I was sure, but because he was in danger of collapsing onto the ground. He put his hands on the back of his head and then put his head between his knees, in the manner of someone doing his best not to faint.

"I let you in," I explained. "Chrissy ... wasn't ready to."

"Mum," she said then, "I want you to leave. This minute. And take shithead with you." She turned and marched off down the narrow corridor that led from the living room. A door slammed and a bolt slid home. Locking herself in the bathroom had been one of her favourite ploys as a teenager. It was obviously back in her arsenal.

"Come on, Gerry," I said. "This is pointless."

He spoke without looking up. "Go on. Say 'I told you so'."

"All right. I told you so."

He dragged himself to his feet, still not willing to catch my eye and went out the way he'd come in not sixty seconds earlier. I followed and closed the door behind me.

"I thought you'd gone," I said to his back.

He kept walking; shuffling rather. "I tried to. Only got as far as the front door."

"Why did you come back? You knew she wasn't going to –"

"I just couldn't believe it, that's all. I just couldn't believe that my little girl would treat me like that. I believe it now."

We were outside before he turned to face me. Even then, he spoke to my shoulder.

"I don't suppose there's any point in asking you to come home."

I shook my head. "No. There isn't."

He barely reacted. "Thought not. So you're going back to Melissa's?"

"For now, yeah."

"Okay then."

He stepped closer and bent down to hug me. I started to back away, then had a change of heart and let him do it. His nose burrowed into my left earhole.

"I'm so sorry," he whispered. "About everything."

"I know you are." It was all I could think to say.

"I love you, Jackie."

"I know you do."

He swallowed and his nose burrowed in a little further. Then he ended the hug and backed away, looking at my knees now. "Give me a ring," he said. "At some stage. When you feel like it again."

I nodded, but I'm not sure he even saw me. Then I got into the car and drove away.

* * *

Back at Melissa's, the story didn't take long to tell.

"'Shithead' …" she said thoughtfully when I'd finished. "I've heard worse."

I shook my head. "It was the way she said it. She didn't just cast it out there, like, in a temper. It's obviously what she thinks of him, what she *really* thinks of him. She's deadly serious about cutting him off."

"I'm sure she'll get over it," Melissa said. "And besides,

it's his problem, not yours. You have to concentrate on getting your own head together."

"But what if it had been me? Would she turn away from me too? She would! Of course she would."

Melissa shook her head. "You're being silly."

"I asked her as much in town the other day and she wouldn't give me an answer."

There was a pause. Then she shook her head again and said, "You're being silly" again.

I found that I didn't have much to say for the rest of the day. My only contribution at dinner was an occasional smile and, as soon as we had cleared up, I retired to a corner of the living room with a pile of Melissa's magazines. While she and Colm seemed to understand that I wasn't in the humour for talking, the point was utterly lost on Niall. He leaned over the side of my armchair as I read and found something to point out on almost every page I turned over. It probably would have been annoying even if his interruptions and observations had been funny or clever, but most of them were along the lines of "Look! A car!" After about ten minutes of it, I began to huff and puff quite audibly, hoping Melissa would take the hint and snatch her son away. She definitely heard me – I saw her glancing over at least twice – but still she failed to intervene. It was something of a relief when my mobile rang at around eight o'clock; I was seriously thinking of putting Niall to bed myself and that might not have gone down at all well.

The caller was Eddie. I excused myself and took the phone into the kitchen.

"Are you all right?" I asked him once I was settled on a stool. "Why are you whispering?"

"I'm in a cubicle."

"You're in a what?"

"A cubicle. A … toilet."

He whispered the word so delicately that he briefly left me behind; I thought I'd misheard.

"You're calling me from a *toilet*?" I asked when I'd caught up.

"Yeah."

"What, have you got a tummy bug for real now?"

"No. No – I'm out with Margaret. I called her, did everything you said. It worked. She agreed to see me again."

"And … you took her … to a toilet?"

He groaned and tutted. "I took her to a pub. Which has a toilet. Which I'm in."

This was as short-tempered as I'd ever heard him. He was clearly feeling stressed. "Sorry," I said. "I wasn't trying to be funny. What's up?"

"Right – I think I've made a mistake. With the venue."

"Why? Where are you?"

"Bright Red."

I'd never been there myself but I'd heard the twins talking about it on several occasions.

"Really? Bright Red? Isn't that a bit …" The first words that sprang to mind were "cool" and "trendy". I discarded both on the grounds that Eddie might find them insulting. Still, it wasn't easy to think of an alternative. "Youthful?" I said eventually.

"Yes. It is. Half the men in here – half the *boys* in here aren't even shaving yet. And the girls! Jackie. You'd want to see the get-ups they have on them. I don't know where to look. It's like a stripping club or something."

"I don't see the problem, Eddie. Why don't you just leave?"

"I think Margaret likes it."

"Well, *stay* then," I sighed. Even though I'd been glad of the interruption, I wasn't really in the mood for Eddie's … Eddieness.

"But I'm not *sure* she likes it. She's been making wee cracks about how young and weird everybody else is compared to us. Is she really joking or is she dropping hints, do you think?"

"Jesus, Eddie, how am I supposed to judge that from here? If I –" At that point, a nearby toilet flushed. I waited for the gurgles to fade. "If I were you," I went on when relative silence was restored, "I'd throw caution to the wind. Get radical. I mean, really go out on a limb."

"I'm listening."

"*Ask her*, for God's sake."

There was a pause. "I suppose I could do that. But what if she takes that to mean that *I* want to go and even though she's perfectly happy where she is, she thinks she should –"

"Eddie! You're over-thinking it – by a long way. I'm telling you. Just ask her if she wants to stay … or leave. You'd be amazed at what you can achieve using simple human language."

He ignored the sarcasm. "I don't know what the hell made me suggest here in the first place. It just popped into my head. I should have –"

"Stop right there. Eddie – just get up off the toilet and go back to your date. Ask her if she's comfortable where she is or would she like to try somewhere else. If she says she wants to move, agree with a smile and go somewhere else. If she says she's grand where she is, then put the idea behind you and get on with enjoying yourself."

"Hmmm."

"Okay? Got it? Are we done?"

"But supposing she does want to go on somewhere else? Where do we go?"

I ground my teeth together and raised my eyes to heaven, determined that I would neither lose my temper nor supply an answer.

"Oh," Eddie said then. "I know what you're going to say. You're going to say I should just ask her where she'd like to go."

"*Plink!*"

"Sorry? What was that?"

"That was the sound of a penny dropping. Goodnight, Eddie. And good luck."

"Okay, okay. Goodnight. And thanks."

We hung up and I went back into the front room.

Colm had gone, at last, to put Niall to bed. I told Melissa that the caller was a work colleague enquiring after my health. Really, I had no good reason to skirt the truth.

It was becoming a habit, I guessed.

I went up to my room quite early. I'd found the day exhausting and was looking forward to being horizontal, if not sound asleep, by eleven. In the end, I managed neither. I'd just kicked off my shoes and was halfway out of my jeans when my phone rang again. When I saw that the caller was Eddie, I seriously considered letting it ring out. Supposing his relationship with Margaret lasted for weeks or months? Would he still be calling me for advice every couple of hours? Despite my doubts, sheer nosiness quickly got the better of me and I picked up.

"Edward. What can I do for you now?"

"Jackie, I'm really sorry to be calling again. You must be sick of the sight of me. Sound of me."

"That's okay. What's up now? Are you in a toilet again?"

"Yes. In Hegarty's."

I'd been joking; I should have known better. "So you moved venue."

"Yes. She wanted to. You were right – thanks. I just asked her and it was no big deal."

"Told you s–"

"But once we got settled in here, we got into a proper conversation – more relaxed, you know, not just small talk."

"Right. That's a good thing, surely?"

"Ish. She asked me about my … past. Girlfriend-wise."

"Oh."

"I didn't know what to say, so I told her I didn't want to talk about it."

"Fair enough."

"Yeah, it was fair enough for a while – about thirty seconds. Then she got all intrigued. Curious. She wanted to know if I'd had a 'bad experience'. She kept saying that over and over again. It must be a phrase that women use, is it?"

Not for the first time, I longed to know what it must be

like to be inside his head, looking out.

"'A phrase that women use'? Eddie! We don't have little sayings of our own that you don't know about. She was just showing an interest."

"Well, whatever. I panicked, Jackie. I panicked and I told her I'd had a serious girlfriend for ages. Lynette. *Lynette*, for God's sake! I don't know where I got that from. Anyway – me and this Lynette were mad about each other. Planned to get married, the whole works. But it all came to an end last year."

"How?"

"That's where I got stuck. I couldn't think of a thing to say. So I said I was too upset to talk about it and ran off to the jacks again."

"I see."

"So?"

"So what?"

"So what am I going to say? I could have Lynette getting cancer or something but that seems a bit morbid. Then again, I can't just say I dumped her because I'm after spending ten minutes going on about how great she was, funny and nice and kind to animals, all that. And I certainly can't say *she* dumped *me*. What kind of an ad would that be? Maybe if –"

"All right, Eddie, stop right there. You don't have to do anything. Just leave it. The way things sit now, she thinks you've got a tragic, mysterious past. That's brilliant. Women *love* a tragic, mysterious past."

"Do they?"

"Of course!"

"Well, even if they do, they don't like being lied to, do they? It's bound to come out ... some day."

"Look ... don't take this the wrong way, Eddie, but this is your first date. There might not be a 'some day'. And if there is, worry about it then. In the meantime, you're not on *trial*. You're not under *oath*. Relax."

He breathed down the line. "Okay. Relax. Relax. Relax. I just don't like lying, that's all."

"No one does," I said with a small cough. "Now go back in and clam right up. No more talking about Lynette. Just refuse. And remember, the less you say, the more tragic and mysterious you'll look."

"Right. Okay. Right. Thanks again, Jackie. Where would I be without you?"

"Look where you are *with* me," I sighed. "A pub toilet."

We said goodnight.

CHAPTER 18

I barely slept at all on Tuesday night. Every time I closed my eyes I saw Chrissy's pinched-up face, spitting venom at her father. I tried to tell myself that he deserved it, of course, but I couldn't make the thought stick. It was just after seven when I finally woke up for good. I lay there staring at the ceiling and eventually heard the others get themselves ready for the day. Colm left at about eight, at which point Niall decided he would give a little performance. Although his repertoire was limited to just one number – if it had had a name, it would have been "Lar Lar Lar" – he compensated by singing it at full volume. Every so often, I heard Melissa asking him to keep it down, but to no avail. I knew I should just get out of bed; the noise would (presumably) be less annoying once I was up and about. But

I felt too leaden to move. I stayed put until almost ten o'clock, growing more and more irritated by the minute. By the time I finally roused myself and sloped off to the shower, I was frowning so hard that my forehead was beginning to ache.

Back in the bedroom, I found that I had trouble choosing what to wear. I didn't have many of my clothes with me and the ones I had suddenly seemed drab and threadbare. After much huffing and puffing, I threw on a pair of jeans and a faded blue T-shirt. When I looked in the mirror, I felt a surge of dread so powerful that my legs wobbled and I had to sit down for a minute. I rested my elbows on my knees and tried to breathe deeply, through my nose.

When I started work in First Premier, I was quite friendly with a woman called Wendy O'Gara. She suffered from depression and talked about it all the time; I think she found it helpful. We used to have great bitching sessions together. I would complain about people comparing my headaches with ordinary ones and Wendy would complain about them comparing depression with a bad mood. What it was really like, she'd say, was being buried alive. When the depression finally went away, it didn't feel like cheering up to her – it felt like being dug out. I didn't really understand what she meant at the time, but I think I got a little taste of it that Wednesday morning. I stayed in my bedroom until eleven thirty, breathing deeply all the while, and gradually I began to feel a little less entombed. Then I went downstairs for breakfast.

"Jesus!" Melissa said when she caught sight of me in the kitchen.

I plonked myself down on a stool. "What?"

"Nothing. You look a bit … awful, that's all."

"A *bit* awful? But not completely awful, right?"

"Did you not sleep very well? You're down very late."

"You could say that."

"Chrissy?"

I shrugged. "The whole thing I suppose."

"It's to be expected."

"Yeah."

Niall came tearing down the hall at that point and arrived in the kitchen like Pavarotti arriving on stage. "LAR LAR LAR!" he roared. "LAR LAR LAR!"

"Niall, please!" Melissa said. "I've asked you a hundred times, please keep it down. Please, honey, for me."

He walked over to her and looked up into her face "LAR LAR LAR!"

I tried to remind myself of the sweet little boy at the zoo, but he was suddenly gone from my memory.

"LAR LAR LAR!"

"Niall! Please!"

I hopped off my stool. "I think I'll go for a walk," I said.

Melissa turned to me with a pained look on her face. "I'm sorry, Jackie," she said. "He'll calm down in a minute or two. Then again, he might not. This might be one of his singing days. He has them once in a while."

"No, don't worry about it, it's not … I just need some air."

"But you're only out of bed. You haven't even had any breakfast yet."

"Five minutes," I said. "I'll get something when I come back."

209

In truth, I didn't just want to get away from the noise; I wanted to get some fags. I smiled at Niall as broadly as I could and slipped away down the hall. Even if I hadn't gone out then, I probably would have found out about Robert that morning anyway – or later that day, at worst. Someone would have let me know. Still, I should have stayed put. It would have been nice to have had another few hours of partial, as opposed to total misery.

One evening when the twins were still in primary school, we were sitting around the kitchen table having our tea (we called it "tea" then, like everyone else – it didn't become "dinner" until a few years later). Gerry was telling me how he'd bumped into an old pal from school who he hadn't seen in years. Last time Gerry had seen him, he'd had a pony-tail that he'd been cultivating since he was a teenager. Now, not only was the pony-tail gone, he was bald as an egg. Gerry said that he'd almost walked straight past the guy but had done a double-take at the last second. I'd never heard that term before and asked him what he meant; he did a mime. The feeling of delight that coursed through me was the same one I'd experienced when I first heard the words "déjà vu" – *there's a name for this!* From then on, every time I saw someone do a double-take or did one of my own, I experienced a fleeting echo of that same delight.

I did the double-take to end all double-takes in the newsagent's that morning, just as the assistant handed me my change. It was a text-book performance. I was saying thanks and happened to glance to my left, to the rack where I'd spotted *Your Story* a few days previously. There were bundles of newspapers on the floor at its base. I saw Robert's face on the cover of one, turned back to the assistant and then almost broke my neck going back to Robert. But there was no feeling of delight, only a violent lurching of the intestines.

"Jesus Christ!" I screeched as I dived down for a closer look.

"What?" the assistant said, alarmed. "Is it a rat? Eh, not that we have rats."

I didn't reply. I was too busy taking in the headline: "SOAP STAR'S DRUNKEN SHAME". The paper – it was *The Irish Sun* – shook so badly in my hands that it must have looked as if I was fanning myself. I tried to read the first paragraph, but the letters seemed to be moving around like tiny insects.

"Are you all right there?" the assistant asked.

I nodded my head and put the paper down on the counter. "This," was all I managed to say. I paid and turned towards the door.

"We haven't got rats, you know," she said to my back.

Outside, I sat down on the shop windowsill and stared at my son's picture. It was one I'd seen before – his first publicity shot for *The O'Mahonys*. He'd begrudgingly thrust it at me in his flat one day and rolled his eyes when I said he looked like James Dean. The caption underneath read *Robert O'Connell plays bad boy Valentine Reilly*. I took another deep breath – my four hundredth of the morning – and started to read.

Actor Robert O'Connell, who plays Valentine Reilly in the hit soap
The O'Mahonys, was in hot water with his RTÉ bosses last night
after getting involved in a vicious night-club brawl. O'Connell,
twenty-one, was drinking with pals in trendy private night-spot
Club Zed on Monday night when the row erupted. The target of
O'Connell's alleged assault was Michael Rice, a twenty-nine-year-
old architect, who was enjoying a night out with his girlfriend.
Eyewitnesses reported that O'Connell approached Rice's table and
began hurling abuse for no apparent reason. A fight broke out at
which point night club staff intervened, but not before Rice suffered
a broken nose and severe facial bruising. He is understood to be
considering the possibility of taking legal action against O'Connell.

The story continued, briefly, on an inside page. There wasn't
much more to tell; it was all background stuff on Robert and
snide asides about life imitating art (if you could call *The
O'Mahonys* art). I read the whole thing twice, half-imagining
that there might be two Robert O'Connells, both of whom
played characters called Valentine Reilly in rival soaps of the
same name. And who also looked identical.

When I finished for the second time, I grabbed my mobile
from my bag and rang Robert, hoping to get some sensible
explanation. There was no answer. When his voicemail
kicked in, I said, "Robert, it's your mother. I saw the paper.
I hope you're all right. Please call me. Please."

I hung up and called Gerry. He took a long time to answer.

"Jackie?"

"Yeah. It's me."

"Are you okay?"

"You haven't seen it then."

"Seen what?"

"*The Sun*."

"The newspaper?"

"No, Gerry, the big fucking yellow thing in the sky. *Yes*, the newspaper."

"All right, calm –"

"Robert's plastered all over the front of it. He attacked someone in a private club. 'Soap Star's Drunken Shame.'"

"You're codding me?"

"Go out and buy one."

"*Attacked* someone? Robert?"

"Yes! Club Zed, wherever that is."

"Has he been arrested?"

My head spun. It was the second time in as many days when I'd discussed whether or not a child of mine had been picked up by the police.

"Apparently not. But the guy's threatening legal action. He's got a broken nose and facial bruising. *Severe* facial bruising."

"I don't understand. Who is this guy?"

"What does it matter?"

"It doesn't, I suppose."

"It says his name's Michael something, wait … Michael Rice. He's an architect. He was out having a drink with his girlfriend when Robert, according to this anyway, just went for him."

There was no reply, but I thought I heard gulping.

"Gerry? Are you there?"

"Yeah."

"What is it?"

"This girlfriend … does it mention her name?"

"No. Why?"

"Eh … Lisa's got a boyfriend who's an architect. I'm pretty sure his name's Michael."

The blood drained from my head and for a moment the world looked very bright.

"Jackie? Are you still there?"

I hung up.

Back at the house, Melissa did her best to be reassuring.

"Let's not go jumping to conclusions," she said. "Let's wait to hear from Robert."

"ROBERT!" Niall yelled. "LAR LAR LAR!"

"We could be waiting a long time," I told her. "He's only just started talking to me properly again. He's hardly going to ring me up to discuss *this*, is he? I'm going over there. To his apartment."

"But he might not even be there. He's probably working."

"If he hasn't got fired …"

"He won't get fired, Jackie."

"I have to do something. I'm going."

"I'll come with you then."

Momentarily, the idea appealed to me. Then I remembered the obvious. "What about Niall?"

"It'll just take me a minute to get him ready. He can come too."

"WE'RE GOING TO THE ZOO ZOO ZOO!" Niall roared. "YOU CAN COME TOO TOO TOO! LAR LAR LAR!"

I had a vision of the three of us in the car, one of us hoarse, two of us deafened.

"No," I said firmly. "You stay put. I'll be grand."

I grabbed my bag and turned on my heels before she could form an argument.

"Aw!" said Niall.

* * *

Robert's latest apartment – his third since he'd left home – was in a new development in Ballsbridge. He was living alone for the first time, which was just as well, given the size of the place; it was like a fully-furnished cupboard. I'd pointed that out to him during my first visit, presuming he thought as much himself. But no. He'd taken offence and another epic row had ensued. I'd tried to calm him down by praising the relative lack of litter and weeds in the grounds – only about half as much as at his sister's – but that was no good either. He went from row-mode to fuming-silence-mode and I ended up leaving him to it, not fifteen minutes after I'd arrived.

I parked on a meter around the corner and took a quick walk (and fag) to help get my thoughts together. It didn't work. My thoughts stayed just the way they were, separate little rubber balls bouncing around in my skull, crashing together only occasionally. I had a call from Gerry as I walked, but I ignored it. A young couple came out the main door of Robert's building just as I reached it and I briefly considered running in while I had the chance. But I didn't go for it. I rang the buzzer instead and waited, wringing my hands together. There was no reply. I buzzed again, with the same result. Then I took out my phone and called him, in case he was in there but not answering the door. I got voicemail again.

"It's me," I said, looking around. "I'm outside ... never mind." I hung up.

Robert was coming through the main gates with a bag of groceries. He was wearing a baseball cap and sunglasses. I might not even have recognised him if it hadn't been for his walk, which was just like Gerry's – sort of John Wayne-ish, but not as comical. He was looking at the ground and didn't see me until he was about thirty feet away. When he did, he turned and started off in the other direction.

"Robert!" I called out. "Don't be silly, I just want to talk!"

He'd only taken a few strides when he slowed to a crawl, then stopped. I guessed he'd concluded that he looked ridiculous, which he did. He turned and came back towards me.

"How are you doing?" I said as he approached.

He didn't reply until he was by my side. "Never better," he said and swiped his card at the electronic door thingy.

"Can I come in for a chat?"

He nodded as the door clicked open, then held it open and did an exaggerated bow like a butler.

Great, I thought. *Sarcasm.*

It had been quite a while since I'd been in Robert's place and I was reasonably impressed. There were no more than a dozen or so plates and cups lying around unwashed and the dust was only millimetres, as opposed to inches thick. He hadn't spoken a word in the lift or the corridor outside and I hadn't gone beyond mumbling pleasantries, so things were a little awkward as we took our seats at his kitchen table.

"Tea?" he said by way of an opener.

"No thanks. I value my health too much."

He shot me a look and was clearly on the point of saying something unpleasant. Then he removed his cap and then his sunglasses, revealing a blackened right eye.

"Robert! Are you all right?"

"I'm fine."

"You don't look –"

"I'm *fine*."

"Okay. If you say so. Do you want to tell me what happened?"

"No."

"Maybe you –"

"It was just a fight, all right? Nothing to get excited about."

"A fight over what?"

"Nothing much. It doesn't matter. Who told you anyway? I didn't have you down as a *Sun* reader."

"I saw it in a shop. It's on the cover."

"It sure is."

I bit the inside of my cheek for a moment. "Robert … was it Lisa? Your man's girlfriend?"

His good eye widened. "How the fuck do you know that?"

"I spoke to your father. He told me Lisa has a boyfriend called Michael who's an architect."

Robert half-turned away in disgust, then brought his fist down on the table so hard that his salt cellar jumped. "He's had conversations with her about her fucking boyfriend? What the fuck's the matter with him?"

"Robert, please don't sw–"

"I'll fucking swear if I want to! It's my house. Apartment, whatever. This is all his fault and I'm telling you now, if I lose my job over this, that'll be both of his kids who are never going near him again. Fucking *asshole*!"

My hands trembled. "Don't say that. Please."

"It's the truth. And why are you defending him, for Christ's sake?"

"I'm not defending him."

"You've been weird about this since the start. I –"

"It's hardly your father's fault that you picked a job where you're liable to end up in the papers when something goes wrong!"

He shook his head. "You're priceless, you are. Unbelievable ..."

"Tell me what happened in the club," I said. "You might as well."

"Why? So you can have a go at me?"

"I'm not going to have a go at you. Tell me about it, please."

He sat back and did his jaw-rubbing thing, saying nothing.

I said, "If you don't give me your side of it, I'll have nothing to go on but the piece in *The Sun*. Is that what you want?"

That seemed to get through to him. Another few seconds went by and then he finally spoke up.

"I was rotten drunk, for a start. I was out with Ginger and Bogie."

"Who?"

"You don't know them, never mind that bit. Club Zed. It's a private, after-hours sort of joint. About one, maybe one thirty, I got up to go for a whizz. Y'know, go to the toilet."

"I know what a whizz is, Robert, I'm not a nun."

"Christ, I'm just saying –"

"All right, all right. Go on."

He shook his head and muttered something indecipherable. "On my way to the jacks, I spotted her. Lisa. Sitting with this greasy-looking gobshite with a fake tan and a bucket of wax on him."

"A bucket of what?"

"*Wax*. On his hair."

"Wax?"

"Jesus, *yes*. It's like gel. People use wax now, all right? What does it matter?"

This was starting to resemble one of our old-school conversations. I told myself that he was under a lot of stress and tried to remain pleasant.

"It doesn't matter. But you don't have to take my head off."

He glanced away for a moment. "Right, so I'm on my way to the jacks and I spot them in the corner. He was all over her, pawing at her, and she was giving it loads, all *that* business." He paused and did a reasonable mime of a woman being pawed and loving it, head back, eyes-a-flutter. "I mean, I'd seen her in there before and all, but I dunno ... for some reason I was sure I'd never see her again. I was kinda staring, I suppose. I don't think I was even planning on saying anything, to begin with. Then she caught my eye and I could see that she was trying to place me. I'd only met her the once, at that barbeque you had. Then she sort of … smirked."

I recalled the look she'd given me through the front-room window and nodded.

"Well, maybe not smirked, but … she certainly didn't look embarrassed or anything. Then the boyfriend turned to see what she was looking at and I caught *his* eye and there was another bit of staring. Then he crooked his finger at me, you know, like he was beckoning a fucking waiter. I knew he was going to start, but I marched over anyway. He says, 'Do you think my girlfriend's attractive?', all cool and sneery. And I said, 'Lots of people do, by all accounts' or something similar. Then he says, 'What's that supposed to mean?' and I ignored him. Then I made some sort of a comment to her."

"Like what?"

"I can't remember."

"Robert …"

"I really can't. But it was something about being a slut or a tramp. Or maybe a whore. Something along those lines."

"Brilliant. What did you think that was going to achieve?"

"I thought you weren't going to have a go at me?"

"This isn't having a go, Robert. If I wanted to have a go, I'd –"

"Anyway. The boyfriend jumped up and punched me. I went back on another table or a person or something – I didn't fall anyway. And when he came for me again, I was ready and I ... beat the shit out of him."

This was said in a challenging tone, with more than a hint of pride.

I said, "Do you expect me to be impressed?"

Robert's face soured. "You? No."

Sensing trouble, I changed course. "What happened then?"

"Bouncers bundled in, I was bundled out. I got in a taxi and went home."

"And this was on *Monday* night?"

"Yeah, why?"

"Nothing. I just didn't know people went to night-clubs on a Monday night."

He tossed his head back. "Jesus, you never listen! It isn't a night-club, it's an after-hours drinking club!"

"But you know what I mean. You're still out at one in the morning. Don't people have jobs any more?"

He ground his teeth at me but didn't bother with an actual reply.

"So what about RTÉ?" I said then. "When did they find out?"

"Yesterday. Paper rang them for a comment."

"Probably would have been better coming from you," I ventured.

"Well, I wasn't out there, was I? I'm not shooting anything until tomorrow."

"Still, you could have called them."

He rubbed his hands over his face and tented his fingers. His lips moved but no words came out.

"I'm sorry, Robert," I said. "I don't mean to be critical."

He dropped his hands to the table. "No, you never do, do you?"

I took a couple of slow breaths. "Have they been in touch? RTÉ?"

"There are messages. Which I haven't returned."

"That's a great strategy."

He made no reply.

I tried again: "What do you think they'll say?"

"*How the fuck would I know?*" he boomed.

That tore it.

"Maybe I should just go," I said quietly.

He gave the tiniest of shrugs, which I took to mean that he agreed. I got up from the table and waited for him to get up too, or to at least say something. When he didn't, I turned and walked to the door.

"See you soon," I said as I turned the handle.

"Yeah," he said from his seat. "See ya."

CHAPTER 19

When I got back to the car, I was shaking so badly that I didn't think it wise to get behind the wheel. Instead, I walked around the corner and up onto Baggot Street, where I went into the first coffee shop I saw. I ordered a pot of tea for one and the unhealthiest-looking bun they had. There was a free table by the window. I took a seat there and in the next hour rose only once, to get more tea. At about two-thirty or so, a short, doughy man came along and sat at the next table. He was a carpenter, I guessed, or maybe an electrician – he had a tool-belt on him at any rate. As well an apple and a bag of crisps, he had before him an enormous baguette that, as far as I could tell, he'd asked the assistant to stuff with every filling available. He read *The Sun* as he ate, holding the paper up so unnaturally high that I wondered if he was doing it deliberately to annoy me. Every time I glanced across and saw Robert's face, the corners of the mouth turned down, the eyes narrowed and the nose twitched, just as they did when he was launching another jibe my way. The carpenter didn't seem remotely interested in the story; he'd taken one look at the headline and moved on to the inside pages. But that was no comfort to me. I could easily imagine what he'd thought when he saw the headline: *Another overpaid so-called "celebrity" wanker throwing his weight around. Boring.* Somehow I think I would have preferred it if he'd read the story avidly, muttering to himself and shaking his head in disgust. If Robert was going to be a tabloid-fodder thug, I thought, let him at least be an interesting tabloid-fodder thug. That was no longer my main concern, in any event. Apparently, Robert's recent change of attitude towards me had been a mere blip. The very moment he had problems of his own, we were back to square one, me and him, as if nothing had ever happened. It was a poor day indeed, I couldn't help but think, when your son's humiliation on the cover of a national newspaper wasn't even the worst thing that happened to you.

I had finished my second pot of tea and was contemplating going for a third when my phone rang. *It might be Robert*, I allowed myself to hope. *Calling to apologise.* But it wasn't Robert.

"Jackie O," said a voice so familiar it was like getting a call from myself.

"Nancy!"

"None other. Je suis back de Paris depuis about an heure."

"How did it go?"

"Fan-*tas*-tic. That was my fifth trip, and I love it more every time. You have to go, Jackie. You just have to, that's all there is to it. Light a fire under Gerry and pack a bag tonight."

My voice failed me.

"Jackie? Are you there?"

"Yeah," I whispered.

"What's wrong? Are you all right?"

"Can I come over?"

"What's the matter?"

"Can I come over?" I repeated.

"Of course you can, but I'm not home yet, I'm at David's. I'll be back at about five. What is it?"

"Five," I said and hung up before I set myself off.

I had time to kill now, but the prospect of returning to Melissa's – and the "Lar Lar Lar" song – was not an appealing one. Instead, I decided to go take a walk on Sandymount Strand. I had some vague idea at the back of my mind about the restorative powers of sea air; the word "bracing" figured in my deliberations somewhere. The word "freezing" did not, alas, but those were the conditions I found when I arrived. Although I began to regret my choice of time-killer within seconds of leaving the car, I did manage a quick stroll (more of a jog, really). I texted Melissa along the way, letting her know that I wouldn't be home for a while and would explain how it went with Robert when I saw her. As I added the bit about my current location, I imagined her sympathetic reaction – *Poor old Jackie, all alone in the fading light on a cold, deserted beach.* A curious shiver ran through me, nothing to do with the weather. I hugged myself even more tightly and tried to think about something else.

The walk didn't last long in any event. I ended up killing most of the time just sitting in the car, staring out to sea – still trying to think about something else.

When we first met in Ashbourne, Nancy liked to say that with her travelling days now behind her, she would never again live in a city. "Concrete's not for me," she liked to say, as if she lived in a quaint farmhouse in the middle of nowhere rather than a large housing estate in a fairly busy commuter town. Her attitude began to change not long after I moved in (coincidence, I hoped). Suddenly, there was a lot to be said for city life. There were theatres and clubs and restaurants, for a start, and you had a sense of being at the centre of things. Why, anything could happen in a city! Nancy was pushing forty at the time, so I didn't take her very seriously. Over the next couple of years, she wheeled the idea out once in a while and didn't put up much of a fight when I shot holes in it. On that hot summer's day in 1994, when she announced that she was finally going ahead and doing it, I simply didn't believe her. She'll snap out of it soon, I thought, when the *For Sale* sign went up. It's a phase, I told myself, when she quit her job. I don't think the penny dropped with me until we were standing by the kerb, having our last official hug as neighbours, while the removal men worked in the background. She vowed to stay in touch, but I didn't believe that either. It was one of the happiest surprises of my life that she kept her promise. If anything, we became even closer because it required a bit of an effort for us to meet up; she seemed to appreciate it when I made the trek into town and I know I was grateful when she came out to visit me.

The house she'd bought in Dublin was smack in the middle of a terrace in Crumlin. It wasn't much to look at – or smell – when she moved in, but over the years she'd gradually turned it into one of those small-on-the-outside-surprisingly-spacious-on-the-inside sort of places for which young professionals were now paying an arm and both legs. She achieved the transformation by more or less gutting the joint, knocking a wall down here, moving a bathroom there. This was another aspect of her personality that I found admirable – her ability to think long-term. It drove me insane to have a plumber in for half an hour; Nancy had every tradesman in Dublin through the house over a period of several years, but she was able to keep her eye on the prize. And, I had to admit, she had indeed made the most of city life. Forty-something (now fifty-something) or not, she was out more nights than she was in, and the job she'd found shortly after the move – she worked as a doctor's receptionist – seemed to give her real pleasure. I was glad for her, genuinely. But I still wished we were neighbours.

She was already on the doorstep as I parked the car that Wednesday afternoon. I waved out at her with such enthusiasm that I almost clipped the Mondeo that I was planning to get in behind. The near-miss played havoc with my confidence and it took me quite a while to get myself into position. I glanced across the street occasionally as I fought with the steering wheel like Johnny Weissmuller battling a rubber crocodile and could see that she was torn between sympathy and hysterics.

"You've had your hair cut," she said when I finally came through her front gate. "Don't worry. It'll grow back."

We busied ourselves with small-talk until we were settled on the sofa with tea and biscuits. This was an old tactic of Nancy's. In times of crisis, she always liked to ease herself in. I usually found that comforting in itself. On this occasion, however, she used the word "romance" about eight times – that was not so comforting. I tried not to change my expression when she did so. It wasn't easy.

"So," she said, as I reached for the Garfield mug that she always gave me when I called around, "tell me."

I drank some tea and placed the mug on the floor by my foot. There didn't seem to be anything for it but to come right out with the big news, the kicker-offer. "Gerry had sex with our next-door neighbour."

Nancy didn't even blink. At first, I put it down to her legendary calmness and was more in awe of her than ever. Then I realised that she thought I was joking, and was waiting for me to tell her the real story.

"I'm not kidding, Nancy," I felt obliged to say. "He did the woman from next-door. Lisa. I caught them at it, Friday lunchtime. Saw them through the window, like in a *Carry On* film."

Her eyebrows slowly started creeping towards her hairline.

"I've moved out," I went on. "For a while at least. I've been staying with Melissa."

At last, Nancy found her voice. "This is a gag," she said.

"No," I insisted. "It isn't."

"But ..."

"There're no buts about it."

She took a moment to let it sink in. "I don't know what ... I mean ... how *could* he?"

"Quite easily, by all accounts."

As usual, Nancy was wearing a cardigan and as usual, its sleeves were far too long. When she raised her hand and placed it over her mouth, only the tips of her fingers showed. This gesture, performed against the background of her elfin frame, gave her a suddenly child-like appearance. I felt as if I'd just told a little girl that there was no such thing as Santa and it wasn't looking good for the Tooth Fairy either.

"Now don't you go getting upset," I said, as her eyes moistened.

"*Gerry?*" she bleated.

"Gerry. He said it was just the once."

"*Gerry?*"

"Yes! For Christ's sake! Gerry!"

She put both hands – or sleeves rather – over her face and started to cry for real. A couple of seconds later, I joined her. She edged along the sofa and grabbed me around my neck, pulling me towards her for what turned into a hug but started out as a head-butt.

"I'm so sorry!" she wailed.

"Me too!" I wailed back.

We stayed in that position for a while until my arched back began to ache and I pulled away.

"I feel like such a shit," Nancy said then.

I dabbed at my cheeks with the backs of my hands. "You? Why?"

She gulped. "David asked me to marry him."

"*What? No!*"

"Yeah."

She tugged her left sleeve out of the way, revealing a fairly hefty rock on a platinum ring.

"Nancy!"

We resumed the hug, and the crying.

"I'm sorry," she sniffled into my shoulder, "but I had to tell you. I couldn't sit here and not tell you ..."

"Don't apologise," I said. "It's wonderful news."

"But Gerry ..." she said and then became incoherent.

When she calmed down again, I said, "I take it you accepted the proposal?"

I felt her nodding. "And have you set a date?"

She drew back from me and shook her head. "Not yet. David wants it to be soon, though. Anyway – never mind me. What are you going –"

I held up my hand to interrupt her. "No. Tell me about this first." In my head I added: *So we can get it out of the way.* I was happy for her. Of course I was. I'd met David several times and he was a lovely man, warm and gentle and caring – everything Nancy deserved after a lifetime of getting turned over by losers and sociopaths. But I hadn't even told her about Chrissy and Robert yet. We had a lot to get through and I wanted her full attention.

"Honestly," I said. "Tell me."

"Jackie, are you sure –"

"Go on. It's OK."

She sighed. "He did it on our first night – what was that – the Friday." Her face crumpled as she realised that Friday had been a pretty big day for me too.

I did a little reassuring. "I want to hear it, Nancy. Really."

"OK. OK, but I'll be quick. Hang on, wait 'til I get a tissue." She got up and disappeared into the kitchen, returning with two wodges of kitchen roll, one for her, one for me. We attended to our noses and she started up again. "We went out for dinner, which was wonderful. Oh, Jackie, the restaurants – I'd forgotten what they were like. You feel like you're in a romantic movie, a *good* one, an old-fashioned one, not some jokey sex thing with, I dunno, Cameron bloody Diaz. David was kind of fidgety all throughout, but I didn't pay much attention. He hates flying and we'd had a few bumps on the way over, so I put it down to that. Then, when the meal was finished, he said we should go for a walk along the Seine, which we did. It was so beautiful, beautiful buildings, beautiful boats, beautiful Parisians strolling past. He kept taking my hand and giving it a little squeeze and then letting go, you know, really nervous. I asked him if he had something on his mind and he said no, his dinner wasn't sitting right, which I found hard to believe because the food was sensational. So light, but full of flavour, you know?"

For someone who didn't want to tell the story, she wasn't long getting into it, I thought but didn't say.

"Anyway. We could see the Eiffel Tower way off in the distance and next thing I know, David pipes up that we should go and see it right then. I didn't want to because I was knackered and besides, we had it on our itinerary for the Sunday afternoon – you know me and my lists. I said all that to him, but he wouldn't take no for an answer. He got almost angry about it, which was out of character for him. So I gave in, not very graciously, and off we went on the Metro – which, by the way, is great. Really efficient."

"Hmmm."

"It never crossed my mind that he was going to propose, I swear to God it didn't. We've only been together for six months. So up we went, anyway, up the stairs out of the Metro station and *Jackie* … it doesn't matter how many times you see it, the Eiffel Tower is something else altogether. First time I saw it, which was thirty years ago – Jesus Christ, thirty years – I couldn't believe my eyes. I thought it was going to be like the Statue of Liberty, which is just, you know … so what? *It's a big statue, whoop-de-doo.* But the Eiffel Tower is amazing, really, really amazing. You don't appreciate how massive it is until you're right up next to it."

"Suppose not," I said, just for the sake of saying something. I was beginning to regret letting her go first.

"We walked around for a while, sat on the grass for a while, watched the light-show – they do this amazing light-show on the hour, the whole thing *fizzes*, it's gorgeous."

"Hmmm," I said again.

"And then I said we should go up, you know, get the view. But David wouldn't. He doesn't like heights of any kind, it's not just the flying thing. And I got kind of stroppy because it had been his idea to go over in the first place and what's the point, I thought, if you're not going to go up the bloody thing? So we got into a kind of a row about it. There were all these other couples walking around cooing at each other and there's me and him with our hands on our hips having a right old go. Well, I was the one having the go, really, he was just standing there looking lost and befuddled. Then I said, 'What's the matter with you? You're being really odd.' And that's when he did it. Dropped to one knee and all, started fumbling around in his pocket. You know what? I still didn't get it. It sounds ridiculous, doesn't it?"

"A wee bit," I said.

"But it's the truth! I was staring down at him, wondering if he was having some sort of fit. Then he produced the little box and opened it and said, 'Will you please marry me?' I said, 'Will I please *what*?' It came out kind of sarcastic, but I didn't mean it that way. He said, 'Uhhh …' – this big long 'Uuuhhhh …' – and then he said, 'Marry me?' I nearly asked him to say it again. But I didn't. I just said 'Yes, I will.' Then I dragged him to his feet and we had the best kiss of my life, which is saying something."

"Wow!" I said.

"I haven't even started yet!" she trilled.

Jesus Christ, I thought. *She hasn't even started yet*.

Fifteen minutes later, Nancy had filled me in on every detail of her remaining time in Paris. The Louvre was "breathtaking". Versailles was "stunning". The Champs-Élysées was "thrilling". I almost told her that I knew all of this already because I was fortunate enough to own a television set. But I didn't. She was excited, which was perfectly understandable, and that was all there was to it. Still, I could have done without the unnecessarily (and for Nancy, uncharacteristically) graphic descriptions of their weekend bedroom activities. Truth be told, I became quite angry as she launched into her third – third! – tribute to David's "tenderness" and "attentiveness". For once in our relationship, I was all too aware that in little more than a decade's time, Nancy would be a pensioner. And besides, try as I might, I couldn't help but conclude that she was being insensitive. I was glad I had come out without my watch because she would undoubtedly have caught me looking at it – several times. Although the story of the trip to Paris seemed to last almost as long as the trip itself, Nancy eventually came to the bit where she and David parted at his house in Maynooth.

"I cried again," she said, "which isn't like me at all. But I'm just so upside-down. In a nice way though."

"Good for you," I said with as much enthusiasm as I could muster. "I'm so glad for you. Couldn't be happier. Now –"

"Let me ask you something, Jackie. And I want an honest answer."

My finger tapped on my thigh. "What?"

"Do you think I'm too old to get married in a church?"

"No, of course I don't!"

"Neither does David. But I do. I mean, look at the cut of me." She ran her hands through her long grey hair which, in all honesty, could have done with a snip. "One of the wee shites at the end of the street calls me 'The Witch'."

"Well, I presume you'd be getting your hair done for it ..."

"Yeah … Yeah, maybe you're right."

"Of course I'm right. Just don't go to the muppet who did mine. Now –"

"But it's not just the hair though, is it? Can you see me in a white dress walking up an aisle? I'm not exactly Cameron Diaz in general, am I?"

My voice rose. "What is it with you and Cameron Diaz all of a sudden?"

She groaned. "David fancies her."

"I'm sure he does. So what?"

"All right, even leaving looks aside – we don't know all that many people. I'd be surprised if we could rustle up a guest list of more than, what, thirty?"

"And?"

"It's going to look stupid, isn't it? Thirty people in a big church?"

"So don't get a big church. Get a little church."

"It'll have to be *very* little. We'll have to get married in a shagging tree-house."

"What's the alternative? A registry office in a health centre? Tripping over sick people on your way to the altar? Oh, excuse me, there wouldn't be an altar, would there? Tripping over sick people on your to *the desk*?"

"Less hassle …" Nancy mumbled.

"Yeah, less hassle and less special. Get married in a church, for God's sake. No pun intended."

"None taken."

"You'll always regret it if you don't."

She mused for a moment, then broke into a smile. "You're

right. You're right. Aw, Jackie, what would I do without you?"
She leaned in for yet another hug, which, frankly, I cut short.

"OK then," I said. "That's that. Listen –"

"Then there's the reception," Nancy said, biting a
fingernail. "That's a nightmare in itself …"

I didn't hear what she said next; I didn't hear it because of
all the blood that was suddenly rushing about in my head.

It was almost a quarter past six by the time she finished. I
knew that because when she finally tapered off, she looked
at her watch and said, "Jesus! It's almost a quarter past six!"

"Good God," I said, just to emphasise that yes indeed, we
had been talking about her wedding for the guts of an hour –
or rather, she had. I'd contributed precious little, apart from
an occasional "Yeah, I agree", the whole point of which was
to hurry things along (it hadn't worked, obviously).

"I'm sorry," Nancy said. "I knew I shouldn't have started.
I'm just so thrilled with the whole thing."

"I know. But maybe we could move on now to –"

"Of course. Of course. I apologise, really, I do."

"That's okay. I'll have to be heading back soon, so I'll try
to be –"

"Hey, listen, I know – why don't you stay here tonight?"

"Well …"

"Ah, go on. I've no groceries in, but I can nip down to the
Spar at the corner. I'll get some wine too, a bit of dessert.
You'll be on the pull-out, mind."

"But I've got nothing with me, no clothes or –"

"It's only one night, Jackie. You'll live."

"Suppose so. Yeah. Yeah – all right then. I'll let Melissa know."

"Good girl. I'll do a quick shopping list."

"Put wine at the top."

"Will do."

She left to get a pen and a notebook. I got my phone out and started texting.

* * *

We opened a bottle of Rioja as soon as Nancy got back from the shop. I sat at the kitchen table while she got to work on a spag bol. From past experience I knew that she hated any interference while cooking, so I didn't offer to help. I just sipped my wine as she chopped and stirred, waiting for her to mention the elephant in the room. But she didn't. She got back on to the subject of Parisian restaurants and stayed there for quite a while. When that topic had been exhausted, she gave me a detailed analysis of the many difficulties facing the user of Dublin airport. From there, she moved on to vegetarianism – a good thing or not? At that point it became clear to me that I would have to do a little subtle prompting.

"Nancy!" I said. "For fuck's sake!"

She turned to face me. "What?"

"I've been here for two hours and we haven't talked about Gerry yet."

"I was waiting for you to start," she said. "I didn't want to be pushy."

"Oh. Yeah, I should have … I'm sorry, I just –"

"Go on. Tell me. I'm all ears." She turned back to her pots and pans.

"Right. Friday morning, I got one of my headaches."

"Oh no."

"Yeah. It was pretty bad, so I left work and went home. Gerry was out doing a wedding, I thought. But halfway up the garden path, I looked in through the front window and there he was. With Lisa from next door. Hard at it."

I paused, anticipating a response. None materialised. Then Nancy half-turned and said, "I'm listening, go on."

"Are you nearly done?" I said. "I'd prefer to talk to your face if at all possible."

"Sorry, just a tick, I'm nearly there." She reached into her fridge and grabbed a tub of parmesan. Then she sprinkled some in (far too much, in my opinion), wiped her hands on a tea-towel and finally took a seat across from me.

"Sorry, sorry," she said. "I'm all yours."

I glugged the remainder of my wine and poured some more. Nancy had barely started hers.

"Okay," I said. "So there they were, over the back of the sofa –"

"But, Jesus, they must have known they could be seen. What were they thinking of?"

"I don't know. I haven't asked him. Yet."

"What did you do? Did you barge in or run away?"

"I barged in. Or I started to anyway. But I didn't even get through the front door before she came tearing out and away up the road."

"What about Gerry?"

"Ran upstairs and puked his socks up."

"No!"

"Yeah. I went in to the bedroom and packed."

"Did you not even talk to him?"

"A wee bit. Just to say I was off, basically."

"And have you talked to him since?"

"A few times. I, eh … I wrecked his jeep …" I trailed off, waiting for her astonished reaction.

She nodded. "What? Took a hammer to it?"

I'd expected a scream at least. I struggled to keep my disappointment off my face and out of my voice. "No. Scraped it against a pillar."

"Least he deserves, isn't it? What about the twins? Do they know?"

"Do they ever! Chrissy says she's never talking to him again. And she means it. Not only that, she put a brick through Lisa's window and sloshed a bucket of paint over her car."

"Doesn't sound like Chrissy."

"There you go. As for the other eejit, he's on the front page of *The Sun* today."

"What? Why?"

"He saw Lisa in a night-club, excuse me, a drinking club, with her boyfriend –"

"Not Gerry? A different boyfriend?"

I thought for a moment that this was a shockingly tasteless joke, but no, it was a real question. "Not Gerry," I said through my teeth. "Her real boyfriend. The point is, Robert went for her, made some sort of smart comment and the

239

boyfriend upped and lamped him. There was a fight, which Robert seems to have won decisively. Somebody called the paper and there he is: "Soap Star's Drunken Shame". He could be in serious trouble with RTÉ. And if anything really bad comes of it, he says he's never speaking to his dad again either." I took a swig of wine and slumped in my chair. "It's such a mess, Nancy."

"And what about you?" she said. "How are you coping?"

"I was doing all right," I said, carefully. "Until the kids went crazy. Now … I'm not doing all right. At all."

She nodded and had some wine. "You're right," she said. "It's a mess."

I waited for her advice. She tucked a strand of hair behind her ear and bit her lower lip, a sure sign that she was thinking hard.

"Listen," she said then. "I'm sorry, but I can't concentrate. I've got something on my mind."

Every muscle in my body contracted. In an instant, I convinced myself that she was about to make some horrific revelation about Gerry – that she'd caught him at it herself one day. Or that he'd tried it on with *her* ten minutes after we became neighbours, all those years ago.

"What is it?" I managed to say.

"My father's been dead for twenty years," she said. "Who should I get to give me away?"

CHAPTER 20

Dinner was nice, I had to give her that. What was even nicer, though, was the wine. We ended up getting through two bottles before dessert. I drank way more than my share. Frankly, I needed it. Although we did indeed have the "nice long chat" that Nancy had promised, not a lot of it was about Gerry and the twins. And the parts that were delivered nothing of any significance. Nancy told me how sorry she was, several times, and while she seemed to mean it quite sincerely, her condolences were of no practical help. I kept finding myself frowning at the space above her head, wondering where I'd gone wrong. In the end, I concluded that I hadn't gone wrong anywhere. A woman who had recently got engaged – even a fifty-two-year-old – was no one's idea of a great conversationalist, and that was all there was to it. By the time we had decided not to bother with coffee and open bottle number three instead, I was finding it all but funny – which is not to say that I was in good humour. I was troubled by so many different negative emotions that I was having a hard time giving them all names. And being categorically pissed wasn't helping any.

During my walk on the beach – technically, during my sit in the car – I had contemplated telling Nancy about me and Tony. I'd decided not to during dinner, but the drunker I got, the harder it became to keep the words down. By the time we had moved back to the sofa, I had resorted to clamping my lips together like a child trying to get out of taking medicine.

"Is your mouth all right?" Nancy asked as she sat down beside me.

I nodded.

"Toothache?"

I unclamped. "Nothing. I'm fine."

"Okay. Will I put some music on?"

"Sure."

She got up – a little unsteadily – and went to her CD rack, which, without being unkind, was mostly filled with albums that had come free with Sunday newspapers. "Christ, I really should get some new stuff. Kenny Rogers? No, wait ... eh ..."

"Kenny Rogers will do grand."

She put the CD on and returned to the sofa. "I had a friend in New York once, Sally, who was seriously into Kenny Rogers."

"Yeah?"

"Not the music. I mean … sexually. She never shut up about him. Made her husband grow a beard and all. But that didn't last. He didn't look like Kenny Rogers, he just looked homeless."

"Pity."

"She was a really sophisticated woman, very stylish, owned her own business, read high-falutin' books, went to the opera a lot – opera! All that malarkey. But plain old country Kenny did something for her."

I took another wholly unnecessary sip of wine. "Strange."

"It *was* strange. But there's no accounting for people and the things they see in one another." She turned to face me. "What do you think Gerry saw in your one?"

I didn't think she had told me about Sally and Kenny Rogers because she wanted a jokey prelude to her question about Lisa; that just seemed to suddenly occur to her. Still, I felt slightly cornered.

"Was it all about her looks?" Nancy prompted when I failed to answer.

"I haven't really thought about it."

"Come on, Jackie. You must have done."

"Looks, then," I mumbled.

Nothing more was said for a while. Kenny Rogers complained to Lucille about her poor timing.

"Not that it matters, really," Nancy said then.

"Suppose not."

"But you'd like to think it was just looks."

"Would I?"

243

"One, I should say. *One* would like to think it was just looks."

"What makes you say that?"

"I mean, it'd be a whole other kettle of fish if it was a proper relationship, wouldn't it? Better if it's nothing more than … sex."

"I never thought it was a proper relationship," I said. "I believed him from the start on that score."

"Yeah. You said. I'm not sure I would have. Not Gerry, don't get me wrong, that's up to you. But if I caught David playing away and he swore it was just the once, I'm not sure I'd be all that convinced."

I shrugged and put down my glass. The room was starting to spin. Kenny Rogers had moved on from Lucille to Ruby, but he still wasn't having any luck.

"Why are *you* so convinced?" Nancy asked.

"Because."

"Was it his tone of voice or what?"

"Yeah. It was his tone of voice."

"How did he sound? Was he –"

"Plus … Plus … I think that sort of thing … can happen."

"What can?"

"A … one-off. Mistake. A one-off mistake."

"Really?"

"Maybe."

"You sound like you've forgiven him already. Have you?"

My confession climbed my throat again. I swallowed it down and faked a smile. "Ah, I'm too sozzled to talk about this now," I said. "Have you thought about anywhere nice for the honeymoon?"

* * *

I awoke next morning to a feeling that I had read about but never personally experienced – complete ignorance regarding my current whereabouts. It was only when I hauled myself up onto my elbows and saw Nancy's framed *Casablanca* poster that the answer arrived. I heard the tinkle of spoon against mug coming from the kitchen and realised that I was not alone. Another realisation followed immediately: I had been drunk, seriously, properly plastered for the first time since my arrest. *Why now?* I scolded myself. *Aren't things complicated enough?*

"Hello?" I called out.

Nancy appeared in the archway.

"Jackie O. You're alive."

I thought it over. It seemed to be the truth. "Barely. What time is it?"

"Almost eleven. I didn't want to wake you."

I placed a tentative hand against my brow. "Christ … my head."

"I'll get you a Resolve."

I sat up properly and tried to reconstruct the evening. The last thing I remembered even semi-clearly was listening to Kenny Rogers. But that had been quite early.

"What time did I go to bed?" I called, greatly resenting having to raise my voice.

Nancy came back into the room bearing a glass, whose contents I swallowed in two noisy gulps. It tasted like fizzy

245

bleach, but I didn't care. There was water in there somewhere and that was the main thing.

"Take a guess," Nancy said.

"Dunno. One? Two?"

"You flatter yourself."

"Earlier? Midnight?"

"Half past ten."

"What? No way!"

"Half past ten. And you didn't 'go to bed', you conked out. I had to get the pull-out fixed up *round* you, which was no mean task, I might add."

"Jesus. Sorry."

"Don't worry about it. I needed the early night myself."

A horrible thought occurred to me. "Um … I was talking complete rubbish, I suppose, was I?"

She wobbled her hand back and forth. "I've heard you in better form, let's put it like that."

"Right. Did I say anything *really* embarrassing?"

"Yes."

My toes curled. "What?"

"You said we should go to Sligo for our honeymoon because that's where you and Gerry went and you had a great time. I reminded you about six times that I'm *from* Sligo, but you didn't seem to hear me."

"Oh. Anything else?"

"You talked about Robert a lot. Gave out about him a lot, I mean. Nothing new there."

"Meaning what?"

"Nothing. Nothing. Listen, Jackie … I want to apologise."

"For?"

"For going on and on about David and the wedding."

"Oh. It's all right."

"No, it's not. You came over here for support and I let you down. But it was such a shock …"

I shook my head, a move that I instantly regretted. "Forget about it."

"OK. If you're sure. Now – do you want to go for a walk or something? Bit of fresh air."

"No. Thanks. I should really get back over to Melissa's."

"Oh. Okay. Whatever you like. But have a bit of tea and toast first. It might help."

"Thanks."

She retreated into the kitchen. I began the long and difficult task of getting off the floor.

Tea and toast and fizzy bleach notwithstanding, my hangover worsened during the drive back to Ranelagh. My visit to Nancy's started to seem like an episode with brackets around it; mentally, I was now back in the Baggot Street coffee shop, feeling stunned and panicked and miserable. I checked my phone along the way, but there were no missed calls from Robert. None from Chrissy, for that matter. Gerry had called three times.

Melissa took a long time to answer my ring at the door. When she finally did emerge, she nodded sharply at me and turned on her heels.

"You're back," she said quietly as she went down the hall to the kitchen.

No missed calls from her either, I thought.

Niall poked his head out of the living room as I stepped inside.

"Hello," he said. "I missed you because you were GONE."

With that, he disappeared inside again, slamming the door behind him.

"I missed you too!" I called out.

I found Melissa furiously scrubbing a casserole dish in the sink.

"Niall seems to be in good form," I said. "Gave up on the singing, did he?"

"Yup," she said, to the casserole dish more than me.

"No more episodes?"

Her shoulders slumped. "I'm sorry I ever used that word. And the answer's no. He's been fine."

I sat on a stool. "And how are you?"

"Fine." More scrubbing.

"So … I met Robert yesterday."

No response.

"Melissa?"

She half-turned. "What?"

"I said, I met Robert yesterday."

She turned back. "And?"

"It wasn't good. *The Sun* had it more or less right. And he blames Gerry for him getting into trouble. He's talking like Chrissy now, never speaking to his dad again, that kind of thing. And, on top of it all, he's back to his old self with me. He was so rude. I was very upset."

"You were probably nagging him again."

I decided to play nice. "Even if I had been, and I wasn't,

it's no excuse. He should –"

"And what did *Nancy* have to say about it all?"

Even though I couldn't see her face, I could tell by her voice that she had screwed it up on the word "Nancy".

"Are you all right, Melissa?" I said. "You seem to be annoyed about something."

She stopped scrubbing and turned around fully, then folded her arms and leaned back against the sink. "Yeah," she said. "Yeah, I am annoyed as a matter of fact. Do you want to take a guess why?"

I felt my teeth grinding together. "How about we skip that part and you just *tell* me why?"

"OK. I will. We've been very good to you, I think, over the past few days."

"Of course you have."

"And when you left here yesterday lunch-time, all agitated and flustered about Robert, *I* was all agitated and flustered too. But you didn't even bother to call me and tell me how it went. I got a bloody text saying you were off to *Nancy's* and you'd call later."

"But –"

"Let me finish. Then, when I was just starting to seriously worry, I get another text saying, oh, you've decided to stay with *Nancy* now."

"Do you have to do that every time you say her name?"

"Do what?"

I pulled a face – and a voice. "*Nancy.*"

Melissa shook her head sadly. "Unbelievable. I'm saying her name wrong now …"

"I could do without the tone, that's all," I said.

"Well, hard luck. It's quite obvious to me that you only came to us in the first place because the wonderful Nancy – did I say it right that time? – the wonderful Nancy wasn't around. And as soon as she was available again, you dropped us like a hot spud. After, what is it, nearly a week, you didn't even think to call me and let me know what was going on. Texts, Jackie. Fucking *texts*."

"You're being very dramatic," I countered. "It wasn't supposed to be a snub, Jesus. Nancy's my best friend. Of course I'm going to want to see her at a time like this. What, do you expect me to apologise for that?"

"No. I expect you to apologise for treating my house like a hotel where you –"

"A hotel! Oh, for –"

"– where you can come and stay when it suits and just bugger off with barely a backward glance when it doesn't."

"Melissa, I don't particularly feel the need to explain myself to you, but the fact is, I didn't mean to stay over in Nancy's last night. But we got talking –"

"Oh, did you now?"

I pulled my lips tight over my teeth. "What's that supposed to mean?"

"Talking. If I was anything more than a B&B to you –"

"Sorry, I thought it was a hotel."

"Don't try to be a smart-arse, Jackie, it doesn't suit you. If I was anything more than a *hotel* to you, then surely to God you'd have had a talk with *me* by now. But no. You've had no interest in talking to me about Gerry and what the hell you're going to do about it. It's been downright weird, frankly. Colm thinks so too. I'm good enough for putting a roof over your head, obviously, but not good enough for actual conversation. You need a Nancy for that kind of thing, don't you?"

In the sink behind her, the casserole dish suddenly fell over from its side, causing me but not Melissa, to jump.

"What I was about to say, before you interrupted me, was that I didn't intend to stay with Nancy, but we got talking and opened a bottle of wine, so before I knew what was what, I couldn't drive." As soon as I said this, I realised it was bad on two scores. Firstly, it wasn't strictly true. And secondly, it gave a serious poke to a sleeping dog. I held my breath, hoping Melissa would resist the obvious come-back. She didn't.

"That doesn't usually stop you," she said.

I closed my eyes for a couple of seconds. When I opened them again, Melissa had turned back to her scrubbing. I didn't know if she had done so with a sense of shame or triumph, and I didn't really care. For a moment, I considered telling her that it was the first time I'd been drunk in almost three years. But that, I decided, was hardly the point.

"Maybe it would be best if I just left," I said and slid off my stool.

Melissa didn't reply. The sound of her assault on the casserole dish filled the air. I waited for a few seconds, then walked out of the kitchen and up the stairs. It didn't take me long to pack.

Niall met me in the hall when I came back down.

"Where are you going?" he said quietly.

"I have to go away for a while," I said. "But I'll see you soon."

I waited for his tears and hug.

"GoodBYE!" he said and ran off down the hall to his mother.

I slipped away.

CHAPTER 21

I was no more than twenty metres away from Melissa's when the tears started to flow. By the time I'd made it around the corner and into the next street, they were coming so thick and fast that I could no longer see where I was going. I pulled in, switched off the engine, and waited for order to be restored. It turned out to be a long wait, twenty minutes at least. Just when I was beginning to get myself under control, an old lady came along. She wasn't the first person to see me sitting there in a complete state, but she was the first who didn't pick up her pace, staring straight ahead. Instead, she stopped and leaned on someone's front wall, squinting at me through Coke-bottle glasses. Her face was a picture of puzzlement. I guessed that she no longer trusted her vision and wasn't sure if this was what it looked like. After a few seconds she let go of the wall and started towards me. I wiped my nose on the ancient tissue I'd found in the glove compartment and tried to stop my shoulders from heaving. When she was a few feet away from the car, she raised her right hand and waved it vigorously from side to side at the wrist. I waved back, with much less enthusiasm. Then she was at my window, tapping with all five fingers.

"Hello in there," she said through the glass.

I wound the window down. "Hello." My voice sounded goopily nasal.

"Are you all right, love?"

"I'm fine."

"You don't look fine."

I made myself smile. "Bad day. I'm grand, honestly. Thank you."

She pushed her glasses up her nose. "Nothing I can do for you, love? A wee chat, maybe?"

For a moment, I considered telling her the whole story. It would be nice to hear a stranger's perspective, I thought.

"Nothing. Honestly. But thanks again. You're very kind."

"All right, love. Take care."

She shuffled off. I burst into tears again. This time they lasted half an hour.

* * *

It was just after two p.m. when I pulled up outside Gerry's studio-cum-shop. He was in there, I knew, because the battered jeep was parked two spaces behind me. I lit a cigarette and smoked it manically, all the while keeping an eye on the front window. Stephanie, Gerry's sole employee, was dealing with a customer who seemed to be having a great deal of trouble choosing a frame for something. I could tell that she was running out of patience with the guy; her occasional smiles formed too quickly and disappeared too suddenly to be genuine. By the time the customer finally pulled out his wallet, I was on cigarette number three. I waited for him to leave, finished the fag, and climbed out of the car.

Stephanie didn't look up as her front door tinkled open. When she did, she gave me a smile that was the polar opposite of the one she'd used on her customer. We'd always rubbed along well together, possibly because she greatly enjoyed telling tales behind Gerry's back and I greatly enjoyed hearing them.

"Well, stranger," she said. "Haven't see you in a while. Where have you been hiding?"

"Around and about," I said. Ordinarily I would have stopped for a chat, or at least enquired after her mother (who had been dying any day now for the past two years). But not this time. "He's in there, is he?"

"Yeah, he is. But he's got someone with him, family portrait. Should be done any minute. Take a seat and I'll make us a cup of tea."

"No thanks. I'll just go on back and hurry him up."

Stephanie was clearly surprised by this. I'd never before entered the studio while Gerry was working, never. "He won't be long, honestly," she said. "I thought they'd be done by now, actually."

"Don't worry about it," I said and marched on through the

Staff Only door. I found Gerry smiling and shaking hands with a woman of about my age. In the background, the woman's husband was scolding their two small boys for what I could only presume had been poor modelling. All four were in their best gear; the boys looked deeply uncomfortable and faintly ridiculous in their little suits and ties. They reminded me of ventriloquist's dummies. Gerry turned in my direction when I closed the door behind me. He stared at me for a second and then returned his attention to his client. I could tell that he had lost the thread of what he was saying.

"This is my wife, Jackie," he said uncertainly as I stepped into the studio.

The couple nodded hello. I'd seen them around town but didn't know their names. Gerry was too flustered to complete the introductions. I nodded back at them and walked across to the desk in the far corner. While they finished their goodbyes and thank-yous I kept my back to them all, pretending I was looking for something in a ledger.

"Okay then," Gerry said after a few seconds. He was speaking unnecessarily loudly now – for my benefit, I supposed, to signal that he was almost done. "Stephanie will sort you out, if you … uh …"

I heard footsteps then, followed by more goodbyes and thank-yous. The door opened and closed. I turned and saw that we were alone. Gerry put his hands on his hips, then wrung them together in front of him, then returned them to his hips.

"Jackie," he said and moved towards me. I started walking too. We met right in the middle of the floor, beside his tripod. "It's great to see you," he said, and then he wrinkled his nose. "Have you been *smoking*?"

I drew my right hand back and to the side, then smacked him as hard as I could across the face. It was like hitting a lump of solid wood. My palm tingled with pain. I rubbed it against my thigh, not caring how that looked.

Gerry barely reacted to the blow itself. But a second later, he staggered back and raised his hand to his cheek. I guessed that this was the result of shock, rather than injury.

"Jackie –" he began.

"Don't you fucking 'Jackie' me!" I snarled. "You stupid shit. You've ruined our family. Ruined it! For some slut who doesn't care whether you live or die. I hope you're fucking happy!"

"What brought this on?" he said.

Now it was my turn to stagger back. "What brought ... *What*?"

"I mean, you seemed fairly ... I thought you were ... y'know ... Why are you freaking out now all of a sudden?"

I tried not to let it show that this was a good question. "*I can freak out whenever I fucking want to!*" I roared.

"Shhh!" he said. "Stephanie will hear you."

"I don't care who fucking hears me!"

"Come on," he said. "At least let's sit down and talk about this in –"

I pointed my finger in his face. "Shut up, Gerry. Just shut up. I don't *want* to talk to you."

He spread his arms wide, angry now himself. "Then what are you doing here? Why did you come at all?"

I didn't really have an answer to that one, so I said the first thing that came into my head. "In the *front room*! Behind a big fucking window! What were you *thinking*? Did you want to get caught, was that it?"

"I thought you didn't want to talk."

"Just answer the bloody question, Gerry!"

He dropped his head and looked at his feet. "Of course I didn't want to get caught."

"Explain it then."

"What, here?"

"Yes. Here."

"Wouldn't you rather –"

"Start talking, Gerry, or I swear to God . . ."

"All right, all right. Look … she took me by surprise. It all happened very quickly. She was at her front door when I arrived home and we got chatting, just … chatting." He paused and took a deep breath. "We really should go somewhere else for this con–"

"*Keep going*," I said.

Another deep breath. "She started telling me about her boyfriend. Michael. She said she wouldn't be around for much longer because she was moving in with him."

"Oh, I get it. So if you wanted to have sex with her, you'd have to do it sooner rather than later."

He winced, then carried on as if I hadn't spoken. "She invited herself in for coffee. I swear to God, Jackie. She invited *herself* in."

"Why wasn't she at work? What does she do anyway?" These were deeply unimportant questions, but I really wanted to hear the answers. I braced myself for "She's a model".

"She's a medical sales rep. She had come home for her laptop charger."

I heard the beginnings of a stinging comeback in my head, something to do with lap-dancing. Nothing came of it, so I nodded for him to continue.

"Jackie, are you sure you want to hear this? I don't feel comfortable talking ab–"

"I don't care about your *comfort*, Gerry. Get on with it."

"We went into the kitchen," he said softly, "and I made the coffee. She asked a lot of questions about my job and then she said she'd like to see some of my pictures."

"And you showed her the Cross-eyed Busker, I suppose."

This was the name we'd given to a shot Gerry had taken on weekend away in Donegal. The subject was a fiddle player we'd spotted on a street corner. When he noticed that someone was pointing a camera at him, he'd struck a pose, a sort of parody, in a way, all eyebrows and elbows. It would have been a decent photograph in any event – "an accident of the light", Gerry called it – but what made it really special was the expression on the busker's face. He'd smiled with the sort of pure and true delight that you normally only see in small children. The dramatic turn in his left eye made the smile seem even sweeter, somehow. Gerry blew the picture up when we got home and gave it pride of place on the living-room wall. It was far and away his favourite of his own photos. And it had been mine too, up until this moment.

"Yeah," he said. "I showed her the Cross-eyed Busker."

"Did she like it?"

"Jackie ..."

"Did she?"

"She said she did, yes."

"So much that she just *had* to –"

"All right, I think that's as far as we should go with this. You can guess the rest."

"I want to hear you saying it."

There was a tentative knock, the door opened and Stephanie stuck her head in. Gerry turned to face her. I turned away.

Stephanie's voice was shaky. She'd obviously heard us raising ours.

"Eh, sorry to … Sorry. Gerry, Mrs Gogan's on the phone about –"

"Tell her I'll call her back."

"I already tried that, but she's called three times and she's really angry, she said she's getting a sol–"

"Stephanie, *please*."

"Okay. Okay." She retreated, closing the door as if she expected it to explode halfway through the manoeuvre.

I faced Gerry again. "You were saying?"

He put his hands on his forehead and let them slide down his face, dragging his lower eyelids.

"I don't know how to describe it, other than to say … it just happened. We were talking about the picture and next thing I knew, she had her … hands … on my waist. I couldn't believe it. I didn't know what to say. And then she kissed me. And that's all I'm saying about it."

"I think you're leaving a bit out."

"Of course I am! What do you want, details?"

I tried to swallow but found that I couldn't. "Did this happen because I'm going to be turning forty soon?" In truth, I'd never thought that it had anything to do with my age. I just wanted to make him feel even worse.

"*What*? Jackie! No. No."

"She's always fancied you. Obviously. Did she tell you that?"

He nodded. "Yes."

"And had you always fancied her?"

"No!"

"Liar."

"Jackie, what do you want me to say? I can't pretend I hadn't noticed the way she looks. But I wasn't ... after her."

"It just happened."

"*Yes*. It sounds pathetic, but it's the truth. I didn't plan for it to happen and I was already regretting it as soon it started. And I'm sorry, I'm sorrier than I've ever been for anything in my life. I know an apology is as much use to you as a chocolate teapot, but it's –"

"As much use as a *what*? You're making *jokes*?"

"No! That wasn't a joke, it's just an expression. Please, Jackie ..."

I tried to think of another question, but nothing came to mind. So I walked away, going through the staff door and the shop at speed, hoping Stephanie would be too mortified to even say goodbye. She was.

CHAPTER 22

When I screeched into the driveway in Ashbourne, I suddenly became convinced that I was going to bump into Lisa, home to pick up her laptop charger again. But there was no one around apart from Keano, the Raffertys' Jack Russell. I got out of the car and stormed in to the house, keeping my eyes dead ahead, never so much as glancing at next-door. Inside, I hit 1985 – the year of our wedding, the year of the twins' birth – on the alarm panel. The kitchen looked pretty much as I'd expected to find it – tidy enough, but hardly clean. There were a few dishes in the sink and the bin needed to be emptied. The microwave door was hanging open and inside I could detect the remnants of several poorly covered soups. There were crumbs and tea-stains on every surface and the air was horribly stale.

I stood in the kitchen for a few minutes, breathing heavily, then grabbed a pair of scissors and went upstairs. The bedroom was a real mess. There were socks and boxer shorts strewn all over the place and the bed looked as if it hadn't been made all week; it looked as if it hadn't been made *ever*. I threw the door open on Gerry's side of the wardrobe and started throwing armfuls of his clothes onto the floor. When I thought the pile was big enough, I went at it with the scissors, slashing and gouging and ripping and chopping, working extra hard on the suits and the more expensive-looking shirts. My attack was what news reporters call "frenzied" to begin with, but I soon began to fear for the safety of my left hand and adopted a more methodical approach.

Ten minutes or more went by before, exhausted and sweaty, I finally dropped the scissors. As soon as it hit the floor, I started surveying the room, looking for something else to destroy. The only real candidate was Gerry's old CD Walkman, which was on his bedside locker. He'd recently upgraded to an iPod, but that was nowhere to be seen. I pulled the Walkman to the floor and jumped on it with both feet. Nothing. It looked as good as new. I jumped on it again – still nothing. Cursing Japanese production standards, I picked it up and hurled it against the wall. A small piece of debris flew away from the point of impact and for a moment, I felt as if I'd achieved something important. On closer inspection, however, I realised that the debris was a piece of plaster; the Walkman was still in perfect shape. I picked it up again and started trying to wrench the CD door off. But my fingers were too weak. I looked around for a blunt instrument. None was available. *Last resort*, I thought and went into the en-suite. I filled the sink with water, tapping my thumb on the edge as I waited, and then dropped my enemy in. The victory felt horribly hollow. The Walkman would never work again, I was sure, but still. I wanted Gerry to see it smashed to pieces, not having a bath. The visuals were all wrong. On the plus side, I spotted his collection of aftershaves, some of which had cost a small fortune, and began to feel a little better as I tossed them out of the window onto the patio below. With that done, I went downstairs again, to the front room. I paused at the doorway and poked my head in, my breath held, my heart thumping. The Cross-eyed Busker stared over at me (and, to be fair, at the sideboard to my left). I stared back for a moment, then walked over and took it down from its hook. Unsurprisingly, it smashed first time when I swung it against the door handle. I snatched a piece of broken glass from the frame and cut an X into the image, corner to corner.

Only then did I take a proper look around the room. It was much cleaner than the kitchen. No crumbs, no dishes. I guessed that Gerry hadn't been in there much, if at all, during the week. After doing a quick lap, I sat down on the sofa and looked out through the front window. *This sofa*, I thought. *That window*. I got up again. The hall floor felt rubbery and unreal under my feet, but I made it down into the kitchen. Sitting at the scratched and wobbly table that a week ago had seemed like a major problem, I tried to focus. Where, for a start, was I going to sleep? It seemed that I had no choice but to go back to Nancy's. She would be perfectly welcoming, I knew. And yet it was not an appealing option. Even if she managed to stay off the topic of her wedding – which I wasn't at all sure she could – I didn't particularly want to talk to her about the mess I was in. Try as I might, I couldn't dismiss the feeling that she had blown her chance. I wished I was back in the car in Ranelagh, talking to the kind old lady. Given another shot, I'd have taken her up on her offer of a chat – although she would have got a lot more than she bargained for.

With a heavy heart, I reached into my bag for my phone, intending to call Nancy. As I started to dial, I noticed that I had missed a call while I was in the studio. This time I recognised the number as Eddie's. I rang my voice-mail and listened to his message.

"Hello, Jackie," he said. Straight away, I knew that things had gone well with Margaret. His voice was so light and bright, so full of life. *"I hope you're feeling better, although I'm sure you're not."* He darkened a little then. *"I mean ... oh, for ... Good man Eddie. You know what I mean. I hope. Anyway. Give me a call if you feel up to it. See ya."*

I stared at the oven, lost in thought. *Eddie.* Could I? He wasn't the complete stranger that I had wondered about talking to, but he was close enough. And, I reminded myself, he had already told me his deepest and darkest. I had told him quite a bit of mine. Granted, he wasn't exactly worldly-wise, but he could listen, after a fashion, and that was what I wanted most. I argued back and forth with myself like this for a few minutes, then went into my Missed Calls and dialled his number. He answered on the first ring.

"Jackie?"

"Hello, Eddie."

"Are you all right? You don't sound all right."

I didn't have the energy or even the will to lie. "No. I'm not all right."

"What's up? I mean … is it something new?"

"Eddie, I'd like to meet up with you. Tonight. Please."

There was a pause. "Of course. Where? What time?"

I gave it some thought. Nowhere public, in case I lost it entirely. That didn't leave us much choice.

"Can I come round to yours?"

"Oh," he said. "Okay. I'll get some buns in."

* * *

We'd arranged to meet at seven-thirty, which left me with a few hours to kill. Not knowing what else to do with the time, I went to the cinema in Coolock. It was handy for Eddie's address in Beaumont, but that wasn't its chief attraction. Its chief attraction was that it would allow me to be alone in the dark for a while. I plumped, more or less at random, for *The Da Vinci Code*. It was rubbish – at least the first half was. I fell asleep after about an hour and had to be shaken back to life by an usher. On the plus side, the nap did wonders for my hangover.

As I emerged blinking from the cinema, I realised that I hadn't eaten since morning and wandered into a nearby pizza joint. I'd almost finished my double pepperoni with extra mushrooms when I spotted a familiar face making her way to a table in the corner. It was Carmel Quinn, a woman who'd left First Premier about six months previously. She was with two other women, one of whom I presumed to be her sister; they were the spit of each other. I hadn't had many dealings with Carmel at work, but I guessed that she would remember me; I remembered her, after all. Although she had always struck me as a perfectly nice person, I didn't want to talk to her. I didn't want to talk to anyone. My best option, I decided, was to abandon the remainder of my meal and sneak away. It was a simple enough plan – couldn't have been simpler, really – but I cocked it up completely. As I pushed back my chair, I somehow managed to take a swipe at my water glass, which shattered on the ground, attracting the attention of everyone in the restaurant, including Carmel.

"Jackie O?" she said with more amazement in her voice than the situation really warranted.

I made a big show of looking all around, as if I had no idea who could possibly be calling me. When I caught Carmel's eye, I tossed my head back in fake delight.

"Carmel!" I said. "Well, well, well."

I walked over to her table.

"Fancy seeing you here!" she said, once again with unnecessary wonder.

"Small world," I agreed. "How have you been?"

"Can't complain, you know yourself. Oh, this is my friend Frances and my sister Julie."

We exchanged nods and nice-to-meet-yous.

"Wrecking the joint, are you?" Carmel said. "Not happy with the service?"

"That's me," I said. "All thumbs and knees."

"I wouldn't be far behind you. So – you escaped from First Premier, did you?"

My thoughts ran away from me, tripped up, ran again, tripped again. I could say that I had, but that would only lead me into further lies. It seemed simpler to tell the one quick one.

"No, no. Day off, that's all."

"Good woman. You'll get as much thanks."

"You said it."

"Jackie works for the same crowd I used to work for," she explained to Frances. (Julie had immediately lost interest in me and was perusing the menu with the look of a woman whose day had involved too much shopping and not enough eating.)

"Oh, very good," Frances said. "The old ..." She mimed fingers tapping on a keyboard.

"Yeah," I said. "Data entry." Even saying the words made my head droop. "It pays the bills."

"That's about all you could say for it," Carmel said. She frowned then, afraid she'd been offensive. "I mean, it's grand and all, you know, it's –"

"No, I know what you're saying," I assured her. "It's not exactly challenging. Where did you move on to, Carmel, I forget?"

"I went back to child-minding. A crèche in Artane. Don't know why I ever gave it up in the first place, to tell you the truth. Just got fed up, I suppose."

I nodded. "A year or two with First Premier changed your mind."

"You can sing that one. Is Jenny still there?"

"Jenny? Jenny will only leave the place feet first. She's my manager now."

Carmel closed her eyes and shook her head, signalling both sorrow and pity. It was as if I'd told her about the death of a loved one. "I thought that was on the cards when I was leaving. Just goes to show you, doesn't it? If you didn't know anything else about the place and someone told you that *that* yoke was a manager, you'd come to the right conclusions, wouldn't you? End of story."

"Yeah. Oh well. What can you do?"

Carmel raised one shoulder. "Leave?"

"Hmmm," I said, pushing my one little lie a bit further. "The day off has been nice …"

"There you go. Sure take a few thousand more of them."

I smiled. Carmel smiled. Frances smiled. Julie kept looking at the menu.

"Anyway," I said. "I'd better head on. Nice to see you again, Carmel. Take care."

"All right then," she said. "Be good."

I nodded goodbye to Frances and the top of Julie's head, and left.

CHAPTER 23

Eddie's street wasn't easy to find. I'd been creeping around the enormous estate for fifteen minutes and had driven down four different cul-de-sacs before I finally spotted the heavily graffitied bench that he'd told me look out for. I swung a left there and imagined I heard a choir of angels when I saw the words "Hanley Gardens" on a kerbside sign-post. The house itself was easier to locate. Even if Eddie hadn't given me the number – which he had, several times – I would have spotted it, no problem. It was the only one with a middle-aged man standing on the front step wearing a pink apron and waving both arms above his head so frantically that he looked as if he might get airborne.

"You found me all right," Eddie said as I approached the door.

"Yeah. Just about."

He stepped around to my side and put his hand in the small of my back. "Come in, come in, please."

"What's with the apron?" I said as I went (or was pushed, rather) inside.

"You don't like my tie, you don't like my apron –"

I turned to apologise and saw that he was joking. "I've been baking," he declared with some pride.

"Not for me, I hope."

"Well, for me too. But yes, for you."

"There was no need to go to any trouble, Eddie."

"The buns in the shop were brutal-looking. And besides, we did a bit of baking in cookery class and I never bothered trying it out at home. I hope they're all right. Scones. They'll be done any minute."

"I'm sure they'll be lovely," I said. "Straight ahead?"

"Straight ahead, that's us."

I moved on down the hall and into the kitchen. Eddie followed so closely behind that he stood on my heel.

"Sorry! Sorry!" he said. "Now, take a seat. What can I get you, tea or coffee? Or wine? Vodka? I think there's gin here somewhere. Beer? Orange juice?"

"Tea's fine," I said. "Vodka and scones wouldn't go so well."

"You might have a point."

I took a seat at his doll-sized kitchen table and tried not to make it obvious that I was having a good look around. There were touches here and there that were just what I would have expected to find – a cutesy kitten calendar, luridly floral tea-towels, a radio from about 1976 – but generally speaking, I was impressed. The place was brightly lit and spotlessly clean.

"This is lovely, Eddie," I said, trying not to sound surprised.

"I make an effort to keep it tidy, at least," he said, reluctant to take the compliment. "And we won't be in here long, we'll move into the sitting room in a minute. I just want to keep an eye on the boyos."

I looked around for a pair of pet cats or a fish-tank. Then I realised he was talking about his scones.

"Don't move on my account," I said. "I'm grand here."

"Okay then. If you're sure."

As Eddie busied himself making tea and getting plates and cutlery together, I found myself turning mute. I wanted to hear how he'd got on with Margaret after our last phone call but was afraid of setting him off the way I'd set Nancy off. He didn't seem to mind the silence. I did.

"So, how did it work out with Margaret?" I asked before very long. "Did she go for the tragedy and mystery angle?"

He put a teapot and two mugs down the table. "That can wait. What about you?"

I could have kissed him. "Me? Ah, you know … Things haven't been … I mean, the last couple of days …"

The oven pinged.

"Sorry," Eddie said. "Won't be a minute."

He was true to his word. The ping was still echoing around the room when he deposited the scones on to the table and sat down opposite me.

"Wow," I said, nodding at his handiwork. "They look lovely. Smell lovely too."

"They do, don't they?" he said with a smile. "Beginner's luck, maybe. Tuck in, tuck in."

I grabbed and quickly buttered a scone, hoping for all I was worth that I wouldn't have to fake a positive review. But there was no danger of that.

"Eddie!" I said, not caring that my mouth was full. "They're *delicious*!"

He took an experimental nibble of his own. "Christ, they are as well," he said. "I don't believe it."

"You could go into business with these."

"Well, now …"

"They're fantastic. Just fantastic."

"I can't say I'm not chuffed."

"Lovely straight from the oven …"

"Yeah."

"Much nicer than mine. You'll have to show me what you did."

"No problem."

"Little hint of cinnamon in there …"

"A wee bit, yeah."

"Not too overpowering though."

"No."

"Just right."

We ran through this exchange at speed. When it was over, I realised that I had been stalling. Eddie seemed to cotton on at exactly the same moment. He gave me another quick smile over the top of his mug. I averted my gaze.

"Anyway," he said. "You were about to tell me something."

I drank some tea and was horrified by the slurp I managed to produce. "Yeah."

"About Gerry, I presume?"

"Yes. No. Sort of. It's about me, really."

He popped a hunk of scone into his mouth and chewed patiently, waiting for me to start.

"All week long," I began, "I've been doing something I'm not proud of."

"Oh?"

"And I want to talk to someone about it. It's … embarrassing."

"You sound like me," he said. "Before I told you about my … y'know."

"Maybe that's why I'm talking to you. Partly at least. Because of the way you confided in me. That and – don't take this the wrong way."

He moved in his chair and straightened his face, getting ready to be offended.

"But you're still practically a stranger to me," I went on. "That's what I want, really. Someone I can talk to who doesn't have any, what do they call it, baggage – I mean, baggage in relation to me. Someone who'll just listen and tell me what they think. Honestly."

"I can do that," Eddie said.

"And you have to promise me that you won't tell a soul."

He crossed his heart. "I promise. Why would I? Sure look at the goods you've got on me."

"I would never tell anyone that," I said solemnly.

"And I'd never tell anyone about your ... whatever it is."

"OK."

I took some more tea and clasped my hands together on the table. "Last Friday," I began, "when I caught Gerry with your woman, Lisa, I was ... shocked. Obviously."

"Obviously."

"I mean, that's not *good news*, is it?"

"God, no."

"That's what any normal person would think."

"Absolutely."

"No one in their right mind would try to look on the bright side, would they?"

Eddie saw where I was going and this time made no reply.

"Well, I did," I said. "I've been ... using it. To get back on good terms with people. My sister. And my son. I fell out with them both, ages ago. I've been deliberately using what happened to get sympathy, to get them on my side. I didn't set out to do it. Not really. Well ... maybe a bit ..."

"And what? You feel guilty about it?"

"Yes. Guilty. And stupid. Because it didn't work. Well, it sort of did, for a while. I got some results. But it turned out they were paper-thin. Now we're back to square one. They're barely talking to me. All week, I've been congratulating myself and now it's ..." I fought for air. "I can't believe I actually ... I actually thought ... *Every cloud* ..."

There was a pause while I regained what little composure was left available to me.

"Is that it?" Eddie said.

"Yeah."

"It's not the worst confession I ever heard. I thought you were going to tell me something really awful."

I thought, *I could tell you something really awful if you like.* "It feels pretty bad from where I'm sitting."

"Listen, Jackie, in a week where you've caught your husband having sex with another woman, this is small potatoes. I mean … oh God! Sorry. That was supposed to sound helpful. Good man, Eddie."

"It's all right. It's not like I'd forgotten about it. I saw him this afternoon. Gerry."

"Yeah?"

"Yeah. I hadn't really had a go at him before today. I was too busy *scheming*. But now that it's all gone wrong, I got furious with him. I smacked him in the face. Then I went home and slashed all his clothes. Christ, it's such a cliché. It was all I could think of at the time."

Eddie was clearly taken aback. "Wow. I can't believe you hit him. I wouldn't have had you down as the violent type."

"Neither would I. Neither would Gerry. He was stunned."

"He probably thought you'd got it out of your system when you vandalised his jeep."

I puffed out my cheeks. "I only did that, really, to get sympathy from my sister. I wanted to impress her with how upset I was."

"Oh."

"See what I mean? I've been a real …" I couldn't think of a word that covered it.

"So," Eddie said. "Your sister, eh –"

"Melissa."

"And your son …"

"Robert."

"You said they're barely talking to you now. How come?"

I shifted sideways in my seat and crossed my legs. But I didn't feel any more comfortable. I undid the move. "My best friend Nancy was away for a few days. She came back last night and I stayed over at hers. Melissa's raging. She thinks I used her house like a hotel while I had no other option and then dropped her when I had. And she's half-right. If Nancy had been around, I probably would have gone to her first. It wouldn't have occurred to me that I could do some … healing, I suppose you'd call it … with Melissa."

"Right. And Robert? What happened there?"

I made a noise with my lips. "He was nice to me for about ten minutes after he heard about Gerry. But he's had some problems of his own the last couple of days. And now that he's got distracted, it's like nothing ever happened. He's treating me like dirt again."

"What kind of problems? Your-fault kind of problems?"

"No. Gerry's fault. Robert ran into Lisa and there was … trouble. In a club. It was all over *The Sun*. Front page."

"Eh? It was in the papers? Must have been big trouble."

"Well, because of *The O'Mahonys* and all."

"What's *The O'Mahonys* got to do with it?"

"What do you mean? Robert's in it. He's Valentine Reilly."

Eddie's mouth formed an O. "You're joking me!"

"What? Did you not know that? You must have heard me talking about it at work."

He shook his head. "Never. Not once."

"Are you sure?"

"I'd have remembered something like that, Jackie."

"Oh. Well I'm sure I mentioned it to Veronica at least." I thought about it and realised that I hadn't done that very often either. "Anyway, he could be in a bit of bother with RTÉ. He's furious at Gerry and he seems to have just … lost interest in being nice to me. Again. I should have known it wouldn't last. He's had no time for me for years."

"What happened between you in the first place? And you and Melissa, for that matter."

My shoulders tensed. "There's no point in getting into it, Eddie. It's not important."

"You did say you wanted to talk …"

There was no anger in his voice – just alarm. I could tell that he wasn't happy with merely listening. He really wanted to help.

"Okay. But I don't think it'll make any difference."

He brightened up. "You never know."

"With Melissa, I can tell you what happened in a few words. Remember in the café, I told you that my parents were killed in a car crash?"

"I remember."

"Well, about a month before that I got banned for drink driving. And the guy who hit my parents was drunk. As far as Melissa was concerned, I might as well have killed them myself. The End."

Eddie took a moment to respond. "That's awful."

"Which bit?"

"All of it."

"Yeah."

"But you didn't kill your parents."

"I know that, Eddie. Try telling Melissa. Driving drunk was the stupidest thing I've ever done in my life. I think about it all the time. Every day of the week. The part that really got to me ..." I closed my eyes in shame. "The part that really got to me was that I didn't even have to get in the car. It was completely unnecessary. I was leaving a DVD back."

Eddie made a sudden involuntary noise, as if someone had dropped an ice-cube down his back. "That was stupid," he said. "I'm not going to sit here and tell you it wasn't. But you learned the lesson, I'm sure."

"Definitely. *Definitely*."

We stared at the scones for a while.

"What about Robert? What happened there?"

I tossed my head back. "Who knows? He just turned into a nightmare at the end of his school days."

"What, cheeky?"

"Cheeky doesn't begin to cover it. He'd take my head off as soon I opened my gob. No one else – just me."

"Why was that, do you think?"

"Dunno."

"Were you giving him a hard time?"

"Not particularly, although there was a lot to give him a hard time about."

"Like?"

"Well, apart from the cheek, there was his *unbelievable* messiness, his clothes, this awful friend he had at the time, the music he had blaring all hours of the day and night –"

"But he was a teenager, wasn't he? Isn't that all par for the course?"

A little bubble of anger rose up in me. "That's what Melissa said," I scowled. "She called me a nag. So did Nancy, more or less."

Eddie gave a little cough. "Maybe you were being a bit of a … I mean, just a wee bit –"

"That wasn't all. He was smoking hash, he had no interest in school, he left a mess everywhere –"

"You said that one already."

"He never said 'please' or 'thank you', he never left the bins out when I asked him because he knew I'd wind up doing it if he waited long enough, he never left his DVDs back either, for the same reason, he never –"

Eddie pointed his finger at me. "Jackie."

"What?"

"DVDs."

"What about them?"

"You said you were leaving a DVD back when you got arrested. Was it one of Robert's?"

The anger bubble grew again and then popped; I almost *heard* it.

"Yes."

Eddie lowered the finger and raised an eyebrow.

"So what?" I said, but I knew. I knew what.

"When was your drink-driving thing?"

"Four years ago."

"You and Robert fell out at the end of his schooldays, you said. When was that?"

"It was about … It was about four years ago."

"You don't think maybe there's a link?"

I didn't reply; *I couldn't*. My voice had stopped working.

"You must do," Eddie went on. "You get caught driving drunk, then your parents are killed by a drunk driver and your sister drops you. It must have been horrible. Do you not think that maybe you started harbouring a grudge against Robert? Because it was his DVD?"

I forced my mouth to open. "It wasn't Robert's fault," I said robotically. "It was my fault. No one else's."

"I'm not arguing with you. But still, you've gotta admit, it's a bit of a co–"

"I have to go," I said and bolted.

I was halfway out the front door before Eddie made it into the hall.

CHAPTER 24

Robert sounded quite cheery when he answered the intercom at his apartment.

"Robert," I said. "It's me. Mum. Can I come in?"

The cheeriness disappeared. "It's not a good time. My mate's here."

"Please, Robert. Please."

"Can it not wait, we're –"

"I'm begging you. It's important."

There was a pause. He mumbled something. Then the door clicked open.

"Thank you," I said, but he'd already hung up.

Inside, I heard laughter as I approached his apartment. When I knocked on the door, the laughter stopped briefly, then started again. It tapered off, slowly this time.

Finally, Robert opened up.

"Hello," I said.

"Hi." He turned, leaving the door open.

I stepped inside and closed it behind me. There were empty beer cans, at least a dozen of them, on the coffee table. The air was thick with smoke. A young man I'd never seen before was sitting on the sofa. He was wearing a multicoloured beanie and a duffel coat, even though the room was stifling warm.

"Hello there," he said.

"This is Bogie," Robert muttered. "Bogie – my mother."

Bogie rose from the sofa. He was ludicrously tall, six-four at least.

"Nice to meet you, Mrs O'Connell," he said and offered his hand.

"You too, eh ... Bogie," I said and shook.

Bogie turned to Robert. "She doesn't seem all that frightening to me."

Robert rolled his eyes. Bogie turned back to me and gently punched me on the shoulder. "I'm only messing with you. Will you have a beer?"

"No, thanks," I said. "Actually ... would you mind very much if I had a word with Robert in private for a moment?"

Bogie said, "No problem" just as Robert said, "For fuck's sake!"

"I'm sorry, Robert," I said. "I know it's your place and all –"

"Damn right it's my place," he snarled. "You can't march in here –"

"It's all right," Bogie said, raising his hands. "I'll run up to the shop, get a few nibbles."

"You don't have to go on her account," Robert said, but Bogie was already moving to the door.

"Good luck now," he said as he departed.

Robert stared at me. I could see his chest rising and falling.

"You sounded like you were in pretty good form," I said. "Before I got here. Did something happen with RTÉ?"

He stared on for another couple of seconds before answering. "We had a meeting. I got my wrist slapped. Not too hard. No such thing as bad publicity."

"What about the other guy? Is he still going to sue?"

"Don't know. Maybe. Probably. Nothing I can do about it, is there?"

"So … does this mean you're not going to cut your dad off?"

"Huh. I was already speaking to him."

"Oh?"

"He rang this afternoon. Very upset. Said you clocked him one."

I didn't want to get into details on that score. "True. Do you mind if I sit down?"

He gestured to the sofa sarcastically, something I wouldn't have thought possible. "Help yourself."

I sat. "Come here. Please."

He groaned and dragged himself across the room to sit beside me. I looked into his eyes. He looked away.

"I suppose you think that was typical," I said. "Me and Bogie."

"Ohhh, yes. Absolutely."

"You think I'm a nag."

He picked at his jeans. "Do you want the truth?"

"Yes."

"Yes, then. I do."

"I'm always giving out to you?"

"Yes."

"Complaining?"

"Yes."

"Finding fault?"

"Yes."

"Would you believe me if I swore I would never do any of those things again?"

He looked at me. "Probably not."

I reached out and took his hand. He didn't snap it away, but his fingers went limp and lifeless.

"Robert," I said. "Do you remember renting *The Mask of Zorro*?"

On the drive over to the apartment, I'd imagined that he would react to what I had to say with extreme anger. I would be telling him, after all, that I'd had the hump with him for a period of years because of something that he hadn't done on purpose – hadn't done at all, in fact. It would be tricky, I knew, but I allowed myself to hope that I'd be able to talk him down from his rage over the course of a few days – or weeks or months, if that was what it took. I would bombard him with apologetic phone calls and visits. I would grovel. I would beg. I would buy him stuff.

It was a considerable shock, then, when I finished

speaking (my head hung low, my eyes half-closed in shame) and he said, "You're fucking joking me." The shock wasn't in his choice of opener; it was in his delivery. There was no anger, no malice, no disgust. There was only surprise.

To my astonishment, the words "Language, Robert" formed on my lips. I left them there.

"I don't know how to tell you how sorry I am," I said weakly. "I know that's a pathetic thing to say. I know it doesn't –"

"And, what? You've just worked this out?"

Again, the tone was merely curious.

"Yes," I said. "I've been doing a lot of thinking these last few days and … yes, I've just worked it out."

I hoped he wouldn't question me any further on this specific point. Bad enough that I had to admit to such a thing without having to declare that it had come to me as news from a third-party.

"Really?"

"Really. I've been kidding myself for years that the problem was with *you*, with *your* behaviour. But no. It's me. It's been me all along. Looking for reasons to be mad at you. Hence the … nagging."

He thought for a moment then moved on to a different element of my news. "Drunk driving … I can't get my head round it. I knew there was something weird going on around then. It wasn't just the mood you were in. It was the staying out of the car – the *walking* everywhere. The health kick or whatever you called it. We used to talk about it, Chrissy and me. You know what we came up with?"

I shook my head.

"We thought you had a disease," he said. "You'd got some sort of terrible news from the doctor, a heart condition or something, and you were trying, too late, to get some exercise. It wasn't a bad theory, really. It also explained why you were being such a fucking wasp."

"Nope. Nothing like that. The whole walking thing was … comical, I suppose. Ridiculous. I didn't just walk to the shops or places I had to go to. I didn't think that was believable enough. So I used to go out in the evenings too, remember? In my new runners and all. Made a big deal of making sure you and Chrissy saw me heading off."

"That's right, yeah. Jesus. I never knew you could be so … devious."

My mouth went dry. "I try not to make a habit of it."

Nothing more was said for a few moments.

Then Robert asked, "So … were you already mad at me before Granny and Granda were killed? Or did you get mad afterwards?"

"Well, I wasn't *aware* of being mad you at all. But I suppose it was both. I was already mad and then it got much worse. It was a horrible few months, Robert. It would have been horrible even if the two things had been separate. But to have them linked up like that … I was all over the place."

He nodded. "Maybe that's why you got that bloody job. Or part of the reason anyway."

"My *job*? What's that got to do with it?"

He popped a shoulder. "Just wondering. I've never understood it. You obviously don't like it. Which is fair

287

enough. Sounds bloody tedious to me. You don't need the money, do you?"

"No. Not really. It comes in handy, definitely. But that's not why I started there."

"Why, then?"

"It seemed like a good idea, that's all. You kids were finishing school. I'd never had a real job, ever. I wanted something to do, I suppose. A new identity."

That was what I'd always told myself. But now that I thought about it, Robert seemed to have a point. Maybe it was just part of the larger crisis. It and the other thing.

"Then there was Jonathon Mullen," said Robert.

My knees knocked together. Was he *reading minds* now? "Sorry?"

"That was around then as well. And you got very involved there, didn't you?"

"What do you mean?" I asked, mouse-like.

"I mean, you took it badly. I know he got better and all, but still. That's fucking hard to watch. A sick child."

I nodded for all I was worth. "That's true. It was tough." In my desperation to change the subject, I blurted out, "And there was something else."

"Oh?"

"Your Auntie Melissa and I fell out after Mum and Dad died."

"I know that. Over the wills."

"No. Not over the wills. Over my drink-driving. I told her about it. She wasn't impressed, obviously, but she wasn't particularly bothered. Then Mum and Dad ..."

"Right. The other driver —"

"Yes."

"It all makes sense now. This was another thing me and Chrissy used to talk about. We couldn't work out how you two could get in such a mess over Granny and Granda's whatchacallit, estate. I mean, they weren't exactly rich, were they?"

"No. They sure weren't."

He reached for a beer and took a hefty slug. "That must have been hard on you too. You used to be so close. But you and her seem to be all right now. You're staying there and all ..."

"Yeah."

"So whats with the sudden thaw? Did she just forgive you out of the blue?"

"Not only has she not forgiven me out of the blue, I don't think she's forgiven me at all. We were doing OK for a few days, yeah. But it went horribly wrong this morning. Things were said."

"What kind of things?"

"Just ... things."

He waited to see if I would add anything else and when I didn't, said, "Ah, don't sweat it. I'm sure you'll make up tonight."

I didn't feel like getting into the uncertainty of my sleeping arrangements. But he had given me a thought. Melissa would be my next stop.

"Maybe you're right."

"Course I'm right. She knows you've been through a lot.

She'll come round."

"Maybe … Robert, I have to ask you something."

"Yeah?"

"Yeah. How come you're not angry? Are you only pretending not to be? Because there's no need. Shout away. I deserve it. I know I do."

His eyes twinkled at me. "Maybe I'll get angry later, when I get over the shock. For now, I'm just … relieved. Don't get me wrong, I'm not *congratulating* you on any of this. But at least now I know there was a reason for you turning on me. It's a fucking ridiculous reason, but it's better than nothing. And for what it's worth, I'm sorry I gave as good as I got."

That last bit was almost too much for me. "Don't you be apologising for God's sake," I told him. "I feel bad enough."

"Yeah," he said with a mock frown. "You're right. I take it back. Why should I –" He was interrupted by a knock on the door. "Bogie. Will I send him away again?"

This conversation had gone better than I could have dared to hope. Here was an opportunity for me to get out while I was still ahead.

"Let him in," I said.

"*Come in!*" Robert roared. "It's open."

Bogie entered. He was laden down with crisps and chocolate bars, enough for a children's party.

"Am I too early?" he said. "I can go out again."

"No," I said, getting up. My legs felt like hollow tubes. "I'm off now. I'm sorry I turfed you out. Family business."

"Nil desperandum," he said. "Here, lookit, I got you a

Snickers. You look like a Snickers kind of girl."

I took the bar. *This is a dream*, I thought. *You'll wake up in a minute.* "Thanks."

"I'll walk you out to the car," Robert said.

"No need. You stay here."

"Sure?"

"The beer's not going to drink itself."

He stepped over to me. Our hug went on for quite a while.

"Nice," said Bogie.

* * *

It had just gone nine thirty when I arrived at Melissa's.

Colm answered the door.

"Jackie!" he said, more startled than delighted.

"Hi."

We looked at each other for a moment. And then he seemed to suddenly remember where he was. "Come in, Christ, come in."

I followed him into the living-room where Melissa was sitting on the sofa. Niall was draped across her lap, his eyes half-closed, his mouth fully open.

"Hello," I said quietly.

"Hiya." She didn't look at all surprised to see me. I guessed that she'd heard me at the front door and had used the warning period to compose herself.

"He's up late," I said, nodding at Niall.

"He had a bit of an episode," Colm explained. "He got upset when he realised you'd gone and he set himself off."

"But I said goodbye earlier. He seemed all right then. Actually, he looked like he couldn't have cared less."

"Well, he did care," Melissa said sharply. Then to Colm: "And we're not calling them episodes any more. They're tantrums, that's all."

Niall's legs twitched. And then, without further warning, he sprang to life. His eyes flew open and with the agility of a gymnast, he launched himself into a sitting position. Melissa issued a muted "Ooof!" as the wind was knocked out of her. Niall looked around the room as if he'd never seen it before, finally settling his gaze on me.

"You came BACK," he said hoarsely and then threw himself off the sofa. He hit the ground running and had wrapped himself around my knees before I could even say hello. There was just no reading that little boy.

"Come on," Colm said to him. "Let's go and get all tucked in."

"NO!" Niall hollered. "I want to stay UP!"

Melissa groaned. She looked exhausted.

"Tell you what, Niall," I said. "If you go up with your daddy now, I'll come and read you a story in a few minutes. *Little Red Riding Hood* – isn't that the one you like?"

He looked up at me, gravely insulted. "No. I HATE that one."

I was thrown, but not for long. "Okay, then. No story."

He thought it through. "Maybe that one then. Maybe your one."

I smiled at him and only just resisted the urge to ruffle his hair. "Great. See you in a few minutes."

Without another word, he sped off into the hall and went thumping up the stairs.

Colm said, "Don't worry, you won't have to do it. He'll be asleep in seconds."

"I don't mind," I said. "Really."

He smiled and left, closing the door behind him.

"Sit down," Melissa said. It was somewhere between an invitation and an instruction.

I took a seat in an armchair. "Sounds like you've had a hard day," I said.

"So-so."

"You must be knackered."

"Sort of."

So much for small talk, I thought. "Melissa, listen. I want to apologise. About the Nancy thing. You were right, I should have called you. Texting was ... insulting."

"Yes."

Evidently, she had no intention of making it easy for me. "And, apart from that, I shouldn't have stayed over there last night. Not without talking to you properly first."

I thought I'd done quite well there, but she obviously disagreed. Before she even spoke, it was obvious from the narrowing of her eyes and the sudden Desperate Dan-ation of her jaw. "Oh?" she said. "Not without talking to me first? And what would you have said?"

In the silence that followed, I noticed for the first time that the television was on. The volume had been turned almost all the way down. Some British politician was saying that this was just a side-show and he wanted to concentrate on the real issues. I knew how he felt.

"I'll start again," I said, feeling faint and disembodied. "You were kind of right this morning when you said that I probably wouldn't have come here if Nancy had been around."

Melissa sniffed dismissively. "Knew it."

"But I didn't come here thinking you were, I don't know, a poor substitute. I came here with the best of intentions."

"Is that so?"

Overhead, something fell to the floor with such violence that the light-fitting shook. The thump was followed by a giggle. The giggle was followed by a raised voice. The raised voice was followed by a short screech. Then all was quiet.

"Yes," I said. "I did. I could have gone somewhere else, you know."

"I'm supposed to feel privileged, am I?"

"I didn't say that. I'm saying …" I paused.

This, I imagined, was the sort of feeling that bungee-jumpers got when they climbed up onto the rail of the bridge. I closed my eyes and asked myself if I really wanted to do this. The answer came back *Yes and no. Mostly no.* But I did it anyway.

"I'm saying I came here for a reason. I came here because I wanted things to get better between us." For the first time, she looked me in the eye. I hurried on, seizing the moment. "And I'm not telling you this because I'm proud of it. Just the opposite. I'm embarrassed – I'm ashamed – that I thought of using Gerry's behaviour as – I can't think of anything to call it but an excuse . . . I'm ashamed that I thought of using Gerry's behaviour as an excuse to kick-start our relationship. But that's what I did. And I want you to know it."

She blinked at me. "*Kick*-start? What do you mean?"

"Oh, come on."

"What?"

"Melissa …"

She said, "What?" again but with a strange click in her voice that told me she was already losing faith in her ability to keep up the pretence. I let the word hang in the air for a second to underline the silliness of her response.

"You know as well as I do," I said then, "that things have been bad between us since Mum and Dad died."

I waited for a response. But she made none. If she'd been lying down instead of sitting up, I would have assumed that she had died. Her eyes had turned to glass and all traces of expression had vanished from her face. It seemed that I had no choice but to keep talking.

"And the reason's pretty obvious. You've never forgiven me for driving drunk."

Again, I waited and again, it was in vain.

"We should have talked about it," I went on, "but we never did. And it just got worse and worse. You can't deny it. So, yeah … I came to stay with you for a reason. I thought that in all this mess with Gerry, we might … pull together."

Her face reanimated. "And what, you're saying now that I let you down? I pulled plenty, let me tell –"

"No, Melissa, *Jesus*. You're so defensive … I'm not saying you haven't been good to me. You've been very good! I said so this morning too. There's only so many times I can repeat it. I'm just saying … we should talk. That's all."

"And what if I don't want to?"

I was surprised by this line, as, apparently, was she. Her eyebrows briefly came together as if she'd spotted a strange and possibly dangerous object on the floor between us.

"I really think we should," I said uncertainly. "I mean, it can't hurt, can it? I've just been over to Robert and I had a talk with him that I should have had a long time ago too. And I'm glad that I did. *Very* glad."

"What was all that about then?" she said. "You and Robert?"

I looked at her, surprised by her sudden chirpiness. She wasn't really interested in me and Robert. It was obvious. She was trying to change the subject, that was all. And I wasn't having it.

"That'll keep for another day. It's you and me that I want to work on now."

The chirpiness disappeared as abruptly as it had arisen. "*Work* on? Christ. Should I get a notebook? Will there be an exam later?"

That tore it. "Melissa," I said thinly. "Why are you being like this?"

"Like what?" she bristled.

"Like *that*. All prickly and defensive."

"I'm not being any such thing."

"Yeah, you are. And you know you are."

She fumed for a moment and then sat back. "All right. Go on then if you're so …. Go on. What do you want me to do?"

"It's just a conversation, Melissa, I know you've had them before. I say something, you say something … You'll get the hang of it."

It was hardly the time for sarcasm, but I couldn't help myself. She folded her arms. "All right," she said gruffly. "Start."

The door opened then and Colm stuck his nose in. When he saw Melissa's posture and my frown, he went into reverse, calling out in a fake-cheery voice, "He's out for the count. Anyone for tea?"

"No, thanks," we said together.

"Grand, so."

The door closed again.

"OK," I began. "First of all, I suppose I should say again that driving drunk was the stupidest thing I've ever done."

Melissa's lips twitched. "You *suppose*?"

I ignored that. "And I know I could have killed someone. You don't have to point that out. I already regretted it before Mum and Dad died and, believe me, I've regretted it a hell of a lot more ever since. I think about it every single day. And I understand why you were disgusted with me. I was disgusted with myself. I *hated* myself. But what was I supposed to do? Curl up and die? All I could do was learn from it and never make the same idiotic mistake again. Which I never will. What do you want me to do or say, Melissa? *It wasn't me who killed Mum and Dad?* You already know that. But still, you won't … you won't give me a break."

I braced myself for her response. It was a while in coming. A series of expressions took turns on her face while she was

297

thinking. I thought I saw traces of anger, fear, and sorrow, amongst unidentifiable others. She considered her response for so long that I eventually began to wonder if she'd decided to give me the silent treatment and was simply waiting for me to lose heart and leave. Then she raised her chin and primly gathered herself together.

"Well," she said. "You've certainly ..." But she ran out of steam immediately.

And then I saw that her bottom lip was beginning to tremble. I was knocked off balance completely.

"Melissa? Are you all right?"

She brought one hand up to her mouth and used the other to steady herself on the sofa, as if she was in danger of keeling over from the sitting position. I shifted my weight, ready to get up and go to her, but she was on her feet before I made it to mine. She walked off – ran, really – in the direction of the kitchen. I stepped after her, unable to believe how quickly things had unravelled.

"Leave me alone!" she wailed as she disappeared around the corner.

I stood still and ran my hand across my brow, wondering what the hell had just happened. Colm was in the kitchen. I heard him speaking in a tense whisper but couldn't make out what he was saying. Then Melissa produced a sort of groan and took off again, this time down the hall and up the stairs. Colm followed – I heard their footsteps thumping past. Then she shouted at him to leave her alone too. Not knowing how else to proceed, I sat down again. After a few seconds, the door to the hall swung open and Colm crept in. He gave me a weary smile and heavy sigh combo, then took the seat that Melissa had occupied not two minutes earlier.

"Is she all right?" I asked. "I mean, obviously not, but –"

"Dunno," he said. "She wouldn't even tell me what the problem was."

"We were just talking," I said, "and she suddenly got all upset. Legged it before I knew what was what."

"Hmmm."

"It was my fault. I brought up the subject of … Mum and Dad."

That was as far as I was willing to go for the moment. I wanted to see how he would react. The answer to that one was: slowly. He didn't say or do anything at first. And then, ever so gently, he started to nod his head. The movement was almost imperceptible at first. By the time I'd realised that he was doing it, he'd stopped. There followed a lengthy silence. And then, at last, he spoke.

"That might not be good," he said.

I stared across at him. "Oh?"

He shook as head with no more vigour than he had nodded it. "No."

"Why do you say that?"

"She's very … sensitive about all that."

"Yeah. I know. That's why I brought it up, I suppose. We can't keep pussyfooting around the way we have been. I mean, you know about all it, don't you? The way it's been between us? And why?"

"I know you've had your problems," he said noncommittally.

ALEX COLEMAN

"We sure have," I agreed. "And I want them to stop. You know what I really hate about all this? She makes me feel like I should be *defending* drunk driving. You know? Saying 'Oh, get over it, it was no big deal'. When it was a big deal. Christ, I know that."

I realised that my voice had risen and flashed a half-smile at Colm to show that I wasn't about to lose my temper entirely.

"It must be hard for you," he said. And then he stared at his knees for a moment. "Has she, eh … Has she ever talked to you about her own feelings? Her guilt? About her … role? As she sees it."

"Sorry?"

"That night. When your Mum and Dad died."

"*Guilt*?" I squeaked. "*Role*? What role? She didn't have a role."

"No," he agreed. "She didn't. But it's hard to convince her of that sometimes."

"I don't follow you."

He puffed out some air. "There's nothing to follow. It doesn't make a whole lot of sense. But they were coming back from our house, weren't they? Your parents."

I waited for him to come to the point. And then I realised that he already had. My eyes widened. "No!"

"Yeah …"

"No! You're *joking* me! She feels guilty because –"

"Because –"

"– they were killed coming back from *visiting* you?"

"Yes. Yeah. Yes. That's about the height of it."

300

"But that's ridiculous!"

"I know that. Try telling your sister."

"They could have been coming home from anywhere. Or been on their way *to* anywhere. She can't possibly think –"

"She does, Jackie. I know she does. She hasn't mentioned it in a long time. But there was a time when it was all she talked about."

"You're *joking* me." I knew I was repeating myself but I found it hard to stop.

"I wish I was. She was very hard on herself for a long time. Back then. Months. And months. If you ask me, she's never really allowed herself to get over it."

"But I'm the one she gives the hard time to. Why does … I don't see … Right, I'm going to talk to her."

I got up but Colm followed suit and with a nimbleness that I wouldn't have credited him with, intervened between me and the door I was heading for.

"Please don't," he said.

"But I have to try to –"

"I've *tried*. Dozens of times. It doesn't work. She won't listen."

I thought it over. And then I rushed past him. He grabbed my forearm and when I turned to face him, immediately let it go again; he really wasn't the physical-action type.

"Jackie," he said. "It would be a mistake. Believe me."

I shook my head. "Colm, I want to know what's going on."

Silently and miserably, he sat down again. I left the room.

CHAPTER 25

My first knock on Melissa and Colm's bedroom door went unanswered. The second was met with a hissed "*Go away.*"

"It's me," I said (as if that would help). "Let me in, Melissa. Please. I want to talk to you."

"Leave me alone," she said.

At least, I thought that was what she said. By the sound of it, she had buried her head in a pillow. Her line might just as well have been "Lob me a bone" or "Lend me a throne".

I turned the handle – the door wasn't locked. "No. I won't. I'm coming in."

She started to protest but I had crossed the threshold before she could properly get going. I thought my unsolicited entry might set her to full-on roaring and screaming but mercifully, it had just the opposite effect. She was lying diagonally on the bed and when I stepped inside, she gave me a quick (and dirty) look before slamming her head back into the depths of her foot-thick pillow. It was a maneouvre that Chrissy had often employed in her teenage years (it was her second favourite, in fact, after the bathroom-door-slam). In Chrissy's case, it was invariably accompanied by frantic, snotty wailing and accusations of betrayal, callousness or cold indifference; sometimes all three. Melissa, by contrast, had no follow-up to the head-slam. She just lay there, breathing so heavily that her entire body seemed to be pulsing.

"Melissa," I said softly, as if trying to wake her. "Come on. Sit up. Let's have a chat."

She made no response, other than to shift the position of her slippered right foot by a few inches.

"I didn't mean to upset you," I went on. "I'm sorry."

Again, nothing – not so much as a twitch.

"Don't you think we should talk? Or, at least, you could talk to me – tell me what I said to annoy you so badly."

At last, she spoke. Her voice was hoarse but calm. "Jackie, I'm not annoyed at you. Please, just leave me alone. Please. Go back down and ... Just go back down."

If I hadn't had my brief but highly informative chat with Colm, then I would have guessed that this was a bog-standard brush-off and would probably have become angry. Instead, I perched myself on the end of the bed and reached out to touch her ankle. She didn't exactly recoil, but she turned her face still further into the pillow. I had two options open to me, I realised. I could feign ignorance and try to tease a revelation out of her gradually or I could tell her that I'd spoken to Colm and cut right to the chase. All things being equal, the first was obviously superior. If I could get Melissa to open up of her own accord, we would undoubtedly be on surer ground. Telling her about my conversation with her husband might lead to a screaming match and, quite apart from that, would be a horrible betrayal of his trust. I weighed it up for a few seconds and then went the potential screaming match/horrible-betrayal-of-trust route.

"I just had a word with Colm," I said. "He's worried about you."

Melissa sniffed. "I'm fine."

"I don't believe you. I don't think you've been fine for a long time. I told him that I'd upset you by bringing up the subject of Mum and Dad, and … he told me something interesting."

She half-turned her face towards me. Her lips twitched but no words emerged. My heart-rate doubled. "He told me because he loves you and he wants to help, Melissa. Bear that in mind."

Now she twisted her torso in my direction and then, after grimacing ominously, sat up, curling her legs beneath her.

"I'm all ears," she said.

"Well," I began, treading carefully, "he says you were very upset when they died … and not just because of the grief."

Her face hardened. I tried to take a gulp of air and found that there was suddenly precious little of it in the room.

"Melissa, have you been feeling guilty about it all this time? Tell me the truth."

"Guilty? Guilty about what?"

"You tell me."

"I don't what you're talking about. If any of us should feel guilty, it's you."

"I do feel guilty. You already know that. I'm asking you if you do too."

"Maybe you didn't hear me, Jackie: guilty about *what*?"

"About the fact that Mum and Dad were coming home from visiting you when they were killed."

I was shocked – absolutely *astonished* – at the speed with which she started to cry. It seemed that I had barely made it to the word "killed" before her eyes were red and her cheeks glistening. It was a very quiet and understated breakdown. There was no wailing, no thrashing about. Her expression barely changed. But the flow of tears was remarkable; it was as if a pair of taps had been given a half-turn.

"What?" she managed to say.

The word itself was all but inaudible. I lip-read it as much as heard it.

"Have you been feeling guilty about the fact –"

"What a thing to say ..." she said dreamily. "What a silly thing to say ..."

Her eyelids rolled shut and then open again. She looked as if she'd just been hit over the head with a blunt instrument.

"Colm seems to think so," I said, wincing internally and hoping he would forgive me later. Melissa's features rippled. She looked so *pained*.

"Silly ..." she said again and shifted her gaze to the floor.

I waited to see if she had anything to add. Apparently, she had not. Thirty seconds went by. A minute. Two. More. The silence was merely tense at first. Then it became excruciating, then morbid, and finally almost comical. As the stand-off dragged on and on, I vowed repeatedly that I would not be the one to end it. I wouldn't speak and I wouldn't move. Not an inch. If she thought I was going to give up just like that, she could think again. I didn't care if I had to sit there staring at her all night long. There was no way –

"They'd been over a couple of days before," she said in a low monotone.

I almost said, "Who? When?" And then I realised that, without warning and well before I'd expected her to, she had given up the charade. I forced myself over the shock, vowing that I wouldn't interrupt until she had unburdened herself entirely.

"And a couple of days before that," she went on. "And a couple of days before that again. It wasn't like they hadn't seen us in ages. Not that there was anything to see ... just a bump. Maybe I'd have felt different afterwards if there'd been a baby to visit. But there wasn't. Not yet. I was full of myself, that was all. The only woman in Ireland who'd ever been pregnant. Colm used to take the piss. I'd had half the country round to see it. Was I going to start charging? All that. He said he was going to put a sign up near the house. One of those big fingers pointing – *This Way To The Miraculous Bump*. Bad enough to have dragged them over to see something that wasn't worth seeing and they'd already seen in any case ...

but I wouldn't let them go when they wanted to. They arrived at about eight and started trying to leave before ten. You know what Dad was like. He was fine to begin with and then once he'd had a cup of tea and a chat, he was itching to go. But no. 'We'll have more tea,' I said. 'Sure it's early yet. Ah, you will. Go on, go on.' Mrs fucking Doyle here. I don't think *Mum* was all that keen, even. We'd said everything we had to say to each other. But I insisted. And then, once the tea was gone, I went and got the scans out – again. The scans they'd already seen at least twice."

She paused for a moment to dry her cheeks. I forced myself to keep quiet and waited for her to start talking again, which she promptly did.

"It was well after eleven when they left. The bottom line, the inescapable bottom line is that the man who killed them was still in the pub when they wanted to go and was out on the road when I *let* them go. There's no way round that. I might as well have ploughed into them myself."

That was as much as I could take. I cast my promise to myself aside. "Melissa … I'm sure the stupidest thing I can say is that it wasn't your fault because you know that. You must do. But I can't think of anything else. Listen to me: *It wasn't your fault.*"

"You're right," she said and almost smiled. "That is a stupid thing to say."

"Why?"

"Because this isn't about what I know. It's about what I feel. I know it wasn't my fault. But I *feel* that it was. And you're exactly the same way. I've made it my business to make sure you're exactly the same way."

A couple of seconds floated by before I caught up with what she'd said.

"You've made it your ... What did you say?"

"You heard me. I wanted you to feel like shit about your drunk-driving. I didn't decide to do it, I swear to God. It just happened. I've been thinking about it all week and I know it's the truth. If *you* felt bad, then maybe *I* wouldn't ... It doesn't make sense when you say it out loud."

"Yes, it does," I heard myself saying. "Deflection ... or projection. Something like that. There's a word for it."

She nodded. "Yeah. I'm sure there is. And that's not even the worst part."

I was still struggling with the current part but felt obliged to say, "Oh?"

"Niall."

"What about him?"

"I've damaged him. I know I have."

"What? How?"

She attended to her cheeks again. The taps had been turned off, I noticed, which seemed like progress of a kind.

"I was such a basket case when they died. That affects a child. All those chemicals rushing around – stress hormones. And don't tell me that's rubbish because I'm married to a doctor."

"I wasn't going to –"

"And I was no better when he was born. You've seen how he is. Episodes, tantrums, whatever the hell they are. He's ... not right. And it's my fault."

She took a gulp and seemed to be on the verge of fresh tears. I stepped in quickly.

"Melissa, I think I can help you on that score. I know exactly what's wrong with Niall. The child ..." I paused for dramatic effect. "... is spoiled *rotten*."

She shot me a look, half-sneery and half-curious. "What do you mean?"

"I mean what I say. You spoil him rotten. Both of you. But mostly you. Maybe you're over-compensating for the way you felt around the time he was born, but I'm telling you, there's nothing wrong with that little boy that wouldn't be put right if he got a bit of a talking-to once in a while."

"A *talking*-to?"

"Yeah. A talking-to. Get tough with him. Tougher, anyway. He isn't *damaged*. He's just learned that the fastest way to get what he wants is by screaming and throwing things."

She tried to give me a how-dare-you look – but she couldn't quite pull it off.

"Look," I said. "This is a conversation for a different day. Right now, let's agree on this: Mum and Dad's death wasn't my fault and it wasn't your fault. It was the van driver's fault."

Her head drooped. It was much too soon for her to agree to that or at least, to voice agreement. I reached out and grabbed her hand.

"I have an idea," I said. "Put your shoes on."

She looked up. "Why? Where are we going?"

"*Shoes*," I said firmly.

309

CHAPTER 26

When I was a little girl, I had a very clear picture of what heaven looked like. It was an enormous green field, dotted here and there with the fluffiest of sheep (I had a thing for sheep back then). Because I had no idea what a soul might look like, I envisioned the inhabitants as Valentine's Day hearts with arms and legs. I mentioned all of this to Melissa one Sunday afternoon when I was about seven. We had just come home from mass and I was in a spiritual frame of mind. Melissa, unfortunately, was not. She almost bust a gut laughing and then adopted a serious, slightly superior expression. How could heaven possibly be anything like that? she asked me. It was supposed to be perfect and everyone in it was supposed to be perfectly happy. What were they going to do all day in a big field? They couldn't even talk to each other (I'd mentioned that my Valentine's Day hearts lacked faces). I sulked for a while and then threw it back at her. What was her idea of heaven, if she was so smart? I didn't think she had ever given it much thought – the answer she came up with seemed to be nothing more than the opposite of my own. Heaven, she declared, was a very busy place. Everywhere you looked, there was something exciting to do. It was like a giant fun-fair crossed with a giant sports centre crossed with a giant toy-shop. Nobody ever got bored. Everyone had a face. There were few sheep. I had to admit – to myself, not to Melissa – that her version did indeed sound more fun than mine. But the conversation got me thinking. Supposing she was right and everyone in heaven looked "just like they did on Earth". What exactly did that mean? Did they look the way they did when they had died? Most people who died were old and wrinkly. They had bad hips and false teeth and ugly, purple veins in the backs of their hands. Surely they didn't go to heaven looking like that? What good would a giant sports centre be to someone who'd lived and died in a wheelchair, like poor old Mrs Farrelly from across the street? And another thing: I knew from experience that fun-fairs were great crack for a while, but the thrill wore out pretty quickly. Heaven was forever. You'd get bored in the end; you were bound to. The toy-shop bit didn't stand up either. I liked toy-shops as much as the next girl, but Mum and Dad didn't. They seemed to prefer supermarkets and bakeries and DIY superstores. It was possible, I supposed, that heaven had a mixture of retail outlets. But if that was the case, then it had bits that some people found boring, which would mean that it wasn't perfect after all. I thought about the problem every day for a week or more before giving up. There was no way to picture heaven that made sense. This attitude was to stay with me throughout my life. It didn't change when my pets died. It didn't change when my grand-parents died. And it didn't change when the van ploughed into my mother and father's beloved Golf, leaving it concertina'd at the edge of a ditch, looking for all the world like a controversial piece of modern art. When I stood by my my parents' grave, which I didn't do very often, I found myself looking not at the headstone or the flowers but at the other relatives scattered around. I imagined that they all had perfectly clear visions of heaven and saw the graves as mere memorials. *Their* loved ones were really somewhere up above, having a whale of a time. I found it hard to shake the feeling that mine were right in front of me.

Late one afternoon in the second winter after the accident, I visited the graveyard, on a sudden whim. It was one of those days that starts out so murky and grim that you barely notice when the light begins to fail for real. As I picked my way through the headstones, I spoke to myself in a voice that I hadn't used for twenty-five years: *That noise was just an owl. That shape is just a tree.* There was no one else around and the only sound came from the wind, which was suitably hollow and mournful. I stayed by the graveside for no more than two minutes – a new low – and then legged it back to the car, desperately trying to turn off the music in my head, which was the theme from *Tales of the Unexpected*. As soon as I was under the comforting streetlights again, I vowed that from now on I would only visit the cemetery at lunch-time. The idea of going there in the dead of night would have filled me with pure dread.

But when I parked the car and killed the headlights forty minutes after leaving Ranelagh after my talk with Melissa, I felt nothing of the kind. All I felt was hope.

Melissa pulled up alongside me and we both got out, closing our doors with a pleasing synchronicity.

We went through the cemetery gates together and turned smoothly, like birds in flight. As I walked along the path, I found myself reciting the path to my parents' plot in my mind – *Through the gate, turn left, fourth row, fifth grave on the right; through the gate, turn left, fourth row, fifth grave on the right* . . . It felt as familiar as the route from my kitchen to my bedroom, despite the infrequency of my visits.

I was about to say as much to Melissa when she gasped and stopped dead. I quickly followed suit. There was activity ahead, movement, voices. We shuffled closer together, breathing heavily. Then I heard a girl's scream, high and piercing. We shuffled closer still. But the scream was followed immediately by laughter, then by a poor imitation of a wolf's howl. The source of the noise, we now saw, was a trio of teenagers, two boys and a girl. They were walking down the row next to my parents'. Although I saw no bottles of cider or naggins of vodka, I presumed they'd been having a sneaky drink.

"Teenagers having fun in a graveyard at night," I whispered. "Have they never seen a horror movie?"

As they drew closer, I prepared to let fly with a tirade about respect and decency and the way things were done in my day. But I held my tongue, largely because I was afraid that they'd ask us what the hell *we* were doing there at that time of night. Instead, I merely nodded at them as they passed. Melissa did likewise. The boys nodded back; the girl said, "All right?" They stayed silent for another few steps and then started laughing again; one of them launched into the chorus of "Thriller" and the others joined in.

Mum and Dad's grave was plain in every way. While its immediate neighbours sported a large angel and an elaborate Celtic cross, respectively, theirs had a simple black headstone with a gentle curve at the top. Both neighbours were grassy and had miniature rose-bushes in all four corners. Mum and Dad were buried under white gravel, through which a multitude of weeds gamely poked. There was a single pot in the centre. The plant inside had seen better days – but not recently. I joined my hands in front of me and slowly read the inscription on the stone.

In Loving Memory of
Martin Flynn
1940-2002
and his Beloved Wife
Theresa
1941-2002

Requiescat In Pace

Sometimes I thought that I expected it to change – that one day there'd be new information to report, or perhaps that some old information would be added: *Martin worked as an electrician* or *Theresa was smarter than she let on.* The last line of the inscription had caused some friction – some extra friction – between Melissa and me. I'd argued that the full Latin looked pretentious. Melissa had thought it looked dignified. She'd won out, in the end, because I simply gave up. It hadn't seemed like a big deal in the grand scheme of things. But it annoyed me every time I saw it. On the other hand, the gravel annoyed me too and that had been my idea. "Less trouble," I'd said. "Easier to keep. If we get grass, we'll have to be out here every week in the summer." Melissa had quickly agreed. *Less trouble* was good. *Easier to keep* was good. *Fewer visits* was good.

I once asked Gerry what he did when he came to see his own parents' grave, which was on the far side of the same cemetery. The question embarrassed him, but he answered it anyway. He said he chatted to them, told them his news. I was astonished. Gerry had never really seen eye to eye with his mother and he was still in nappies when his father died of a massive heart attack. I said as much; Gerry looked at me as if I'd lost my mind. What did it matter if he'd never known his dad and hadn't been close to his mum? They were *dead*. They couldn't answer him, could they? He talked to them because it helped him to get his ducks in a row in his head – to see where he was coming from and where he was going to. It was something to do besides reciting prayers, which he knew was boring and suspected was pointless. (I followed up by asking him if he had a clear image of heaven. He answered the question with a question: had I been sniffing glue?) I'd tried to copy his example myself, a couple of times. But I'd just felt silly and had gone back to what

315

I was used to – reading the headstone and feeling empty. Tonight, perhaps, would be third time lucky. I closed my eyes and brought my parents' faces to mind. Then I lowered my chin and thought about those strange and terrible months almost four years ago. The images swirled and tilted, fell into and out of sequence. The Guard on the street saying: "Blow into this for me, love." The Guard at the door saying: "Prepare yourself for a shock." Melissa avoiding my gaze. Robert rolling his eyes. Chrissy biting a fingernail. Gerry slamming a door. Tony kissing my tummy. Then I thought about more recent events. Gerry and Lisa in the front room. Melissa greeting me at her door. Chrissy denouncing her father. Robert giving me a hug. Melissa crying on her bed.

It was a while before I managed to frame my opening bit of chat. This is what I came up with: *Mum? Dad? Hello. It's been a while.* I'd no sooner thought that thought than Melissa spoke up for the first time since we'd arrived.

"It doesn't look too good, does it?" she said.

"No."

"Uncared for ..."

"Well ...."

"Neglected, then."

"Yeah. Neglected."

She became lost in thought for a moment. Then she said, "You know what I've just realised? Apart from the funeral, this is the first time you and I have been here together. The very first time ..."

I reached out in the darkness and took her hand. "That," I told her, "is the whole point."

CHAPTER 27

I didn't stay in Melissa's that night. I went home.

Twenty metres from the house, I took my foot off the accelerator and allowed the car to coast, as was my habit. There were no lights on inside. I pictured Gerry in the foetal position right in the centre of the bed, gently shivering as he caressed his wounded cheek. Then I realised that his jeep was nowhere to be seen. I parked in the drive and let myself in. Everything seemed to be just as I had left it. The ruins of the Cross-eyed Busker hadn't been disturbed. There was no new rubbish teetering atop the kitchen bin. Upstairs, however, I found a clue. The pile of slashed clothes was exactly where I had left it – but the plug had been removed from the sink in the en suite. The Walkman was still sitting there, its surface beaded with water; he hadn't even bothered lifting it out. I shuddered at the feebleness of my Angry Wife tactics.

Downstairs, I made myself a cup of tea, then sat at the kitchen table and didn't drink it. I looked at the wall clock. It was half past eleven. I very much doubted that Gerry was out drowning his sorrows. His interest in drinking had started to wane when he was in his early thirties. I couldn't remember the last time I had seen him drunk. And besides, he wasn't the sorrow-drowning type. Alcohol had always been a social lubricant to him, at best; it was never medicinal. He could have been visiting someone, I supposed, but that seemed just as unlikely. Although Gerry had several close friends, I couldn't see him calling around to any of them late at night to pour his heart out. He wasn't the type for that either. I flicked the edge of my cup with a fingernail and rested my chin on my hand. And then my mobile rang. It was Chrissy. As soon as I answered, I could tell that she was upset about something.

"Chrissy?" I said. "Are you all right?

"Hi. Yeah, sort of. I'm … I'm fine."

"What's going on?"

She didn't answer. I heard a muffled ruckus of some kind. My heart raced. "Hello? Hello?"

Her voice returned. "Yeah, I'm here, hang on." More muffled ruckus. I heard her say, "Go back in, I'll be with you in a minute." Then: "Mum?"

"What is it?"

She breathed down the line. "Dad's here."

"*Is* he?"

"He was on the front doorstep when I came in from work.

Miserable. Babbling."

I fought hard to keep the smile out of my voice. "And you took him in ... "

"I certainly did not. I walked right past him."

"Ah, Chrissy ..."

"But a while later some eejit held the front door for him. He started babbling outside the apartment then."

I tried again. "And you took him in ..."

"It was embarrassing, that's all. I could hear people sticking their heads out into the corridor for a look. He says you punched him in the face."

"Slapped," I said. "I *slapped* him in the face."

"And wrecked his clothes. And his Walkman. And the Cross-eyed Busker."

"Yeah, well ..."

"About time too. He's in bits in there. 'I'm a bloody fool, I don't deserve to live, blah blah blah!'. Same old shite. I don't know what to do with him. He says he can't go back to the house – he wants to stay here for the night. Jesus."

"But you're talking? The two of you are talking?"

"Don't get excited. I haven't really got much choice in the matter, have I?"

"It's a start," I said.

There was an unpleasant pause. "I just don't get you, Mum. I really don't. After the way that man –"

"Let's not get into it now. Please."

I thought quickly. My conversation with Gerry could wait. It was more important that he and Chrissy made some sort of headway while the going was good.

"Are you going to let him stay?" I asked.

"I don't want to," she said. "That's why I'm ringing you. Can you talk him into leaving? Please? If I was fit to lift him and throw him out, I would have done it by now."

"No," I said, immediately and firmly.

"What do you mean, *no*?"

"I mean no, Chrissy. I'm not doing that."

She sighed so hard the phone line crackled. "Fine then. I'll go and stay on someone's floor for the night. Maybe I'll join you at Melissa's, she's got nice thick carpets …"

This was an empty threat, I was sure of it. Chrissy hated any kind of discomfort, however temporary. The threat – the entire phone-call – was a last roll of the dice. I didn't bother pointing out that my stay at her aunt's was over. The news that I was close by would only add fuel to her fire.

"It's up to you," I said and let the words dangle.

She made no reply.

"Okay then," I said with an air of finality. "Go on back to him. Tell him you were ringing one of your pals or something. And try to be nice."

"I have no intention of being nice," she said.

I didn't push it. The ball was rolling and that was enough. We said goodnight and hung up.

* * *

About a fortnight after Tony and I slept together (to use the TV way of putting it; there was, of course, no sleeping involved), I started hassling Gerry for a new bed. He didn't put up much of a struggle; luckily for me, we'd had our current one for fifteen years, and it showed. I was sure that the sickly, sweaty feeling that had engulfed me when I lay down every night would vanish as soon as the swap was made, but I was wrong. The problem, it turned out, was not the bed but the room itself. It took many months for me to stop thinking of it as a crime-scene. Even then, no matter how hard I wiped and scrubbed and dusted – it was the cleanest room in the house, by far – I was never able to shake the feeling that it was indelibly tainted. For some reason, it never bothered me during the day, even though that was when Tony and I had committed our sin. I could only guess that the guilt became stronger when I was in there alone with Gerry, lying side by side, oblivious husband and callous wife. When I got off the phone from Chrissy that night, I decided to hit the sack straight away. As soon as I walked through the bedroom door, I noticed that the space felt different, more comfortable than usual – this, despite the pile of sabotaged clothes on the floor and the damp and useless Walkman in the en suite. I got myself ready in record time and dived under the crumpled duvet.

It was probably a good thing, I told myself, that I wouldn't be seeing Gerry straight away. Even though I knew now what I wanted to say to him, the extra thinking time would be useful. The ideas and sentiments were all in place – but the words were not. I thought about Tony too, about how strange it had been in those few months between our encounter and his move to Galway. It had been hard to pretend that nothing untoward had happened while knowing that he was sleeping on the other side of the wall. And now Lisa was in there, laughing it up with her boyfriend for all I knew. I made myself think about her, forced myself to, and still I couldn't raise any strong feelings towards her. She was a non-person to me, a sort of silhouette.

Sleep crept up on me surprisingly quickly. As it did so, an idea lodged in my tired mind and refused all of my efforts to shift it. My last waking thought was that before I spoke to my husband, I had one more visit to make.

CHAPTER 28

I woke early on Friday morning, and was pulling out of the drive within twenty minutes of opening my eyes. Gerry might well have been going to work straight from Chrissy's, I thought, but I didn't want to take the chance of bumping into him. Traffic out of Ashbourne was heavy, even though it was not yet eight o'clock, and only worsened as I approached the M50. Every morning during my commute to First Premier, I heard the horror stories on the radio and thanked God that I didn't have to go near that particular stretch of motorway. Still, I was totally unprepared for the scene that confronted me when I finally joined it. The phrases that I'd heard so many times in the traffic reports – *It's bumper-to-bumper*, *It's choc-a-bloc*, *It's like a car park* – seemed woefully inadequate. I'd been driving on it for ten minutes when I felt a giddy little rush and couldn't understand why. Then it dawned on me – I'd made it into second gear. I'd driven faster in funeral processions.

Shortly after nine o'clock, I pulled in at a service station and rang directory enquiries. The woman who answered sounded as if she'd just finished a giggling fit and was looking forward to starting another as soon as she'd dealt with me. Her good humour was so infectious that I found myself smiling as I asked for the numbers of every Bank of Ireland branch in Galway city. To my surprise, there were only three. I wrote them down on the back of an old receipt and thanked her for help. She told me it had been a pleasure and seemed to genuinely mean it. *This woman's in love*, I thought. *Or on drugs. Probably drugs.*

The first branch I rang was in the shopping centre.

A male voice, implausibly young, said, "Bank of Ireland, can I help you?"

I cleared my throat. "Hello. I was wondering if I could speak to Tony Mullen?"

"Sure. I'll put you through."

I hung up. Right first time.

* * *

I arrived in Galway at eleven-thirty and found my way to the shopping centre with relative ease. The bank was smaller than I expected it to be, but busier too; there were eight people in front of me in the queue. I felt completely calm as

I shuffled towards the counter. And then I saw him; he emerged from an office at the back, holding a sheet of paper in one hand and a biro in the other. His stride was easy, purposeful, confident. He approached a colleague, a moon-faced young woman and began pointing out something or other on the page, periodically tapping the biro against it for emphasis. When he'd finished speaking, he playfully elbowed the woman and said something out of the corner of his mouth. She laughed and he turned to leave her.

"Tony!" I said – loudly, it turned out.

Every eye in the bank swivelled towards me. He looked right at me, half-smiling. Then he realised who he was looking at and the smile vanished; in fact, his whole face seemed to collapse in on itself like an overcooked soufflé. I stepped out of the queue and went to a vacant spot at the counter. Tony's lips moved. I presumed he was swearing to himself. Then he came over to join me. The sheet of paper was shaking in his hands.

"Hello," I said. "Long time no see. Sorry for shouting."

He leaned forward on his side of the counter the way bank staff sometimes do when they're trying to keep your business confidential. I guessed that Tony was doing it for physical support.

"Jackie," he squeaked. "What, what, eh, what –"

"Brings me here?" I said for him. "Don't worry. Nothing much, really."

"Are you … living here now?"

"No, no."

"On holiday?"

"No. I came for the day. To see you."

That was the wrong thing to spring on him. His eyes bulged in their sockets.

"It's all right," I told him. "I won't take up much of your time. And I'm sorry for not calling ahead. I thought maybe we could have lunch somewhere?"

"Not today," he said with something like relief. "Honestly. I can't. There's a Chamber of Commerce thing on, there's no way I can get –"

"Coffee then. Ten minutes, Tony. That's all I need."

He looked doubtful.

"Look," I said in a low voice, "I'm not going to pretend I drove the whole way across the country just to say hello. But if you're playing *Fatal Attraction* in your head, you can stop now. I've got two questions to ask you. Two. Then I'm gone. And chances are, you'll never see me again."

"It's not that I'm sorry to see you," he said and for the first time, gave me a smile – half of one at least.

"Two questions," I repeated.

He glanced at his watch. "There's a place called Beans 'n' Biscuits a few doors away. Go out of here and turn right. I'll see you there in a few minutes."

"Thank you. What'll I get you, coffee-wise?"

He looked at me as if it was the strangest question he'd ever been asked. "Latte," he said, "please."

I smiled as reassuringly as I could and left.

* * *

Beans 'n' Biscuits was one of those coffee-shops that made me feel old. I'd grown up thinking of coffee-shops as places where furry-hatted old dears came together to talk about who had died in the past week. They had sturdy square tables and straight-backed, no-nonsense chairs. Apart from ordinary tea and ordinary coffee, they offered sticky buns and Black Forest Gateaux, served by red-faced and invariably fat menopausal women. Beans 'n' Biscuits, on the other hand, had a menu that filled two large blackboards. It sold eight different types of coffee, only a few of which I'd ever heard of. All of the staff were young and good-looking, and most of them were elaborately pierced. It had a few stools by a narrow bar and was otherwise exclusively furnished by battered sofas. If a furry-hatted old dear ever managed to get into one, I thought, she'd have a hell of a time getting out again.

"Hey there," said the Tom Cruise look-alike who served me. "What can I get you?"

"Two lattes, please," I said.

"What size would you like?" he asked, and then said some words I'd never heard before.

I stared at him for a moment and then said, "Medium-ish", hoping that would be the end of the conversation. It was. After I'd paid and collected the drinks, I lowered myself onto a free sofa with clear view of the door. No sooner had I placed the mugs on the magazine-littered table than Tony appeared in the doorway, looking like a man who'd lost something valuable and was slowly retracing his steps. I raised my chin – as if that would make me more visible – and he came over, doing his best to smile.

"Latte, as requested," I said.

He sat beside me – not close, but not as far away as he could have – and said, "Thanks." There was a slight sheen on his face. I guessed that he'd been splashing water on himself. It was either that or sweat – either way, it spoke of nerves that needed to be calmed.

"Don't panic," I said. "You're not going to regret talking to me."

"You look great," he said, too quickly. "Your hair is … different."

"It sure is," I said, raking my fingers through it. "You look great too."

That wasn't exactly true. He looked the way he'd always looked, even when Jonathon had been well – tired and run-down. And balding. And long-nosed. And pale. *My former lover*, I thought and marvelled at my own existence.

"How's the family?" he asked and I saw him gulp.

"Fine. They're fine. How's Jonathon?"

"He's fine too. Shooting up. Getting on well at school, playing a lot of football."

"Is he still mad about cars?"

"Oh, yeah. I think he always will be."

"And how's his health? I'm dying to know."

The word "dying" had been poorly-chosen. Tony didn't seem to notice.

"Good, good. Not a bother on him."

"That's fantastic," I said. "I'm delighted."

We smiled at each other, briefly.

Then Tony turned business-like. "I don't mean to be rude," he said, "but I'm really under pressure. You said you had two questions?"

I was a little taken aback. We hadn't even done the "How's work?" bit. He really didn't want to be there. That was fair enough, I thought. I could only imagine how I would have reacted if he'd shown up at First Premier.

"Okay," I said. "If we had time, I'd lead into this more gently. But since we haven't ..."

He went for his coffee and took a fortifying mouthful, as if it was brandy. "Yes?"

"Don't get alarmed now."

"What is it?"

"I don't want you to have a fit or run off in –"

"Jackie. What is it?"

"I want to ask your permission. To tell Gerry. About us."

He sucked air through his nose. His fingers went rigid. "Are you nuts?" he whispered, leaning in. "No. No! Absolutely not. No way. No."

"Why not?"

"Why *not*? Because he'll fucking kill me, that's why not. Have you seen the size of him?"

"He won't kill you, Tony. I promise."

"Oh, you *promise*, oh, well then!"

"I know he won't kill you because he's in no position to. He's just done it himself. Been unfaithful."

This seemed to have an effect. The panic-stricken look slid off his face for a second – but then reappeared, good as new.

"That's awful," he said, still whispering. "I'm sorry for you, I really am. But the answer's still no. *Why*, for God's sake? Why would you want to tell him?"

I told the truth. "I'm going to be having a long and serious talk with him and I want it to be 100 per cent honest. This has to be part of it."

"No, Jackie. No, it doesn't. You can be as honest as you want about anything else, but not that. It's not *necessary*. What's done is done. Leave it alone. I'm with someone now –"

"Oh! I'm glad."

"– and I don't want anything to interfere with that."

"What's her name?"

"Patricia."

"And how did you two meet?"

"Why do you … Wine-appreciation. I'm doing a wine-appreciation course."

"Really? I know someone in Dublin who got fixed up doing a cookery course. The two things seem to go together."

His nostrils flared. "I really don't have time for this. You can't tell Gerry. Absolutely not. Now what's your other question?"

I realised then that he wasn't just panicked; he was angry. Maybe I reminded him of bad times with Jonathon. Or maybe he regretted that afternoon as much as I did. Either way, his past had come calling and he didn't like it one little bit. I tried not to let his reaction annoy me. "Okay, Tony. Okay. When you and I … I never know what to call it. What do you call it, in your head?"

"Sex," he said bluntly. "We had sex. Once."

I took a little sip of coffee to give my mouth something to do. "When you and I had sex, once, I was all over the place. Mentally. I've been wondering how ... Well. I've been ... My second question, Tony, is this: with you and me ... who started it?"

His mouth fell open. "You drove from Dublin to ask me *that*?"

"Yes. That and the other one."

"Have you lost your memory or something?"

"No. I want to hear your version of events."

"*Version of events*, Jesus!" He leaned closer still. "What are you getting at? Are you accusing me —"

"I'm not accusing you of anything, Tony," I cut in before he gathered further steam. "The whole thing was entirely consensual. I just want to know who started it, that's all."

He pouted like a four-year-old. "I don't understand what difference it could possibly —".

"Tony, please, it —"

"*I* did, all right? I started it. Is that what you wanted to hear?"

I'd thought it was, actually. I'd thought I wanted confirmation that he'd started it with me, just as Lisa had started it with Gerry. I'd thought it would make me feel better. But now I realised in an instant that it didn't matter who had started it. I'd gone along with it. I was every bit as guilty as I'd always imagined I was.

Tony glared at me, awaiting my response. "Well?"

"It turns out," I said slowly, as if chewing the words, "that it doesn't matter."

This statement was too much for him. He stood up and straightened his jacket. "I have to go now," he said. "It was nice to see you again."

I smiled up at him. "I have a niggling feeling that you don't mean that."

"Goodbye, Jackie." He took a step towards the door.

"Tony?"

He stopped and turned. "What is it now?"

"They weren't really two questions. The second one was a question. The first one was … a courtesy. I'm telling Gerry."

He fumed at me in silence for a few seconds then stormed off, muttering something. I didn't quite catch it, which was probably for the best.

I watched him go past the shop window and turned my attention back to my drink. Piercings and all aside, they did a very nice latte.

CHAPTER 29

I took my time on the way back to Dublin, stopping in Athlone for a late lunch. While I was there, I made two additional calls. The first was at a newsagent, where I bought my final packet of cigarettes. I performed the same ritual that I'd used the last time I'd quit forever. Standing over a rubbish bin, I gave a little speech, telling the fags that we'd had some good times, but it was over between us; it wasn't them, it was me. Then I dropped them, unopened, in among the chocolate wrappers and apple cores. My second stop was at Dunnes Stores. I spent longer in there than I meant to but was happy with my small purchase.

According to the clock in the car, it was five precisely when I turned off the engine in the First Premier car park. I rang Eddie on his mobile and asked him to come down and meet me. He said he wasn't sure, he had a lot of data to enter. I didn't realise that he was joking; he had to tell me. Five minutes later, he appeared, looking slightly nervous. I waved to him from the bonnet of the car, where I had taken a seat.

"Hello, Jackie," he said, sitting down next to me. "Sorry – do you mind?"

"Of course not. How are you, Eddie?"

"Oh, I'm fine. It's you I'm worried about. Are you … fine?"

"Yeah. I am. So – full circle."

"Uh. I don't –"

"The car park. This is where we got started, you and me."

"Oh! Right. Yes."

"Not even a week ago."

"I know. Imagine. It's been eventful."

"You can say that again."

He scratched the end of his nose. "About last night, Robert and the DVD. I'm sorry if –"

"No need to be sorry. I'm glad you said what you did."

"Was I right?"

"Yup."

"Sorry".

"And I want to thank you." I put my hand on his and squeezed. For a moment, I thought he was going to die of embarrassment. Then he smiled and squeezed back. "I feel terrible," I said then. "I ran out of your house last night and didn't even find out how it went with Margaret. So …?"

His smile broadened to epic proportions. "It went well. *Very* well."

"Great. So you stayed tragic and mysterious?"

"Yeah. She *loved* it."

"I'm delighted, Eddie. Delighted."

"But I'm going to come clean soon. Next time I see her, in fact. It's not me – lying like that."

"No," I agreed. "Lying isn't easy. Well, it's easy enough to start – but it's hard to keep up."

"Yeah. Y'know, the whole thing would never have happened if it hadn't been for you. Me and Margaret, I mean."

"Ah, now …"

"It's the truth."

"So we're mutually grateful. Good for us."

"Exactly. And, y'know … I've made a bit of progress."

"Have you now?"

"Yup. I mean, you know, one thing at a time. But she has the lips wore off me."

I felt the happiness coming off him in waves. "You must be so chuffed …"

"I feel fucking brilliant!" he declared.

I'd never heard him swear before. It felt like a little treat. This, I decided, was a good place to end the conversation.

"OK, Eddie," I said. "I'm going to scoot."

"Yeah, I should get back up there. Will I see you on Monday?"

"I'll be here."

I declined to add a detail – that I'd be handing in my notice.

"See you then," he said.

I held up my hand. "Wait! I nearly forgot." I slid off the

bonnet and went round to open the door on the passenger side. When I handed Eddie the Dunnes Stores bag, he looked at it as if might bite him.

"What's this?"

"Little present," I told him.

He reached in and withdrew the tie that I had spent twenty minutes choosing.

"Should be an exact match," I said. "Or as near as makes no difference."

He held it up against his own and confirmed that they were indistinguishable.

"One to change the other," I said. "Always good to have a spare."

Eddie nodded his thanks and turned away. God bless him, I think he was getting choked up.

* * *

I hadn't intended to call on Lisa right away, but when I saw her paint-spattered car outside the house, I decided I might as well talk to her now. In Tony's time, the sound of the doorbell had been a long, low buzz. It was different now, a classic ding-dong. There was no answer to my first ring. The door opened on the *dong* of my second. Lisa was still in her work gear, a beautiful black trouser-suit over a crisp red shirt. She looked, as they say, a million dollars. I knew that I looked about a hundred and fifty, but I didn't give a damn.

"Hello," I said as she half-closed the door again, a barrier,

I presumed against physical assault. "I've been away for a week, but I'm back now. I just wanted to drop by and let you know that you mean absolutely nothing to me, so you don't have to worry about being axe-murdered or anything. I understand that you're moving out soon?"

This was all too sudden for her, and too strange. I could see it in her eyes; they didn't seem to be under her voluntary control.

"Yes," she said quietly. "Just over a month from now."

"Good. Moving in with your boyfriend, is that it?" She nodded. I nodded back. "Marriage on the cards?"

She looked at her feet. "Maybe."

"He probably thinks he's a lucky man. And I suppose he is, in some ways. In others, not so much, wouldn't you say?"

She didn't reply. I wouldn't have either.

"You're not going to let him sue my son, are you?"

"It's not up to –"

"Because if you do, it'll all have to come out, won't it? The reason why Robert stopped at your table in the first place. I presume you told him – what – old boyfriend?"

Again, she didn't reply, but her expression gave her away.

"Thought so," I said. "That lie wouldn't last long once the lawyers got involved. But, I don't know, maybe you're thinking of toughing it out. I'd say you've a neck on you for anything. Just to be on the safe side, take a note of this: if Robert gets as much as a solicitor's letter, I won't think twice about telling Michael – that's his name, isn't it? – about telling Michael the full story. Won't take me half an hour to track him down. Do you understand?"

She tossed her hair back, trying to compose herself. "Yes."

"Same goes for my daughter. She never hears from you about your car or your window. That remains an unsolved mystery. Correct?"

"Yes. Correct. I told Michael but I said I didn't know –"

"Good. OK, then. That's all I have to say. See ya."

I walked away. Her door still hadn't closed when I put the key in mine.

CHAPTER 30

Gerry had come back to the house at some point. I knew that because the Cross-eyed Busker had been cleared away. The kitchen bin hadn't been emptied, but that was a different kind of mess.

I sat on the sofa in the front room and, one last time, ran through what I was going to say. It boiled down to this: there was no excuse for infidelity. Maybe he'd done it because he was going through some private crisis of his own. Maybe he'd done it to prove a point to himself. Maybe he'd done it because she was gorgeous and he just couldn't resist. I didn't particularly care; I was going to give him hell all over again. Then I was going to tell him that I'd forgive him if he'd forgive me.

Things seemed clearer now, clearer than they'd been for years. I'd always felt that I had coped well with my parents' deaths; as well as could be expected, at any rate. Now I saw that I had simply looked the other way – to a job I couldn't stand and, briefly, a man I hardly knew. I'd been so busy looking the other way, in fact, that I had allowed my relationships with my son and sister to fall apart for want of a little common sense.

The question now was: what next? I would have a lot of free time on my hands and that would be nice, for a while. I had my restored relationships to explore, for a start. I could take up new hobbies. I could travel. But in the long-term, I would need something else. And I thought I knew what it might be: I could start a little business. The idea was not yet fully formed in my mind, but I had the gist. Cookery lessons for lonely hearts; learn a new skill and maybe meet that special someone while you're doing it. Students could be paired up, male and female, swapping partners each week. There would be dating show-style games and quizzes along the way, and plenty of wine to loosen tongues. I could start small – in my own kitchen, if necessary – and see how it went. If it took off, somewhere down the line I could hire proper facilities. I might even need an assistant; a certain pink apron sprang to mind. The more I thought about it, the more excited I became.

Gerry's key turned in the door at twenty past six. *He's a good man*, I reminded myself. *A good man who did a stupid thing. But we're none of us perfect.* I sat up straight and practised my opening line aloud, but ever so softly.

"First of all," I whispered, "this sofa's got to go."

THE END